This was

Kather
clear surpr
and then go
with short, shaky jerks. She detested the betrayal of her body, hated that she reacted so strongly to him.

He remained on his side, propped on one elbow, his gaze roaming over her face. A battle of expressions—perplexity, frustration, and finally the familiar coldness—crossed his features. He stood. "I was only being flippant with my suggestion to leave by the ledge. You seemed fool enough to try."

She was more of a fool for allowing him to seduce her. She looked around for her slate to write a terse message concerning her intention to never again let him near her.

"Since you do not find my presence pleasing, I'll be sure to remain distant from you whenever I can," he said. "I wouldn't want you to suffer more than necessary until you leave here."

Katherine wheeled toward him, greatly wishing to tell him exactly what she thought of him, how she wanted him—no, *didn't* want him—and demand an explanation of the past.

Then, she looked into his eyes and saw the desperate need beneath the mockery.

Lord Drayton placed a finger under her chin and lifted her face. His touch lit another warm flush inside her, and as his eyes dropped to her lips and lingered there, she thought for a dazed second he would kiss her again.

To her mortification, she knew she would welcome him.

"Listen to me," he said in a voice gruff with emotion. "If your suitor refuses you, nothing will happen between us. You will make no requests of me or think of me as anything but your guardian. You may eat at my table and sleep in my house. Beyond that, my deepest wish is to find you a husband and get you out of my life."

Oh, such vile words, and from lips that had kissed her so fervently only moments ago.

Katherine jerked away before he could see her tears.

Contest finals:

Low Country Romance Writers 2006 Jasmine Contest

Land of Enchantment Romance Writers 2006 Rebecca Contest

Tampa Area Romance Authors 2005 First Impressions Contest

On Silent Wings

by

Pamela Roller

To Susan -

Hope you enjoy the

Story!

Pamela Roller

On Silent Wings

Contact Information: info@thewildrosepress.com

Cover Art by *RJMorris*

The Wild Rose Press
PO Box 706
Adams Basin, NY 14410-0706
Visit us at www.thewildrosepress.com

Publishing History
English Tea Rose Edition, March 2007
Print ISBN 1-60154-054-X

Published in the United States of America

Dedication

I dedicate this book to my husband and family, to Beth Trissel, a good friend and talented writer, to my buddies at Virginia Romance Writers, to Deborah Dutton, my first critique partner, to all those who have helped me along the way,
and to the teens whom I've had the privilege of teaching.

Chapter One

England, April 1667

"She's here," Alexander Fletcher said to the lanky rider beside him. "Would that I had declined the king's request." From his vantage point on the hill facing Drayton castle, he scowled through the misty rain at the coach halting before his door.

"At least she'll be silent," his neighbor Robert Cooke said. "She'd make a perfect wife."

"To anyone but me." Alex shifted in the saddle to conceal a sudden, ridiculous loneliness that banded his chest. Crushing the feeling, he studied the prize sent to him by King Charles II, noting she alighted from the coach with no companion. One pale hand at her throat clutched a cloak that covered her from head to knees. She paused, and her upper body bent and shook with what looked like a bout of coughing.

Even at this distance, Alex sensed her desperation. Useless sympathy sparked, and died, within him. "She looks sickly. Perhaps 'twas another reason fat Rochester made her cry off their betrothal after she became destitute."

"Mmm. Ailing, poor, *and* mute." Robert shook his head, causing the drop of rain on his hooked nose to fall. "And likely mindless from the fire. You have the luck."

"'Twasn't luck that brought her to my doorstep." Alex didn't explain further. Despite what her father had done, there was no cause to invite malice toward her from others. He watched his cousin Elizabeth appear at the door to greet the woman. "Forsooth, I'll rid myself of her without delay."

Robert glanced at him. "You won't act on the king's suggestion?"

"No."

"'Tis well you do not," Robert said. "Taking a woman

like that to wife—God knows she would cause you no end of trouble. And your pain over Mary's death still runs deep."

Alex was silent, his hands fisting around the slippery wet reins. Abruptly, he pivoted his horse toward the open fields. "Enough. We'll check the north end for your runaway mare. But I'll wager she's returned to her stall by now." He pressed in his heels. "Fly, Neos!"

In seconds Robert's mount galloped beside his. Alex stared straight ahead and allowed the wind to whip back the hood of his cloak and the rain to slap the bitter past from his thoughts.

****

Lady Katherine Seymour followed a servant across the withdrawing room while smoothing down her travel-worn dress. After making her wait an intolerable period of time—it was already one of the clock, more than an hour after her arrival—Lord Drayton had finally summoned her. In one damp hand, she clutched her slate.

The servant gave a tentative knock on the door.

"Come," a deep voice spoke from within.

Katherine stepped into a dim, unadorned room, her startled gaze at once drawn to the striking profile of the man writing at a massive desk. She wondered that the slender white quill he held didn't snap in two within his large hand.

"Sit." Without glancing up, he flicked his free hand toward a wooden chair near his desk.

Despite his rude greeting, Katherine approached and sat, back straight and head high. She laid the slate in her lap and pulled the chalk from its holder, ready to answer his questions about her circumstances. How much information had the king given him?

She wanted no sympathy or pitying looks from this man. Only shelter and security. And to keep her pride. It was all she had left.

Pausing in his writing, he glanced at her from beneath furrowed brows. Briefly his features went slack. "You are the Lady Katherine?"

Katherine swallowed at the sudden dryness in her throat.

Blue eyes, lonely and steady and deep, engulfed her

senses, emptied her lungs, made the chalk slick in her damp hand. An odd heaviness stirred within her. Stranger still was the sudden yearning that filled her, a desire to reach out to him.

At her hesitant nod, surprise—and something else she couldn't identify—flickered in his eyes. For too long he stared at her while ink bloomed black on his paper from the tip of his quill.

Then, scowling, he returned his attention to his work.

Taken aback, Katherine glanced around the austere room, warmed by a crackling fire in the hearth. Candles atop the desk added more illumination, but heavy drapes over the windows shut out whatever light could be gleaned from the gray, rainy day outside.

While the scratch of his quill filled the room, she waited, holding herself erect, the chalk clutched in her fingers.

Where was the widower? This man's intense concentration on the bookwork signified he might be the steward, here to help with the ledgers. From the appearance of the papers piled in disarray on the desk and a nearby table, Lord Drayton needed help.

She fell to studying him, the way his dark blond hair fell in damp waves to his shoulders, the ends curling as they dried. An aquiline nose led to sensually curved lips over a strong cleft chin, on which a scar nestled within a light shadow of beard.

After a few moments, Katherine began to nibble at her lip in mounting perplexity. Did his confirmation of her identity sum up her introduction? Had she been dismissed?

She waited. He continued to write. Perhaps he wanted to complete a letter for her to read. It wouldn't be the first time someone thought she was deaf as well as mute. She leaned forward slightly to see, but his arm, which looked strong enough to toss a horse into the air, blocked her view.

At length, Katherine released a thinly disguised, impatient breath. Indignant heat rose to her cheeks and a little knot of anger balled in her stomach. He was ignoring her!

No more.

Her chalk's shrill screech could bring boisterous chatter in Whitehall's banqueting room to an abrupt halt. Now, watching him with narrowed eyes, she set it to her slate and dragged it hard across the surface.

The man's head jerked up and his shoulders hunched. Ah, now she had his attention, grimace and all. And she would keep it. With raised brows she wrote, *And you are?* She turned the slate for him to read.

A heartbeat passed. Two. Then, he locked crystal eyes with her. "I am Lord Drayton. Your guardian."

Oh, mercy. The chalk slipped through Katherine's numb fingers and dropped to the wood floor. With her defiant action, she had just compromised her chance to be sheltered, and the king would not likely attempt to help her again.

Even so, she held Lord Drayton's gaze and fought to breathe. In turn, he scrutinized her as if searching her mind for some secret she might hold.

"You are trembling," he said. "Have you a chill?"

No. Not a chill. The shiver was due to something else entirely, a restlessness that heightened all her senses. She shook her head—more in confusion over the new sensation than in answer to his question—and leaned forward to pick up her chalk.

"Wait." He reached down, fetched the chalk, and held it out.

Careful not to touch his long fingers, Katherine took it, then wiped her slate clean with an attached cloth. When she began to scribble an apology for her discourtesy, he put up a hand. The hostile distrust in his eyes made her draw back in alarm and almost drop the chalk again.

"No games. I want the truth. Do you know why you're here?"

Through her bewilderment at his harsh tone, she tried to keep the chalk steady in her trembling fingers. *The king wished to provide for me,* she wrote.

The slight narrowing of his eyes indicated his disbelief. "I will make myself clear only once, Lady Katherine. Had I refused the king's suggestion to send you here, he would not look favorably upon me. That is the sole reason you are in my home." He leaned toward her and his voice slowed, but rose in volume. "Do you understand what I am saying?"

She drew back from him, frowning. *Of course*, she wrote. *I am not an idiot. Nor deaf*. She tapped an index finger on the last word for emphasis, wondering if Lord Drayton was aware of how stridently his voice had echoed in the bare-walled room.

Indeed, she would go deaf if he kept that up.

Contemplation passed over his features as he read. Then, his face became impassive, his voice low and cold. He stood. "Your opinion of yourself is of no concern to me."

Katherine couldn't voice her sharp retort regarding his disgraceful conduct, and writing it would diffuse her point into a petty, time-consuming reaction. Her head felt suddenly heavy and she lowered it, trying to will away the familiar weary despair. His statement summed up her existence since the fire that had raged through London and consumed everything dear to her, including her voice. No one cared to ask what she wanted. None of her opinions mattered.

She became aware that Lord Drayton's snug rust-colored breeches, buttoned up his thighs, were directly in her line of vision. No fashionable loose petticoat breeches hid the powerful lines of his legs. In the midst of her stunned hurt at his discourtesy, Katherine felt heat blaze her cheeks.

Rising to her feet, she found her eyes level with his broad chest. She tilted back her head and ran her gaze to his face.

The man was a castle unto himself: tall, formidable, all hard lines and impenetrable fortitude. No one, to her memory, seemed packed with more strength. What was such a man doing out here in the countryside? He should be in London, where the women of the Court would drink him up like fine Madeira wine.

The rapid cadence of his pulse revealed itself on his neck above the unlaced collar of his white linen shirt. Warmth emanated from his body. Breathing him in, Katherine found his clean, masculine scent pleasing. Stirring.

She couldn't pardon his insulting reception, however, and returned his scowl with a glare.

"I sympathize with your loss," he said. "You've suffered a great deal." He turned, and with a grace that belied his size, walked to the door. "Whatever the past, you are safe in my home, and may make yourself comfortable while you're here. I will find you a suitable husband who will treat you well. But try to understand, my lady, that as soon as I make the arrangements, you will leave." He opened the door.

It seemed he would waste no time in passing her off to someone else. Struggling for composure, Katherine remained rigid by her chair and waited for him to speak further.

Instead, he left the door open, returned to his desk, sat and picked up his quill.

His dismissal came without words.

****

God's nails!

When the door clicked shut behind her, Alex dropped his sweat-dampened quill, slumped back in his chair, and let out a ragged breath.

Sweet heaven, she was beautiful.

Golden-brown hair. Small hands that gripped her slate against her slender body. A ramrod posture and proud tilt of her chin suggesting inner strength, which she had needed after losing everything in the fire.

Could she ever regain her voice? Had anyone tried to help her?

Her brown eyes, ablaze with vitality, had awakened something deep within him and stirred his heart into an unwelcome gallop. But those eyes revealed nothing about the knowledge of her circumstances.

Did she not know why she was here? Someone had to have informed her that Lady Castlemaine, the king's jealous mistress, had plotted Katherine's ruin upon discovery of Lord Seymour's treason.

A pox on that. Alex wanted nothing to do with the scheme. Cromwell's men had destroyed his family, but that was years ago and had nothing to do with these circumstances. He had no wish to ravage a dead spy's daughter in the name of retribution. The very thought sickened him.

The door opened a crack. "My lord?"

Alex straightened in his chair, cleared his throat, and slid a ledger toward him. "I'm working, Sam."

Ignoring the obvious hint, his old manservant entered and sent a cursory grimace toward the unruly papers piled on Alex's desk. "Well?"

"She's no softheaded mouse."

"I took notice." Sam leaned his gnarled hands on the back of the chair that Katherine had vacated. "What does she know?"

Alex sighed and rubbed the back of his neck. "She said—wrote—the king sent her here to provide her a home. She's lying."

"To protect herself, mayhap," Sam said. "She doesn't know you. But Lady Elizabeth might discover something if she befriends her."

Alex shook his head. "I've said nothing of Katherine's father's treachery. I just want her out of here."

Sam straightened. "'Tis almost mealtime. Shall I see to your dining clothes?"

"Don't bother. I'll dine alone in the withdrawing room off my bedchamber."

"Again? Even though you have a guest?"

Alex wouldn't have tolerated the servant's bold question from any other, but he owed his life to Samuel Peele. Even so, he bristled. "She's no guest. And tomorrow's meal with the Cookes will garner enough socializing to last me through the rest of April." He opened the ledger to another error-filled page, and muttered an oath. "Damnable steward. Should have killed him myself." He heard the door shut as Sam departed, and paused in dipping his quill. His gaze slid to the chair Katherine had occupied.

Despite his attempt to remain unresponsive when she had leaned down to pick up the chalk, Alex had felt his face grow heated with the glimpse she unwittingly gave him of the creamy tops of her breasts. He'd no choice but to glare at her. It was the only way to hide his desire. And he would desire no one, least of all the daughter of a spy.

Hadn't he promised himself? Had he not shut away his heart, created an iron wall around it to stave off the agony of loving a woman who seemed to hate him so much she had taken her own life?

Impatiently he raised his fist and pounded once on his desk, sending his inkbottle into a drunken spiral that nearly spilled its black contents onto a stack of papers nearby.

He would never lose sight of the pact he had made with himself the night his insane wife died.

With grim finality, he shut away Katherine's image from his mind. He grasped his quill, hunched over his ledger, and returned to his task.

Chapter Two

Katherine willed her heart to slow its pattering after meeting the handsome but brusque Lord Drayton. How clear he had been in his declaration that he only sheltered her out of obligation and would be rid of her as soon as he could. The rogue. She tried to summon anger to replace her despondency, but to no avail.

This vast main Hall she followed the servant through made her feel small and insignificant. Her steps echoed on the dark planked floor beneath a high arched ceiling with wooden beams that, in her current humor, appeared as though they might plunge and slice her to pieces.

She looked to her left and paused in dismay at the disjointed images of herself in a grouping of small mirrors over an ornately carved table. Like the fragmented reflections, she was here but not here, a specter with no refuge to call home. She was trivial, irrelevant, an unwanted object tossed about.

Here...yet not here. A surreal emptiness overcame her and, suddenly light-headed, she staggered to one of two nearby chairs flanking an old wooden chest.

Through her haze she saw a figure limp toward her, seemingly a ghost in pale gray.

"Lady Katherine...."

Katherine forced herself to focus on the woman standing before her—Elizabeth Hopkins, Lord Drayton's cousin, whom she'd met upon her arrival. A frown creased Elizabeth's delicate brow, and she gazed down at Katherine with worried gray eyes.

Katherine stood and forced herself to smile.

"Will you not join us in the parlor for refreshments?" Elizabeth asked.

Katherine glanced back through the Hall to the door that led to his study. Who else would be in the parlor? Not Lord Drayton, she hoped.

She would rather be shown to her own bedchamber where she could at least pretend she belonged. Instead, she nodded her consent.

Elizabeth dismissed the servant and led the way through the Hall. Her left hip lifted and twisted to the right with each slow, awkward step.

The vast, echoing Hall seemed to fit the aloof temperament of its owner.

Stretching from the massive front door to the back corridor, the Hall must be situated at the center of the old fortress. Between enormous tapestries the stone walls peered, dark and cold.

Katherine and Elizabeth entered a parlor as dim as Lord Drayton's study. A fire burning in the hearth threw vague, dancing shadows on dark drapes that completely masked the tall windows Katherine had seen from the carriage.

A woman with light yellow hair sat on one of the couches. For just an instant, Katherine caught a glimpse of pursed lips and narrowed eyes before the woman smiled. But it could have been the play of light on her face.

Elizabeth led Katherine to a chair, but Katherine hesitated with her attention drawn to the drapes, willing them to open.

Why on earth did he close off the daylight? Had the king informed him of her affliction with closed, dark spaces since her entrapment in the fire? Surely Lord Drayton wouldn't be so cruel as to play on her fear. Her chest tightening, she took a seat.

"Lady Katherine Seymour, may I present our neighbor, Mistress Agnes Cooke," Elizabeth said. She anchored both hands on the chair arms and sank onto the seat.

"More than just a neighbor I would hope, Lizzy," Agnes replied, and arched blond brows.

"Yes...forgive me. Agnes is also my friend." Elizabeth lowered her eyes and plucked at her dress.

"To you *and* to Alexander," Agnes said.

Katherine forced herself to maintain a pleasant expression. Although Agnes held a sweet smile, her words denoted possessiveness. She must be betrothed to Lord

Drayton. Why else would she refer to him in such an informal manner?

Katherine's gaze again slid to the heavy drapes. Feeling smothered in the dimness, she took a deep breath to calm herself, and this brought on the familiar long, drawn-out cough that had assailed her since the fire. Swallowing hard and relaxing her shoulders, she forced herself to concentrate on the two women before her.

"My family will dine here tomorrow," Agnes announced after a moment.

Elizabeth's hand stilled with her cup halfway to her lips. Her voice barely carried. "Yes, I am aware of this."

"Edward is quite smitten with you, Lizzy," Agnes said.

A blush crept up Elizabeth's cheeks. "He is nice enough." Her cup clattered a little as she set it onto its matching saucer.

Agnes tapped a finger to her lips. "I do hope his feelings don't change upon meeting Lady Katherine."

Elizabeth shifted in her seat. "That would be Edward's choice, of—of course."

Katherine frowned. Who was Edward? And what was Agnes implying?

Agnes again turned toward Katherine, her brows creased in apparent compassion. "Lizzy has informed me you lost your voice in the fire. What a pity. Were the situation different, you could tell us of your interest in the curtains."

Elizabeth looked up quickly. "Agnes, please."

Rude woman. Katherine's body tensed, but she lifted her chalk to explain. Perhaps Elizabeth could ask a servant to open them.

Agnes waved a dismissive hand. "No need. I have always found reading an unnecessary burden for a *true* lady."

Katherine returned her slate to her lap and lowered her head to hide her smirk. True lady, indeed.

At a soft knock on the door, Elizabeth, with clear relief in her voice, bade entry.

A servant entered and curtsied. "Lady Katherine's things have been taken to her room. She has no maid."

Elizabeth turned to Katherine with wide eyes. "No

maid? Certainly you did not make this trip alone!"

Embarrassment heated Katherine's face as she wrote, *No, borrowed servant. She returned to London.* Ellis Potts, her ex-betrothed, had spared all expenses and not bothered to procure a maid for her when he sent her away.

Elizabeth read the words aloud, slowly.

"Well, that is quite odd," Agnes said with a laugh. "I suppose you'll have to curl your own hair and lace your own shoes. Do your dresses button in the front? Gads, I cannot imagine doing anything without my maid, can you, Lizzy?"

"You are in need of a lady's maid," Elizabeth said, her sudden decisiveness surprising after her former hesitation. "I'll accompany you to your bedchamber and try to remedy this. If you'll pardon me, Agnes, I will return shortly."

Katherine rose on stiff legs. The two-day jostling of the coach during her journey from London to Chiswick had taken its toll on her body, and a short rest would surely quell her weariness. Perhaps later she could request a warm bath.

Despite Agnes's friendly smile, Katherine shivered with a wary chill as she passed.

The servant walked ahead of them back through the Hall toward the stairs, her pace slow to accommodate Elizabeth's limp.

Katherine imagined Lord Drayton at his desk. The memory of his broad shoulders and the heat of his powerful masculinity even now triggered something unbidden deep within her.

She scoffed at herself. How shameful and improper that her body should respond in this way to a man who resented her presence.

Her reaction, she knew, stemmed from the profound forlornness she'd seen in his eyes despite his terse manner. Perhaps the widower had loved his wife and missed her very much.

The servant led them up the wide staircase and then down an oak-paneled passageway that stretched in both directions, interspersed with an occasional bench or table. Closed doors stood like shadowy sentinels as the women passed by them.

At the end of the corridor, the servant turned right and headed down another. It seemed strange that Katherine's bedchamber would be so far from the main stairs. Perhaps the doors they passed opened to rooms for overnight guests. Lord Drayton must entertain often.

The thought did not cheer Katherine, whose former lively banter with the other courtiers at Whitehall Palace had been reduced to listening to the talk around her. By the time she added her comments to a conversation on her slate, the subject had moved on.

"Your room looks out at the front," Elizabeth said, panting slightly with her uneven steps. "I do hope you'll enjoy it."

Ahead of them, the maid's shoulders tensed. She stopped at the end of the passage and opened a door.

The chamber was spacious, but the gloom made it difficult to see many details. Katherine rolled her eyes in frustration. Was every window in this home darkened with heavy curtains? What was so wrong with letting in some light?

Without delay, she set her slate on the writing table near the door, crossed over to the window, and grasped the drapes. The metal loops skating across the rod sent a relishing ring throughout the room.

Although gentle rain still fell, the grim daylight added a measure of brightness to the room. Katherine hadn't realized just how tense she had become in this gloomy fortress until relief washed over her. She turned with a smile, and then stared in dismay at the monotony before her.

Gray tester around the bedposts. Mud-gray quarterpane. She glanced at the rug. More gray. And surrounding her, plain walls with no hint of decoration save for a thin border of pale yellow flowers that seemed to cry out in desperate cheer.

Katherine winced at the dreary sight. Had a blind person decorated the room?

"Lady—Lady Katherine," Elizabeth stammered from the doorway. She stood wide-eyed, her white hands pressed to her lips.

Unasked, the servant ran to the window. The metal

loops clanged as she jerked the drapes closed.

"You must never open them," Elizabeth choked out in a whisper. "Never!"

Katherine's heart lurched at Elizabeth's frightened expression. What was she afraid of? Or whom? Nervously, she retrieved her slate and wrote, *What is wrong?*

"There are reasons, but I am forbidden to discuss them." Tension filled Elizabeth's voice.

Exasperation trickled through Katherine's unease. All families had their secrets. But to keep the drapes closed at all times? What the devil was going on?

"Now, we will discuss acquiring a lady's maid for you." Elizabeth raised her chin and turned to the servant, but her voice still trembled. "Millie, you were Lady Drayton's personal maid, were you not?"

Millie nodded. "Yes, m'lady, until the melancholy—" She gasped and stepped back. "Forgive me. I meant no offense."

Elizabeth's hand fluttered to her throat. "Take heed of what you say, Millie."

"Yes, m'lady." Millie sounded close to tears.

Katherine's fervent curiosity had flared. She wished to know more of Lord Drayton and his late wife, and Millie was her best hope.

"Well then," Elizabeth said, her voice again hesitant, "I will leave Millie with you and return to Lady Agnes. We eat a light meal at five of the clock."

After Elizabeth left, Millie removed and shook out Katherine's dresses one by one from her large trunk and placed them on her bed. Katherine had brought none of her black mourning dresses from London. She wanted to forget the past—the fire, her family's deaths, and the callous man she foolishly thought had loved her.

"So beautiful," Millie murmured, holding up a crimson satin gown with gold lace over its pink frilly underskirt. "Lady Drayton had a new dress made every now and then, but none were as fine-lookin' as these."

Katherine nodded her thanks at the compliment and carried her hairdressing case to the table.

"She was never happy. But she wasn't at fault."

Surprised, Katherine turned toward Millie, who stood holding a dress of sapphire silk.

The maid's gaze roamed the room. "So sad, these colors. This was her room."

Lord Drayton made his wife sleep in this drab bedchamber? What was wrong with him? Shaking her head in disgust, Katherine removed her curling iron and brush from the small case.

Millie continued, albeit in a faltering voice. "Lord Drayton never wanted to hear her name again after she died. And Lady Elizabeth won't talk about her because she fears him so. He's not the same as he used to be." The maid removed the last dress and set it on the bed, where it settled with a rustling sigh of silver lace and turquoise satin. She looked toward Katherine, but did not meet her eyes. "The quarrels between my Lord and Lady Drayton...loud and fierce they were. My lord got to be as broodin' and angry as a bull pawin' the ground. And over the years, every time Lady Drayton's babe died in her womb, she blamed him."

Katherine dropped the pearl hairpiece she had been holding, and stared at the maid.

"Just her talk, mind ye," Millie said with a shrug. "Each time she got with child—four times it was—the babe would die. She had a wanderin' womb, y'see."

Katherine had heard about this occurrence, when a mother's womb rose to her head and caused mental fits of hysteria. Still, she couldn't shake the idea that perhaps Lady Drayton had been in some kind of danger. Morbid curiosity riveted her attention to the maid's conspiratorial whisper.

"And then, one night after she started screamin' he was tryin' to kill her...she fell."

Katherine followed the maid's pointed gaze to the window. She touched a hand to her throat and tried to swallow the sudden dryness that had settled there.

Dear God. Had Lord Drayton pushed his wife from the window?

Millie sighed and closed the trunk lid with an echoing bang. "Take care, m'lady. Ye've come into only sorrow here at Drayton Castle."

Chapter Three

"Bloody hell!" Alex shoved around the papers on his desk.

Misplaced letters needed responses. His ledgers contained inconsistent numbers. The documents he'd tossed onto the nearby table for later perusal were only building upon themselves like grains of sand in an hourglass.

Damn his steward, who'd pocketed much of Drayton Castle's profits before getting himself killed last month in a drunken brawl at the tavern.

Alex had only himself to blame. His inattention to household matters during Mary's sickness and the months after her death had necessitated all management of his books to the steward, and the man had taken advantage of it.

The lack of order and mistakes could be remedied over hours of careful study, but Alex had little patience for bookwork. What he wanted to do, right now, was find the missive from the king.

He already knew about Katherine's circumstances. Her father, the noble Thomas Seymour, had died in the London fire. During rebuilding last month, a trunk had been found in the cellar of his burned townhouse containing treasonous documents and gold for bribing.

Alex wasn't concerned with this information. His only reason for finding the letter was to read the king's description of Katherine. Had His Majesty mentioned anything of her astounding beauty?

She must have used those wide brown eyes and full lips to try to convince Charles not to send her here. But of course, he would have conceded to Lady Castlemaine, who governed his political affairs as she did his body.

A lying wench, was Katherine. Since Alex would see her tonight, he'd have to work hard to go along with her pretense that she knew nothing of the reason she was here. After all, she surely waited in fear for him to vent his rage on her.

He would have to settle her mind, but that meant he would have to speak to her. Alone.

With a scowl, he shot up from his chair and stormed toward the door, but paused when he heard a faint knock. It could only be Elizabeth. No one else dared bother him while he was working.

Elizabeth shrank back when he jerked opened the door. Her clear gray eyes, so like his mother's, stared up at him.

She used to have such mettle when she was younger, before the disease of rickets had twisted her back. Although she'd come to live in his house over three months ago, she still held some bizarre fear of him.

"Come in." He gestured to a brown leather chair. When she hesitated, he added gruffly, "I'm sorry if I startled you. I was already at the door when you knocked."

She hobbled into the room and sat, taking a fold of her pale yellow dress in one hand and kneading it. "Agnes awaits you in the parlor," she murmured.

Alex gave an inward groan and crossed his arms. "Has her family arrived?"

"No. I believe she—she arrived early to see you."

"I'm busy." He indicated the piles of papers on his desk. At least the mess gave him an excuse for avoidance. "Is Katherine in there with her?"

"Yes."

The question had been offhand, but Alex's feet moved toward the door as if on their own accord. "Come, then," he said, ignoring the heated ball of anticipation in his gut. "We will converse with them while we await the rest of Agnes's family. I'm sure you're looking forward to seeing Edward."

****

"Do tell me, what *is* your strange fascination with the curtains?" Agnes asked Katherine. Then, she gasped in apparent surprise and flashed a contrite smile. "Oh, yes. I forgot you cannot speak."

Katherine gritted her teeth and gave the woman a cold stare. She wanted little to do with Agnes. How could Elizabeth have befriended her? She was like a cat—

always waiting for a chance to pounce on her prey.

Now, her feline stare traveled over the sloping shoulders and full sleeves of Katherine's satin gown. "Your dress—I must say that peach color is stunning. And so very fashionable. The lace over your underskirt is exquisite. It must have cost a fortune."

It had, but she wasn't about to let Agnes know this. After the fire, Ellis had bought her a new wardrobe. Keeping the expensive garments after he broke the betrothal had been Katherine's only means of reprisal.

"How on earth did you pay for such a dress?" Agnes asked. "Have you a...friend?"

Katherine jumped to her feet, temper blazing. How *dare* she speak thus?

Voices outside the parlor doors heralded the arrival of other guests. Katherine froze, chest heaving, fighting the mounting cough-tickle in her throat. Lord Drayton might enter at any second. Since they hadn't crossed paths since their first meeting yesterday, it wouldn't do for him to see her coughing into one hand while raising the other to slap his betrothed across her white, cerused face.

"Gramercy! Alexander is coming in and I'm a mess." With a satisfied pucker of her lips, Agnes smoothed her blue dress and patted her shining curls.

Katherine dropped back into her chair and attempted unsuccessfully to control both her temper and her cough. Lord Drayton had little taste in women if he courted this one.

Seconds later, a young man dressed in bright blue petticoat breeches and matching embroidered jacket strolled into the room with Elizabeth. Following were a thin older gentleman and a short, wide woman, both of them dressed entirely in green. A stalk of celery with an artichoke, Katherine mused.

Lord Drayton entered last, tall and arresting. Indeed, a most pleasing sight.

His gaze stopped and remained on her far too long, his eyes sending a silent question she couldn't discern.

Her heart's leap had nothing to do with seeing him again, of course. He was most certainly a passionless man, full of wasted virility—even if he did emanate a primal strength that made her quiver. To regain her poise, she studied his attire.

His taste in clothes confirmed his status as a country dweller. That dark blue shirt needed more lace at the wrists. He'd bothered with neither waistcoat nor petticoat breeches, but instead wore another pair of those plain leg-hugging breeches, these the color of dead weeds.

Not one ribbon festooned him. Even his golden hair hung unbound. And in those ancient brown leather boots, he would be laughed out of Court.

Yes. He was an unruly savage, completely lacking in fashionable taste.

Had he really had something to do with his wife's demise? The rumor had to be simple servant gossip, else these perfumed vegetables wouldn't be visiting.

When at last she could tear her eyes from him, her gaze happened upon Agnes, who had brightened, cocked her head, and set a charming smile to her red lips.

"How do you do, my lord?"

A smile touched Lord Drayton's lips when he answered, "I'm well, Mistress Cooke. And you?"

"*Very* well, thank you." Agnes's predatory eyes shone with some emotion. Lust, perhaps.

There. Agnes and Lord Drayton must be, if not betrothed, in earnest courtship.

Katherine fought to relax her throat when Lord Drayton again turned his attention to her. He seemed to take in all of her with that penetrating gaze, as if she were the only other person in the room with him.

"Lady Katherine, may I present Sir Robert and Lady Sarah Cooke, and their son, Mister Edward Cooke," he said.

She gave each of his guests a polite nod. Edward's smile was friendly but cautious, whereas his parents regarded her as if she were an animal on exhibit. A silence ensued while they seemed to decide how to deal with her.

Katherine had grown used to others' awkwardness toward her lack of speech, but it didn't ease the deep pain within. She was different now, something curious to stare at—or ignore.

Again the cough threatened, and again she desperately swallowed it away.

Then, Lord Drayton stood beside her, and somehow his towering nearness calmed her. "May I present Lady Katherine Seymour. She will be staying here for a fortnight or so."

Katherine tried to maintain her smile. Only a fortnight, and then tossed to another destination. Would she ever find a home?

Alex wished to hell Edward would hurry up and ask his cousin's hand in marriage. The man's eyes did not leave Elizabeth as she seated the Cookes around the parlor after they finished their rude stares at Katherine.

Sarah Cooke settled her round self, leaned toward Katherine, and shouted, "Did you meet with much rain on your journey here?"

"She's mute and dimwitted, Madam, not deaf," said Robert as he plucked a goblet of wine from a servant's tray. "You can ask, but she won't answer."

Sarah sat back and touched her fingers to her lips as if self-conscious. Her gaze flitted to Agnes, who raised her brows and gave a bored shrug.

Alex watched Katherine's aggravated, rhythmic tap of her fingers on her slate, and wondered why anyone, including himself, had assumed she'd be daft. She seemed perfectly attuned to the activity around her. The slight smirk on her face as she examined everyone's clothing confirmed his initial suspicion of her arrogance; a product of London nobility she was. Had she been even haughtier before the fire? Was she a bit more humbled now by the new knowledge of her past?

His mind snapped to attention when she lifted the chalk to write, and he involuntarily tensed and clenched his jaw. "'Tis an annoyance to hear that sound."

Brows furrowing with indignation, she waved him off with a quick flick of her hand. Alex glared at her, but knew her reaction was justified. The slate was her only means of communication.

Beside him, Robert's angular features creased into a smile. "Your acquisition seems lively. And she's not old after all, is she?"

Alex grunted under his breath and drew a scowl. "Not old. But a burden nonetheless." No need to tell Robert how she affected him.

The statement had been meant for Robert's ears only, but Agnes caught it and giggled. "Lord Drayton, you mustn't be cruel to poor Lady Katherine. She may be a burden, as you said, but she certainly admires your drapes."

Across the room, Katherine glowered at Agnes, then turned darkened eyes, etched with hurt, on him.

Alex hid both his annoyance at Agnes and regret at his words. She had just caused him the need to apologize to Katherine.

"A highwayman lurks along the woodland path to Chiswick," Sarah said. "My maid told me she heard he attacked a lone rider last week and left him for dead."

"He's a coward," Robert said. "He hides in the woods, and only shows himself when there's one rider."

"I would be afraid to go to town without at least two footmen," Elizabeth said with a shiver.

Edward sent his easy smile toward Elizabeth. "Just stay on the main road away from the forest, and you should be fine. 'Tis what I'd do."

"That's you, Ed," Robert said. "You'd steer clear of him. Agnes now, if she were a man, she'd run the rogue down and run a sword through him before he got a chance to yelp."

Agnes flipped open her white fan and began a swift flutter, her eyes on Alex above the lacy edge. "But I am a lady, Father. Not a man."

"Must've been a mistake," Robert growled.

The usual gleam of Agnes's eyes faded. Edward, perhaps used to such talk, sent a dispassionate glance toward his father.

Alex silently acknowledged a brief empathy toward Robert's children, and then returned his attention to Katherine. Had any doctor inspected her throat? He dismissed the question. The king had no reason not to have aided Katherine as her father's traitorous trunk had only been discovered in the past month. Not only that, but she was a noblewoman formerly betrothed to a man holding the prestigious position of gentleman of the king's bedchamber. Surely even a worm like Lord Rochester would pay the best doctors in London to heal her before he grew tired of waiting and shook her from his pudgy, bejeweled hands.

The best doctors. And in London, too. Before he could crush it, a ghost of an idea took shape in Alex's mind.

"And the dog leaps, I tell you, leaps as high as my head to catch the dried sheep dung the groomsman's children throw," Edward was telling them, his eyes now bright with amazement. "I watched it myself this morning."

"Pish, Ed," Robert said, holding out his goblet for a servant to refill. "You spend too much time on your poems and herb potions to discipline the workers. They should be putting the shit in bags instead of throwing it around. Those brats need a stick to their backs."

"Well," Edward finished, his smile fading, "I thought it rather funny."

Curious, Alex watched Katherine stiffen over Robert's comment. Betrothed to a man like the earl, and doubtless a regular at Court, she should be used to such vulgar talk.

A servant announced the meal. Alex rose without further thought and performed his customary duties whenever the Cookes came to dinner. He approached Agnes, who rose regally and placed her hand on his offered forearm.

Robert and Sarah would take their places behind himself and Agnes, followed by Edward and Elizabeth.

But now there was Katherine to consider. She rose and stood with clasped hands. Although she held her head high, from the look on her face, Alex knew she fought humiliation over having no escort.

Blast it all. He couldn't make her walk alone to the dining room. And she would be a quiet diversion from Agnes's aimless chatter. "Excuse me, Agnes," he said pleasantly, and extracted her hand from his arm while noting the slight narrowing of her eyes. Approaching Katherine, he asked, "May I also escort you to dinner, my lady?"

She regarded him doubtfully and must have considered his act one of forced politeness, but walked with him toward the parlor door.

A delicate lavender scent wafted from her smooth, soft looking skin. Deep warmth from her hand on his arm caused a wild thump of his heart. What was she doing to him?

With effort, he raised his other arm so Agnes could lay her hand on it. That arm remained cool.

How strange.

As they left the parlor, Alex had an overwhelming urge to stop and grasp Katherine's entire body against his to see just how warm the rest of her felt. As quickly as he repressed the thought, perspiration beaded his forehead. He would draw attention to his reaction if he released either woman's arm to wipe it off.

What the devil was wrong with him?

Chapter Four

Katherine carried her slate curled in her left arm, determined to use it despite Lord Drayton's admonishment. He had no idea of the painful agony she'd endured in the sudden loss of her voice. Although the slate was a poor substitute, it was her lifeline in expression.

While those walking behind them spoke quietly among themselves, Agnes's tongue ran on wheels, maintaining a strident prattle that echoed through the Hall. Although Lord Drayton responded in polite tones, he didn't elaborate on her words. Once, he glanced down at Katherine, who had just noticed a sheen of moisture on his forehead.

The moment Agnes stopped talking long enough to take a breath, he said quietly, "Lady Katherine, I apologize for my comment about your being a burden. I know you cannot help your circumstances."

Agnes gave an annoyed click of her tongue.

Lord Drayton continued, his tone a curious mixture of hope and reluctance. "Doctors examined your throat, did they not?"

Katherine nodded. What did Lord Drayton care about her throat?

"'Tis odd they couldn't diagnose the cause of your silence."

What was odd was the heat that sizzled from his forearm. If they didn't reach the table soon, her hand would catch fire. Once, his elbow—unintentionally, she was sure—grazed the side of her breast as they walked. A shiver rippled through her. She swallowed against the ridiculous drumming of her heart and struggled to maintain even breaths.

"You have a competitive spirit, Agnes," Lord Drayton said, and Katherine's attention was immediately drawn to his baritone voice as quickly as it had dismissed Agnes's high-pitched tone. "Edward and Elizabeth won the last game of cribbage. We shall play tonight, if you wish. Or, I could read from *Paradise Lost*, the book I received the other day."

Lord Drayton read books the likes of *Paradise Lost*?

To her chagrin, he caught her amused reaction. "Even country dwellers such as I enjoy reading," he said with a smile that complemented the unexpected twinkle in his eyes.

Then, Agnes resumed her blathering, and Katherine shut her out.

They passed a long table that would easily seat twenty-five people. Directly beyond, they turned left and entered a dining room that held a round oak table surrounded by red-cushioned chairs, their backs carved in intricate patterns. Although the windows in here were also draped, the late afternoon sun stole around the edges of the cloth, and a large iron candelabrum lit the room.

The rising steam from a platter of savory roasted meat on the sideboard was no rival against the smolder of Katherine's hand on Lord Drayton's arm.

Alex's arm grew cold after Katherine removed her hand to stand behind her chair for prayer. Afterwards he helped Elizabeth with the carving, serving his guests the choice pieces of meat. When he sat, he tried to focus on what Agnes was saying, but found himself drawn to the silent messages Katherine sent his way.

She was forming opinions of him, of his house, and had stolen glances at him during their walk to the dining room. For some foolish reason, Alex cared about what she thought.

"Even so, I do hope Lord and Lady Allerton's Ball in June will be well-attended by London gentry," Agnes was saying. "Will you be going, Lord Drayton?"

"Perhaps," he replied.

How did a mute woman keep up with conversation at a social gathering? She'd have to be constantly writing with that squeaky chalk, and the discussion would slow to a crawl in order to include her. How exasperating for all.

They ate and talked, and Katherine ate and listened. She reacted to the topic at hand with some facial gesture—raised brow, nod, charming smile. Several times she leaned forward or lifted her hand as if to respond. Frustration creased her brow during those moments. Alex mused once again on his unorthodox idea, one that could anger the king and his Anglican physicians.

"I'd like to discuss the London fire with her if she's not too softheaded," Robert said to Alex.

"Then do so," Alex replied with a touch of irritation.

Katherine sent an alert, expectant look Robert's way, as if she were ready and able to discuss the fire. However, Robert spoke to everyone but her. Alex's opinion of his blunt neighbor began to sour.

"I heard the strong east wind made the flames jump houses like a leaping horse," Robert said. "'Tis amazing so many buildings were lost in just a few days."

"And all those churches," Edward put in. He turned to Katherine, and Alex was glad to see it. "Is the fire how you lost your voice? I do hope you can understand my words."

Of course she understood, Alex thought, watching her lift the slate from her lap. She would have plenty to say about the tragedy that had changed her life, especially now that her father's treason had been exposed.

Alex couldn't hide his frown thinking she knew all along about it. At that moment, their eyes met. Her face reflecting uneasy annoyance, she lowered the slate.

Gadzoks. He was a toad, no better than Robert.

Sarah, cutting her meat, said quietly, "Edward, perhaps 'tis best not to speak to the simpleton. You'll only confuse her."

Katherine bent her head. Her hand trembled as she took a knife and spread honeyed butter on her bread. She blinked as if fighting tears.

Something hot and pulsing and fiercely protective within Alex roared to life and kicked him hard in his gut.

"Try her, Edward," he said, keeping his voice pleasant but yearning to shout. "I think you'll find her quite astute. And I'll provide you with pen and ink, Lady Katherine." He gave the orders to a servant, wondering why he hadn't thought of the simple solution already.

She peered at him—as did Agnes beside her—clearly gauging his intent. Katherine's moist brown eyes indicated disbelief, whereas Agnes's green ones gleamed with suspicion.

"Lady Cooke," murmured Elizabeth to her plate, "I doubt she is a simpleton. She cannot speak, 'tis all."

Surprised, Alex turned his attention to his timid cousin.

"Well then, that's that," said Edward with a cheerful pat on Elizabeth's hand.

"My apologies, Lady Katherine," said Sarah, her angry eyes on Robert. "My husband evidently misunderstood his information when he told me you were dead from the neck up." She thrust a forkful of beef into her mouth and scraped the pewter prong between her front teeth as she drew it out.

Alex winced. Sarah only made that sound with her fork when she was upset with Robert, which was quite often. More than once, their quarrels at his table had extended to the parlor after the meal and into their carriage when they left. It was one more reason to never take another wife.

"I did not misunderstand," Robert said in clipped tones. "We assumed the fire had taken her mind as well as her voice."

"Then you must learn your facts before you cause my embarrassment and Lady Katherine's discomfort," Sarah shot back. Bits of brown food flew from her lips and added visual impact to her heated words.

Katherine's round-eyed gaze flew from Robert to Sarah.

"'Tis true we were mistaken," Alex said through the tight muscles clenching his jaw. "The king informed me only of her entrapment in the fire and her father's death, as well as her broken engagement to the Earl of Rochester. We assumed the rest, as Robert has said."

No longer looking as if tears threatened, Katherine sipped her wine and regarded him, as he did her. How would her voice sound? Low and musical, he mused. Full of elegance as was her walk, yet with a vibrancy like the glossy curls that graced her shoulders.

"I did assume the rest," Robert muttered. "How was I supposed to know she can think? Why in damnation would anyone care—"

"Fie, Robert, do hush!" Sarah said. "Your words tonight are deplorable."

"Silence, woman!" Robert snapped. "Would that *your* voice could—"

"Enough." Alex's voice, low but hard, silenced the Cookes. There would be no games or reading after the meal. Inviting his nearest neighbors to dinner so Katherine could meet them had been a terrible mistake.

Robert turned to Alex with a pained, set smile. "We apologize, Drayton."

Alex nodded, resisting the urge to order them all to leave right now. "We all misunderstood Lady Katherine's difficulty."

As if relieved, Katherine closed her eyes.

Robert tipped up his wine goblet and drank, and then wiped his mouth with the back of his hand. "I suppose it will be harder now to convince the king as to why you didn't pursue his suggestion."

Katherine's eyes flew open.

Agnes's sharp eyes speared her father. "I'm certain Lord Drayton will succeed."

Puzzlement filled Katherine's features. She arched her brows at Alex, clearly expecting an explanation.

"'Tis not important," Alex said to her, and watched her eyes narrow.

She raised her slate to the table.

"'Twas nothing, Lady Katherine." Damn Robert! The man couldn't keep a straight head when he drank. And it was too late now to tell him the king's suggestion of marriage was a ruse. He'd built the lie to avoid telling Robert the real reason she was here, that her father had been Cromwell's spy.

As she neared her chalk toward the surface, Alex felt his throat constrict. He did not need further association with this woman. "'Twas only a suggestion. I shall discuss it with you in private."

Elizabeth said, "Shall we return to the parlor for—"

Katherine slammed chalk to slate. Each swift, screeching stroke of letters drove needled pain into Alex's ears. Then, she swung the slate around. *You will tell me now.*

Alex swore under his breath and slapped a hand on the table. "Fine. Anything to stop that sound. The king suggested I take you to wife."

Katherine's jaw dropped. Her slate clattered to the table. She stared at him in wide-eyed shock, and shook her head.

"You needn't concern yourself, however," Alex continued. Why did she grimace so? "As we discussed yesterday, I will—"

Katherine rose, her back stiff and straight.

"I did not excuse you," Alex said.

The command gave her pause, but only for a moment. She raised her chin and arched a haughty brow at him before turning heel and sailing out of the room.

Alex maintained a vigilantly stern countenance. He should be satisfied she objected to the marriage suggestion. Instead, a band of iron seemed to tighten around his neck and a strange, sinking distress over her reaction weighted his heart.

Did she, too, think him the fiend that his wife had?

Agnes lay a hand over her deep cleavage. "I am shocked at her willful behavior, my lord," she gasped. "*I* would never think to do such a thing."

Alex dragged his gaze from the empty doorway to Agnes. To his knowledge, she had never raised debate over anything he said, but was drearily agreeable with him. "I'm sure you wouldn't." He forced a smile that felt like a grimace, and Agnes cocked her head in that annoying manner that reminded him of a bird listening for a worm in the ground.

Robert dipped his fingers into the small bowl of water set before him and then wiped them dry on the tablecloth. "I'd say a beating is in order for that vixen."

Alex turned to Robert and held no check on his displeasure. "I'd say you will not give your opinion of how to handle a willful woman in my household."

"I'd offer to do the job myself, but I know you'll put her in her place." Robert leaned back in his chair and lifted his cup to his host.

Alex stood to lead his guests into the adjoining withdrawing room for dessert. He fervently wanted everyone gone.

Elizabeth caught up with him at the door. "What will you do, Alex?" she whispered, her eyes bright with worry.

Alex paused with one hand on the doorframe. What would he do? What he'd like to do. Catch Katherine before she got to the stairs, swing her hard toward him, and grasp her head in his hands. Taste her luscious mouth. Run his hands down her damnably sensual body.

His hand on the doorframe clenched. "'Tis not your concern, Elizabeth," he said, wanting to drive his fist to his forehead and pound some sense into himself. "She will soon learn I have control over her and will demonstrate it fully if need be."

"You don't mean—"

"I will do what is fitting to Lady Katherine Seymour," Alex said. "And since she cannot speak, I will not have to listen to her futile protests."

****

"M'lady, do ye require help—"

Katherine slammed the door, leaving Millie standing in the corridor. Yanking out hairpins and tossing them onto her dressing table, she began a rapid pace across the room and back.

She didn't know at whom she was angrier—King Charles, Lord Drayton, or Sir Cooke. Charles would not care for a complaint after so generously finding her a guardian, yet she felt compelled to pen him a letter anyway and remind him of her father's many years of service during His Majesty's exile. Out of deference to her father, the king should have told her of his suggestion. Instead, she had to hear about it at the dinner table in front of Lord Drayton's guests.

She shook out her hair until it fell loosely down her back, then strode to the window and flung aside the curtains. She would marry Lord Drayton when hens made holy water! Thank heaven he agreed with her way of thinking.

He was just as much to blame. Had he only told her during their first meeting, she would have tolerated the unpleasant duration of the meal. As it was, now he knew her forced silence had done nothing to dampen her tendency to speak her mind. He would have good reason now to remove her from his house at once.

She should apologize to him for leaving his table. The idea, however, made her stomach twist into disagreeable knots. No matter what else she'd lost, she must keep some semblance of pride.

She glanced behind her at her closed bedchamber door and then opened the window. Breaking the silly rule would no doubt cause another flurry of alarm from Elizabeth, but Katherine didn't care. The breeze felt good, and it dried her unbidden tears.

Lord Drayton had been so quick to discount the king's suggestion, telling her it meant nothing. *She* meant nothing.

If only she knew what her future held.

She leaned out and gazed at the pebbled carriage drive, imagining his big hands grasping his wife, shoving her out, and watching her body fall.

A sharp rap came at her bedchamber door, and, with a shiver, she jerked the window closed.

Millie curtsied when Katherine opened the door, and the maid's round eyes were wide. "M'lady, Lord Drayton is finished with his meal and wants ye to come to his study."

He would rebuke her now. Or banish her from his house. Perhaps both. Sudden trepidation made her feet refuse to move. Where would she go?

"He said at once, m'lady. I'm sorry." Millie's eyes lowered.

Gripping her slate in her trembling hands, Katherine followed the maid downstairs.

Chapter Five

Lord Drayton's fierce expression and harsh tone made Katherine, legs shaking and arms hugging the slate to her chest, unable to respond to his words with even a simple nod. All coherent thought now centered on Millie's words of his vicious quarrels with his wife.

He stood in the middle of his study, arms akimbo and feet wide apart. "The Cookes are in the parlor, so I shall not keep them waiting. Should you dine at my table again, you will wait to be excused before leaving. Your abrupt departure, regardless of the cause, was unpardonable."

Was he finished? Would he punish her?

He followed her furtive glance to the thick rod hanging on the wall to his right. To her utter surprise, the hard set of his lips relaxed into wry amusement.

"You could never do anything to warrant that," he said. "'Tis dusty from disuse."

Relieved, Katherine wetted her dry lips. Nonetheless, she remained stiff and still in front of his study door until an itch in her throat made her turn and spend the next moment coughing into her hand.

"Are you ill?" he asked when she at last straightened and moved her loose hair back from her face. "Should I send for a doctor?" His hands, loosely clenched, had dropped to his sides.

She lifted her slate and then studied his reaction.

"Go ahead. I understand your frustration. I could not speak for a week after my parents—" He stopped as if catching himself, and shook his head. "Go on, answer me. Do you wish for a doctor or not?"

Although his voice had once again become firm, his eyes held a searching quality.

She wrote, keeping her strokes light to minimize the chalk's squeak. *Doctors are useless. I have coughed since the London fire.*

"Ah. Well." He seemed almost disappointed. "I won't send for one, then. Have you tried lozenges?"

She nodded. Why did he care?

"Edward Cooke knows his herbs. Perhaps he could suggest something."

Perhaps. Katherine nodded once more, watching the play of candlelight on the bristles of his jaw. How would they feel against her neck?

"Very well. I'll ask him." Lord Drayton once again crossed his arms, took a breath, and leveled his chin. "And there is one more thing I wish to make clear, Lady Katherine. 'Tis only a ruse that the king suggested we marry. If he truly had, I would have taken you to wife yesterday—out of loyalty to him." He turned away and lifted the single candle from his desk. With his back to her he added, "Forsooth, I saw by your reaction in the dining room that you are as against the idea as I."

Katherine's insides took an odd tumble at his declaration. When he again faced her, however, she raised her chin and arched one brow in question. Why had he lied to the Cookes? She didn't want to look away from him to write the question, however. There was an intensity in his eyes that stilled her.

Lord Drayton's mouth opened, then closed and tightened. As he walked toward her holding the candle, the room shrank behind him in the darkness.

Since he hadn't dismissed her, Katherine did not move.

He stopped and scrutinized her, his features flickering in the candlelight. "Must you always tremble like this? I don't wish to frighten you. Whatever the past, you may be assured of your safety."

There it was again, his reference to the past. She hadn't met him before now, had she? Insulted him during a party at Whitehall? Perhaps Ellis had done something.

No. She'd never seen Lord Drayton before. She would have remembered his height, the span of his considerable shoulders, those blue eyes, that jagged scar on his jaw. Her overwhelming draw toward him.

"Would that you could speak," he said softly. "We would have much to discuss."

Indeed they would. She'd question his paradox of behaviors toward her, protecting her from others while maintaining a simmering animosity. She took in a slow breath then, and caught the clean masculine scent of him, warm citrus and spice.

At once, everything about him stood out in more vivid detail than a single candle could possibly provide. Katherine heard his intake of breath with clarity, felt the air around them crackle.

His eyes darkened as they drifted to her lips. He stood so very near.

The sleeve of his linen shirt rasped as he moved his hand toward her waist. His tongue wetted his lips, and Katherine feared her heart would burst from her chest.

An odd, aching warmth stole into the most private part of her.

Now he would take her in his arms and kiss her. Baffled at the thought, she knew she would let him. She closed her eyes.

His hand brushed her waist. She heard a click at her side, and her dazed mind registered it as a latch.

"You're blocking the door."

Her eyes opened. His tone, impassive and flat, matched the expression on his face. Gads! She was a fool to think Lord Drayton could feel any emotion.

The man had a heart forged from iron.

****

In her bedchamber once more, Katherine allowed Millie to help her change into her nightclothes, and then dismissed her with a wave. She walked to the window and once again opened it to let in the breeze. Below her, the Cookes made their noisy way to their carriage. Sir Cooke stumbled and cursed, and Lady Cooke fussed at him. Edward seemed unperturbed.

Agnes glanced up. Her head angled to the side as she stared at Katherine as if contemplating something. To be polite, Katherine waved, and after a moment, Agnes returned the gesture.

Katherine turned away from the window and then crossed the room to sink into the chair at her writing desk.

Lord Drayton provoked a swirling cauldron of emotions within her that she'd never encountered in her life. She should detest him for his coldness, or fear him because of what he might have done to his wife. Instead, she couldn't help the undoubtedly lethal heat that made her breath come short and her hands damp whenever she was near him. What was behind that aloof, handsome face, and why did he affect her so?

She balled up her fists and hit her thighs in frustration, and then rubbed her legs briskly against their protesting ache. His references to their tied past mystified her. She could not fathom how they knew of each other before her arrival here yesterday afternoon.

Unable to dispel her agitation, she pulled her journal from the drawer of the writing desk and opened it to a blank page. Only here could she express her innermost thoughts.

Moments later, a ponderous creak behind her made her drop the quill with a gasp and whip her head around. Her closet door was opening. She stared, hand pressed to her chest, as if expecting someone to step through the door into her room.

Another breeze billowed in through the window, and the door creaked back toward its frame. Shaking her head at her folly, Katherine turned back to her journal and picked up the quill. Seconds later, she startled again at the creak of the closet door opening again.

This wouldn't do.

She went to the door to push it shut, but then paused. A cloth-covered furnishing the size of a small chest had been shoved far back against the wall, away from prying eyes. Strange that she hadn't noticed it before.

Inside might simply be stored linens. Or, perhaps it held a trove from the past that could tell her the story of Lord Drayton and his dead wife, or give her a reason for his contradictory disposition.

She stood, biting at her lip, trying to still her growing curiosity. It mattered not what it was, really. She could wait for Millie to uncover it because it was too far back in the closet, and she didn't want to go in there.

But—she leaned down, squinting—it wasn't a chest, but rather a painting, or a group of them. She could see the dull gleam of a carved gilt frame where the dark cloth didn't quite cover it.

She had seen no portraits on the walls. Some were hidden right here. Why?

Her breathing quickening, Katherine hurried to her bedside table and grabbed the candleholder before she could talk herself out of going in for a quick look. But when she stepped a foot in the doorway, she hesitated as anxiety battled inquisitiveness. Perspiration formed on her upper lip as the familiar fear of small spaces swept over her.

She blew out a slow breath. By the heavens, it was time to get beyond this dread that had begun during her entrapment in the fire.

Armed with light, Katherine edged into the room with her eyes riveted on the object. Four steps took her there. The floor creaked under her weight, and she sneezed and rubbed her nose at the musty smell.

She set the candleholder on the shelf in the very back, grabbed the cloth, and yanked it off.

Five paintings stood facing the back wall as if in forgotten punishment.

Quickly she hoisted the first painting with both hands and turned it around, then knelt in front of it. A chill charged down her spine.

A black-haired young woman with an ashen face and a thin, tormented smile stared at her. Her dark eyes were too wide, as if shocked at some horrible news. Yet they held no emotion.

Was this Lady Drayton? Katherine touched tentative fingers to the woman's pale painted cheek, and then withdrew her hand. Hurriedly, she stood and moved the painting to the side in order to look at the next one.

Cool air tickled the back of her neck, and a creak of hinges brought her back to her surroundings. She whipped her gaze to the door.

It was closing.

Dear God! She had left the window open.

Stomach clenching, Katherine leaped toward the door. Her toe caught the hem of her nightdress. Tumbling to her knees, palms slamming onto the wood floor, she stared through rapidly blinking eyes. Through the closing door, the dull gray tester over her bedposts flapped merrily as if bidding farewell to her with appalling, colorless hands.

A detached voice in her head, something one might mention over a cup of chocolate and biscuits, spoke of the quickly changing weather, and wasn't it just like the English springtime to fling a sprightly gust of wind at any moment?

The door clicked shut.

In the light of the flickering candles on the shelf, Katherine saw an inside handle on the door. She wetted her dry lips and staggered to her feet.

But it was too late. At once, the walls tilted and closed in around her. She stumbled backwards and struck the wall beside the paintings. The closet door skewed and shrank as it drifted away from her. She held out her hands toward it, begging it to return. The door faded to a pinpoint and disappeared.

No way out.

Bands of steel wrapped around her chest and throat, and she gasped for breath. Twisting, she slapped her hands against the rough planked wall as a cough ripped through her chest.

The memory of the fire slammed into her. In her mind she grasped the doorknob, relenting only when intense heat seared the flesh of her palm. On the other side of the door, the children's terrified wails faded to silence.

Katherine covered her face and gasped at the blistering inferno that scorched her throat.

As the memory of thick, acrid smoke engulfed her nose and mouth, she raised her hands in desperate panic and scratched wildly at the splintering wood of the closet wall.

Dragging her torn and bleeding fingertips down, she slumped to her knees. To her right a woman stared, her mouth contorted into a grimace, her dark eyes fathomless yet vacant.

With shaking hands pressed to her face, Katherine collapsed. The scream that resounded in her head only emitted in a thin breath.

All thoughts faded as her eyes closed.

Chapter Six

It had to be only the dampness of the spring weather that sent the sudden chill through Alex.

He sat huddled in an enormous armchair with his stockinged feet stretched toward the roaring fire. The heat in his large bedchamber grew, but the strange coldness within him would not let up its rigid clench.

As he lifted the mug of ale from the small round table beside him, he realized something else held him in its frigid grip. Whatever it was stretched powerful, icy fingers deep inside him and scraped at his carefully wrought, self-imposed numbness with razor-sharp claws.

Alex tensed and growled inwardly, giving a silent warning to whatever dared try to breach the fortress in which he hid his emotions.

Oh, but he had wanted so badly to lose his hands within her soft-looking, fragrant curls. And when she had closed her eyes, as if waiting for him to kiss her....

No. Katherine Seymour was a liar, the daughter of a spy, using her beauty as a means for manipulation. Tomorrow he would begin inquiries of eligible men to choose as her husband.

Alex drained his tankard of ale and slammed it down on the table. He would not touch her. He took strength in the promise he'd made to himself last year—a promise based on a series of horrid circumstances, the details of which not a soul would ever know.

A crisp rap at his door became an outlet for his frustration, and he jumped to his feet. His servant, having just pulled out the truckle bed for himself, straightened and sent a silent question to Alex.

"Just see who it is, Sam," he snapped.

"Yes, m'lord." Sam shaped his face into an annoyed expression similar to Alex's and opened the door with a yank. "Yes?"

The servant standing in the doorway looked past him to Alex, and bowed. "A messenger is here. A company of the king's soldiers is traveling this way and seeks shelter for the night. Shall I direct them to the barn when they arrive?"

"That will do," Alex said from across the room.

Sam closed the door and walked on silent feet to the blue bowl and pitcher on the washstand, where he lifted a clean towel and stood watching Alex expectantly.

"Are you telling me it's time for bed, Sam?" Alex asked. Still, he pulled off his shirt as he walked toward the washstand, gave it to Sam, and washed his face.

"You seem tired," Sam said. "Tired and quite tense."

"Something is amiss with me," Alex conceded as he took the offered towel and dried his face, "but it will pass."

"When the woman is gone?"

Alex hesitated. "Yes. When the woman is gone."

The network of stout ropes holding up the wool undermattress and its feather top mattress creaked and groaned when Alex lay down a few minutes later dressed in his long nightshirt. The large bed molded comfortably to his body, and he sighed and closed his eyes. Perhaps a night's rest would quell the strange feelings that plagued him.

His thoughts drifted for a while, and eventually settled on the image of Katherine at the table rising, her brown eyes flashing fire. But this time, Alex stood and went to her, and eased away the determined line of her beautiful mouth with his lips.

Another knock came, this time gentler yet rapid.

Alex sat up in a fog. "By the devil," he muttered.

"I have it," Sam sighed, and rose from his truckle bed.

"Wake the cooks and give the soldiers food, if that's what they want." Alex lay back down and rolled over onto his side. Vaguely, he heard Sam open the door.

"Lady Elizabeth, what ails you?"

Instantly alert at Sam's alarmed voice, Alex leaped out of bed and dashed to the door.

"Alex!" Elizabeth cried. "Lady Katherine is missing!"

Alex grabbed Elizabeth's thin shoulders. "How do you know this?"

"I—I went to bid her goodnight. She didn't answer her door. When I looked in, she wasn't there. I searched the parlor. I don't know where else she could be!"

Alex released Elizabeth, fetched his candle from his night table, and began a fast pace down the corridor with his hand in front of the flame to keep it from blowing out. Elizabeth was soon left behind, and he stopped at the stairs to wait for her. The pierced iron lantern she held by its top handle swung crazily left and right as she limped toward him. Sam, following behind her in his own shuffling gait, puffed for air.

"Slow down. Both of you!" Alex ordered. "Where is Millie?"

"She's searching the unused rooms," Elizabeth said. "She said Lady Katherine dismissed her. We thought perhaps she walked through the house and couldn't find her way back to her room. Oh, Alex, where could she be?"

She could be anywhere in this rambling fortress. Beneath the castle wound a labyrinth of passageways where one could become lost in minutes. And the ancient keep behind it was dangerous with its tumbled rocks and fallen floors. If she ventured off and hurt herself, no one would know.

Alex's heart wrenched in his chest.

He tried to keep his voice calm, yet his words sounded too rapid. "Tell Millie to alert the servants to a search. And look downstairs in the buttery. Perhaps she was hungry. She barely touched her meal."

As Elizabeth hobbled down the steps, Alex dashed down the hall toward Katherine's bedchamber, slamming open doors of the rooms near hers as he went, pausing, shouting her name.

Nothing.

His feet slowed of their own accord when he drew closer to Katherine's bedchamber. He could almost hear the nightmarish screams tearing from the room as they had on a night like this a year ago.

His mouth dry, he stopped at her door. Going in here now, at night, was much worse than it had been in broad daylight when he'd inspected the room for her arrival.

But he must find her, and he forced his legs to move. He opened the door, trudged in like a man ascending the gallows, and set his candle on the writing table next to a brown leather journal.

He envisioned Mary crouched on the floor, her wrists bruised from the ropes that had bound her to the bed. He'd hated to restrain her like this, but it was the only way. Except this time, someone had let her loose.

He drew in breath between clenched teeth as her shrill voice filled his head.

You killed them, didn't you. Didn't you! But I won't let you murder this one. Do you hear me? I hate you, Alexander! I detest you for what you did to my babes!

"No," Alex whispered, lowering his head and bringing his fists to his temples. "I would never hurt my children."

Swallowing hard, he brought himself back to the present. He ran unwilling eyes over the seemingly empty room and saw the curtain move on a current of air.

Like the gaping mouth of hell, the window was wide open.

He felt the blood drain from his face. "No. Not again. Please." His muscles seized and he ran on stiff legs to the window. It took everything he had to peer out to the darkened ground.

Soldiers of His Majesty's Guard milled about below, talking, removing gear from their horses, and ambling to the lofts in the barn.

No shouts of alarm. No blood-pooled body lay shattered on the cobbled drive or earth packed yard.

Alex sucked in forgotten breath.

Then, he looked more closely at the men. Had one of them enticed her to go outside? Would she be so foolish? He turned to race for the door. Grabbing the candle, he glanced down at the open pages of her journal. And froze.

I need to leave this place. He does not want me here. He holds something against me. Perhaps he is embarrassed to be seen with me, as was Ellis.

He will find someone to marry me, but I wish to marry someone I can love. Someone who will treat me well.

Alex stared at her words in apprehension. She had left him, at night, because of his treatment of her.

Then, his eye caught a thin yellow light along the floor. The closet. He set down the candle, dashed across the room, and whipped open the door.

There she lay near the back, crumpled on her side with her legs drawn up to her chest. With a harsh cry, Alex went to her and dropped to his knees. He lifted her hand and saw her raw and bleeding fingers. Gently he touched her warm cheek.

"My God, what happened to you?" he whispered.

To his right, he caught a glimpse of black hair. Mary stared at him from her portrait a few feet away, her pale face shimmering in the light of the flickering candles on the closet shelf. He looked into the startled vacancy of her eyes and felt the familiar hopelessness of saving her.

Gathering Katherine in his arms, he lifted and carried her toward the bed. Her face turned toward his chest and her loose hair swung over his arm. Her breasts moved softly beneath the lace of her white nightdress.

The feel of her warm, supple body through the gauzy material roused a sudden passion and tenderness within Alex that he had thought quite dead. Unwilling to let her go, he stood cradling her to him.

She was hurt and in a faint. But he couldn't stop his body's craving for her, couldn't stop himself from lowering his head and touching her soft lips with his.

She sighed and stirred, and then opened eyes cloudy with confusion. Slowly she raised one injured hand and caressed his cheek with her palm.

Oh, but to have her awake and doing this! He stayed perfectly still, waiting, willing his heart to slow its relentless hammering.

She sighed again and lowered her hand. He moved forward and lay her on her bed, and then held the candle near her hands to inspect them. Her nails were intact, thank God. The small splinters beneath them could be removed, and her fingertips would heal.

As he pulled the counterpane over her, his fingers unintentionally brushed over her breasts. He couldn't stifle the guttural moan that emitted from deep within his chest.

"Katherine." His throat felt full of grit that made his voice rough and unsteady.

He watched her eyes flutter, then open fully and focus on him. Distress tightened her features. She scooted away and seized the counterpane to pull it to her neck.

Gasping, her face contorting in pain, she glanced at her wounded fingers and then darted confused, frightened eyes at him.

Alex stepped back and raised his hands. "All is well, my lady. Don't be alarmed. You fell while in your closet."

She looked toward the closet. Shame filled her face. She lowered her head but continued to gaze at him with wide eyes. Wisps of her hair floated over her cheek and he wanted to brush them away with the gentleness of a lover.

"No need for embarrassment. Perhaps you were over-tired and went in there by mistake." Feeling powerless to help her, Alex glanced around for her slate, and saw it on her chest of drawers. "Would you like to write? If you can?"

She shook her head.

He considered pressing her for information. It could wait until morning. With great effort, he shook off his desire and cloaked himself with habitual indifference. "Good night, then. I will tell the others you've been found, and send Millie to bandage your fingers. And someone will come in the morning to look at the closet door. The handle is old. Perhaps it became stuck."

Alex stepped over to the window to shut it. "I don't know if anyone informed you," he couldn't help but add, "but I do not allow the windows in this house to show." He jerked the curtain into place. "Ever."

Even with her narrowed look of annoyance she was stunning, lying there with her hair flowing over the pillow and the lace of her nightclothes caressing her breasts with each breath she took. The memory of her firm warm body in his arms made him remain, unmoving, until she looked pointedly at the door.

"Yes. Goodnight." He left the room and strode down the corridor with his hands balled into tight fists. He must be hard, unbreakable. No emotion.

He would absolutely begin sending word tomorrow that there was a marriageable woman of nobility under his guardianship.

Chapter Seven

The pulsating pain in her fingers woke Katherine, and the feminine snore resounding from one corner made her sit up hurriedly. She slipped out of bed, crossed the floor, and moved the drapes with her thumbs just far enough to see Millie asleep in a chair with her ample chin resting upon her chest.

The maid puckered her brow and smacked her lips. "Toll ye t'fetch th' blasted hot water," she mumbled.

Katherine turned back toward the window and blinked at the sunlight that soaked into her face like a welcome poultice. The incident of the night before seemed now only a dream, but her throbbing fingertips confirmed that it wasn't. How shameful that Lord Drayton had found her in a faint in her closet. Her misfortune would only quicken his removal of her.

She examined her hands, wrapped in cloth to anchor the pad of cotton wadding at the ends of each of her fingers. Communicating through written words would be difficult until her fingertips ceased their throbbing ache.

In the meantime, golden shafts breaking through the clouds bathed the green hills outside her window. The bright, open space pulled at her spirit. She would never grow used to this dark, depressing castle, her somber room, the portrait of the wretched woman in the closet.

One hour later, Millie helped Katherine into a blue skirt and then laced it at the back. She waited while Katherine eased her hands through the sleeves of a loose jacket, and then she fastened the tiny pearl buttons up the front. "Poor lady," she cooed. "Stuck in yer closet. Wish I'd stayed in here at bedtime. It's me own fault, y'know." She stared ruefully at Katherine's hands.

Katherine shook her head and patted Millie lightly on her plump shoulder, then stepped into heeled leather shoes. Her fear of small spaces was her own foolishness and nothing more.

"Lady Drayton, she never wanted me in here," Millie continued as she folded Katherine's nightclothes. "Specially when Lady Agnes came over t'help her. They would whisper and laugh, and I think there was drinkin' goin' on. I found empty brandy goblets." She turned to Katherine. "So I didn't know if ye wanted me t'stay with ye or not. I told Lord Drayton as much, but I fear he'll put me out because of what happened to ye."

He would do no such thing. Katherine watched Millie, shoulders slumping, put her nightclothes into the cabinet. She must let him know right away that the maid was not at fault for what happened. Taking a deep breath, she walked to the door.

Her remaining days in Lord Drayton's home simply could not be as dreadful as these first few.

She gestured for her slate, and Millie picked it up. No matter that she wouldn't be able to use it until her fingers healed, the slate had become such a part of Katherine that she couldn't bring herself to leave it behind.

Nearing the stairs, she heard heavy footsteps. At the sight of Lord Drayton below on the first landing, Katherine wasn't sure whether the sudden fluttering in her stomach meant hunger or anxiety. She strongly suspected the latter and paused at the wooden balustrade overlooking the stairs to watch him complete his ascent.

Dark blond curls peeked through the loosened laces of his brown linen shirt. Wetting her dry lips, she forced herself to meet the inquiring gaze that heightened the tremor in her gut.

He glanced down at her hands. "Good morning. I trust the remainder of your night passed without incident?"

Was there the slightest mockery in his expression? Not to be intimidated by his sarcasm, she held her head high and gave him a proud nod.

"Good."

Now he would declare his intentions of sending her away. She steadied her gaze with his and waited while her insides fluttered like a frenzy of wings.

His voice was flat and unapologetic. "I read your journal last night. I respect your desire to leave here and plan to act on it as soon as possible." His lips curved up, but his eyes showed no amusement. "And your desire to marry someone whom you can *love*, as you put it, is absurd. Love is a useless waste of time. Don't look for me to bring around a parade of eligible men and wait for you to fall in love with one of them."

Katherine's mouth moved to speak, and she felt the color rushing to her face. Gads, but it would take too long and cause too much pain to write the hot retort that should pour forth from her lips.

"Did you love your betrothed? Ellis Potts?" he asked unexpectedly.

Ellis? Of course. Hadn't she? She nodded.

The cynical twist of Lord Drayton's mouth took her aback. "There you have it. Look where it got you. He threw you away like so much garbage." He began to turn away with a disgusted shake of his head. "Don't look for love in marriage either, Katherine. I can tell you that it doesn't exist."

Katherine threw up her hands in vexation. She glared at him and tried to will away her tears of frustration.

He didn't understand. She wanted sanctuary, that was all. A life with someone who would accept her for who she was.

Lonely despair spilled through her.

He glanced back as he walked away, and stopped. The sarcasm on his face altered to genuine puzzlement. "Tears? Why? Do you truly think you'll find what you're looking for?"

She brushed by him and headed for the stairs. Explaining herself to this bitter man wasn't worth the pain in her fingers.

"Don't go downstairs. I'll have a servant bring you breakfast."

Resenting the authoritative tone of his voice, she stopped and whirled to face him with her hands on her hips, but lowered them at the resulting sharp twinge.

"Soldiers are coming into the house for the morning meal," he said. "'Tis a large group, and some are unruly. 'Twould be best for you to stay out of sight until they're gone. Elizabeth is in her bedchamber. Perhaps you would like to join her."

Katherine almost refused out of defiance, but common sense told her he was right. She shrugged and looked at Millie.

"I'll take ye there, m'lady," Millie said.

She felt his eyes on her as she walked behind the maid down the corridor.

Moments later, Katherine watched Elizabeth's face crumple at the sight of her bandaged hands, as if she herself had caused the injuries.

Elizabeth set down her cup and a little of the black liquid splashed out onto the saucer. "Oh, Lady Katherine, I'm so sorry you had to go through that horrible event," she said with a waver in her voice. "This house is so very old. The inside handle of your closet should have been inspected to be sure it was working. Alex has instructed Millie to never leave you alone."

I am not a helpless child, Katherine wanted to write on the slate that Millie had set on the table near her. Since she would be leaving soon, though, it was best to keep her feelings to herself.

Elizabeth's bedchamber was plush, colorful, and comfortable looking, with dark pink walls and a pink and yellow coverlet. But in here, as in Katherine's room, the heavy rose patterned drapes were pulled tightly shut to keep out the light.

"Would you like coffee?" Elizabeth asked, indicating the blue and white ceramic pot the servant held, "Or have you taken to drinking the tea that Queen Catharine so enjoys?"

Katherine raised her brows in interest and pointed to her cup. She had indeed come to appreciate tea as well as coffee, but this morning, she needed the strength that only a hot cup of coffee could offer. On the table, she noticed paper, quill and a small bottle of ink. How nice that Elizabeth had procured the items for her.

Feeling obligated to write her thanks, she placed her bandaged fingers on the thin quill, but only managed to slide it around instead of lifting it. She blew out an exasperated breath and glanced down at the thick square of chalk nestled in its holding place on her slate. Perhaps, if she managed to pry it out, she could palm it in her hand as would a young child. With her thumb, she tried to lift it.

"Would ye like me to help, m'lady?" Millie asked, sounding just as frustrated as Katherine felt.

Katherine raised a hand in impatience and shook her head. She would thank Elizabeth later, when she could write again.

She concentrated on lifting her coffee cup to her mouth using both hands. Even so, too much of the hot liquid stung her lips and tongue. Gritting her teeth in frustration and pain, she eased the cup back into its saucer.

"I doubt you would like to be treated as a baby and fed," Elizabeth said with moist eyes, "but is there anything I can do to help you?"

Katherine forced a smile, shook her head, and managed to slide her thumb under a piece of bread and lift it to her lips.

It was a stupid thing she had done, getting stuck in her closet. No matter what happened, during the remainder of her stay at Drayton Castle she would control her curiosity, a vice which had caused her to lose her voice and now injured her hands.

Lord Drayton must think her a clumsy, prying fool. For some silly reason, his opinion of her mattered a great deal.

She ate her bread and, determined to succeed, wielded spoonfuls of pottage to her mouth, spilling most of them in the process. Although Millie placed a cloth on her bodice, Katherine knew she would have to change her dress after breakfast.

Elizabeth must have shaken her head and murmured "Poor thing" twenty-odd times, so that by the time a knock came to the door, Katherine was ready to run from this smothering pink bedchamber back to her sparse, colorless room. Elizabeth's maid opened the door.

Lord Drayton stood there, his shoulders spanning the doorframe. "The soldiers have gone." His cool gaze lowered to Katherine's soiled dress, and then to her hands. A fleeting compassion crossed his annoyingly handsome features. "Millie," he said decisively, "you will feed Lady Katherine her meals until she is able to handle...."

His voice trailed off as Katherine gave him a fierce

stare and shook her head. Would he allow her no dignity!

Lord Drayton's face resumed a mask of indifference. "As you wish. I came to tell you that I leave for Chiswick this morning to meet with a lawyer and draw up a marriage contract for you."

Katherine's eyes widened in stunned surprise. So soon? Livid now, she brushed at the quill until the end of it extended off the edge of the table.

"But she-she is injured," Elizabeth said.

Katherine finally grasped the quill between her thumb and palm and thrust the point straight to the bottom of the inkbottle.

"I said I would meet with him. I did not say she would leave immediately. I know what's best for her."

And now he was speaking as if she weren't in the room—as if she were a mere child. She struggled to keep the pen from slipping around in her bandages as she wrote.

"Who is he?" Elizabeth asked.

Lord Drayton hesitated, and Katherine glanced up to see him looking down at his boots as if expecting their worn leather toes to answer. "I would rather not say in case he refuses her," he said.

"Oh," said Elizabeth meekly.

Katherine finished, straightened, and jerked an aching finger toward her words, which were barely legible and dotted with black splatters.

Lord Drayton walked to the table, picked up the paper, and read, "I meet him. I decide." A deep rumble in his chest suggested a chuckle, although his lips revealed his scorn and his eyes became icy. "No, you will not decide. You will marry whomever I choose for you."

Katherine shook her head and glared at him while the quill slipped from her hand to the floor.

He tossed the paper onto the table, and his derisive laugh sent chills through her body. "Yes, I know. You want only to marry for love. But as I told you, there is no such thing." He walked to the door, then turned to face her. "Tolerance, yes. Perhaps dislike, or in my case, pure hatred. But never love."

Such bitterness! What on earth had happened to the man? Katherine followed him out the door, but his long legs had carried him quickly down the corridor.

And he was gone.

Chapter Eight

Riding east, Alex detoured to Robert's house to leave his copy of *Paradise Lost* for Edward to borrow. A man near Robert's barn pointed to Edward's herbarium.

Alex dismounted and ambled down the pebbled path to the small, squat building, and stopped with his hand on the door latch. Edward wasn't alone. Heated words carried through the glassless window to his right.

"I can't believe it. Are you sure he wants to court you?"

"He would like to. Why do you doubt his intentions? Am I not good enough for him?"

The voices belonged to Agnes and Edward. Disinclined to interrupt their private conversation, Alex released the latch and turned to leave the book with Sarah, but the next words rooted him.

"His year of mourning for Madcap Mary has ended," Agnes said. "At last."

"Has he expressed interest? Spoken to Father?"

"Not yet. Likely Alexander is as slow as you in your courtship. He doesn't wish to offend me by moving forward too quickly." A slight hesitation, and then Agnes added, "You know, Ed, I think you should court Katherine instead of Elizabeth."

"What? No, I don't think—"

"She's pretty, you know," Agnes said. "Almost as pretty as I am. Father said so. Her clothes sit on her like a saddle on a sow's back, and she cannot talk, and she's stupid no matter what anyone says, but you'd have plenty of time to dry your herbs and write love poems."

Alex instinctively stiffened at the insult to Katherine.

"Bear in mind that I mean to continue courting Elizabeth."

Agnes laughed. "Tell me. Have you kissed her yet?"

"No. We're in no hurry."

"So you say."

A clatter echoed from inside. Edward must have dropped something. "What? Has Elizabeth said something to you?"

"Only that it's your decision whether you wish to turn your attentions to Katherine," Agnes replied. "Apparently, Lizzy cares not what you do."

Edward's voice grew stronger. "Don't touch that, Agnes. It's mandrake root. Makes one sleep like the dead." A moment later he said, "What does Elizabeth want? Does she not care for me?"

Alex leaned against the wall and shook his head. What was that vixen doing to her brother?

"Oh, I suppose she does," Agnes said. "She doesn't speak openly about her feelings. Katherine speaks not at all, yet her face and body reveal much. It's how I know of her desire for Alexander. This is why you must turn your attentions to her before he does."

Almost bellowing his surprise, Alex jolted from the wall. Katherine desired him?

Agnes continued in a plea. "I want to be Lady Drayton. It's always what I've wanted. *Will* you court Lady Katherine?"

"No. Alex isn't going to marry her, Ag. Or anyone. You heard what he said at his dinner table. He doesn't want another wife."

"Yes, he does," Agnes said with clear irritation. "He just doesn't know it yet."

Footsteps approached the door. Feeling rather foolish for his covertness, Alex slid around the corner until Agnes had left the herbarium.

It mattered not what she said about Katherine. They were the words of a jealous, possessive woman. Nothing more.

****

Such a dark home, full of misery and loss.

Three days ago Lord Drayton had left for Kensington where there lived a prospective suitor.

Whom did he so eagerly seek to procure as Katherine's husband?

She had to feel the sunlight on her face. A few minutes later, she was in her light summer cloak and outside.

Light. Warmth. She stood for a moment with her eyes squeezed shut, her face tilted to the sun. Here, she was at peace, could breathe without scrutiny.

A soaring hill beyond the barn beckoned to her with its height and open green span, and, gathering her skirts between her open hands, she slowly climbed it.

At the top, she turned and looked at the castle, a masculine splendor in gray stone. The late afternoon sun made jewels of the leaded window panes, so different than they had appeared on the rainy day of her arrival. Then, it had seemed that they had stared at her like so many hooded eyes.

On the front lawn, the shoddy boxwood cluster she had seen was actually an unkempt maze, clearly not enjoyed for many years. Beside it sat an almost unrecognizable knot garden, and further on, a dilapidated flower patch choked with weeds. It could be beautiful, with a little care. As could, perhaps, its owner.

Here on the hill, Katherine had a better view of the towering twin battlements flanking the castle in the back. The stones there were ancient and crumbling.

Millie stood at the bottom of the hill with her hands on her hips, plainly reluctant to climb it. Finally, she turned and walked to a stone bench in the middle of the flower garden, and plopped down on it.

The air up here held a delicate warmth. Katherine tugged off her hood with clumsy fingers, then shook out her hair in a rippling spill down over her shoulders.

It mattered not that she was outdoors with her hair loose and tangled. No one would see her, and no one cared.

She draped the cloak on the ground and sat down with a contented sigh. A quiet breeze caressed her cheek, and the sun swathed the top of her head like a warm hat.

The stillness out here, broken only by the twitter of birds and occasional far-off bleating of lambs, contradicted the steady racket that pervaded London's busy streets. Perhaps the tranquil peace would work its way into her heart.

But it only made her loneliness worse. She almost preferred London.

Lord Drayton sheltered her out of some favor to the

king, but would be rid of her as soon as he could. When would that be? And who would want a destitute woman with no voice?

She swallowed at the lump in her throat and blinked back sudden tears. Raising her face to the sky, she took a deep breath, then lowered her head and coughed.

Damnation! Without warning, frustration and hopeless rage engulfed her at the fire that killed her father, at the heated smoke that stole her voice.

She closed her eyes and tried to quiet her thoughts, but only heard the screaming of the two children trapped in the townhouse next to hers. She crossed her arms over her knees and lowered her head.

The cries of the children trailed away as they had on that day. The silence on the hill became absolute.

No city noise, no plague, no fire, no one to tell her she had become an embarrassment or a burden.

No sanctuary, anywhere. She was utterly alone.

****

Alex rode Neos up his drive at the slowest possible pace. Even after three days away from her, taking his time both there and back, he couldn't shake Katherine from his mind.

Thomas Bliss, Lord Wiltshire, would suit her perfectly. The baron owned a country estate as well as a London residence, and he and Katherine had probably met at one time or another. Since they no doubt socialized within the same circles, Wiltshire would be able to keep her in the lifestyle to which she'd grown accustomed.

She probably couldn't wait to return to fashionable London and its parties. As someone's property in marriage, Katherine's punishment for her father's crimes would become invalid, and Wiltshire would treat her well.

Yes. Alex had done his part and could now let her go.

He glanced up at the top of his favorite hill, and then reigned in sharply.

There she sat, still and pensive, the wind caressing her long, beautiful brown tresses.

After a moment, he opened his mouth and gasped, and realized he'd stopped breathing.

She reached up and back, and brought her hair around to one shoulder. Despite the bulky bandages covering her hands, the movement was graceful and feminine, and it captivated him.

He hoped she wouldn't look to her left and see him watching her because he knew he would continue staring. He simply couldn't look away.

Then, she lowered her head, and her shoulders shook.

God's nails. Was she weeping?

Alex's hands tightened on the reins as pangs of guilt slammed into him. Her tears were his fault. She had lost her voice, her family, her home, and whatever dowry she'd had, and all he had done was to add to her misery by making her feel as if she were nothing but a burden to him. He'd even voiced this to Robert within her hearing. It was probably what had made her wander around and become trapped in her closet.

When had he become such an insensitive, heartless man?

Her father had been a spy, yes, and his death in the fire put the burden of punishment on Katherine to bear. But did she know what he'd done? Or was she pretending ignorance? Should Alex find out or just leave her alone?

While he pondered what to do, his horse whickered to another in the field nearby.

"Ah, Neos, you cannot be quiet, can you," he murmured, and patted the horse on his silky gray neck as he looked back up at Katherine.

She had seen him and jumped to her feet. Hiking her skirts to her shapely ankles, she descended the hill.

Alex trotted Neos toward her. "Katherine."

She stopped and looked up at him. Her face was pink from weeping, and in her eyes shone a tender vulnerability that twisted his heart into a knot.

He dismounted, unable to take his eyes off the sunlit copper glints in her hair. "You're the first woman since my mother to climb that hill. I go up there when I need to think."

Katherine, looking tired and forlorn, nodded her understanding.

"You've lost a great deal." Alex stared at the ground and struggled for words that he'd never spoken to anyone. "I also know of grief. Last year, I lost my wife when she killed herself."

A guarded concern, and puzzlement, flickered in her eyes.

He went on, the words falling from his lips like a halting confession. "My parents died under the hands of Cromwell's men when I was twelve." Alex looked at an area of grass just beyond the drive. "There they were murdered. Then, one of the men came for me. While the others watched, he beat me and threw me onto my parents' bodies. I suppose he thought I would die."

Katherine stood very still, deep compassion now evident in the softness of her lips, the moist intensity of her eyes.

Alex touched the white scar along his jaw. "He wore a ring with some hard edge that cut me. Perhaps that saved my life, because my face was covered with blood."

Why was he telling her all this? These memories only brought forth the surge of anger that he tried to keep locked up. But now it was too late, and his long-buried fury spilled forth. His voice became a growl in its intensity and he clenched his hands. "I've always wanted to find that man. I want to find his family and make him watch while I run them all through with my sword. And then I want to kill *him*."

Katherine stumbled back with a frightened grimace, tears glistening in her wide eyes.

"No. Wait," Alex said, walking toward her, hating himself for fouling this up. "I'm sorry. 'Tis an old boyhood wound within me that has never healed. I just need to forget about it." He speared his fingers through his hair. "I'm not doing so well in helping you lessen your pain, am I?"

In answer, Katherine shook her head. For a frozen moment she wavered. Then, she moistened her lips, slowly reached out her hand, and folded her bandaged fingers over his.

Her gentle brown eyes and tender touch made Alex take a sudden, ragged breath. He looked down at her small hand in his and then enveloped it, gently and completely, with his.

And by the heavens, he wanted to take her in his arms and kiss away all her hurt. "Katherine, I—"

A sudden flap of wings and angry chirping broke the moment. Overhead, two birds carried on an in-air brawl, mayhap over some female.

Katherine blinked then, seeming to awaken from a dream, and pulled her hand from his. Without a glance back, she whirled and fled toward the house.

Alex stood staring after her with a mixture of bemusement and relief. Then, shoving out a breath, he remounted Neos and trotted the horse toward the barn.

He hadn't asked her what she knew. But her acute compassion told him he didn't have to.

Until she was protected by marriage, he would keep her safe.

****

That evening, as Katherine finished dressing for dinner, she frowned with concern at Millie's despondent countenance. She placed a light hand on the maid's shoulder.

"It's yer hands, the bandages. Reminds me of Lady Drayton. She often—" Millie abruptly turned to the dressing table. She busily straightened the brush, comb, and ribbons in their case.

Katherine stepped closer to Millie and met her eyes in the mirror.

Finally, Millie spoke. "She bit her nails, tore at them until her fingers bled. I tried to keep them wrapped, but it didn't help. She just took off the bandages. Two of her fingers lost the nails completely."

Katherine's fingertips stung afresh. In the mirror she caught her wince, but also saw the same sorrow she had felt this morning after Lord Drayton had shared his grief. Briefly felt, anyway, until he had gone into his tirade of revenge.

Did it matter that his heart could shatter, that he was not the unemotional boar he strove to appear? No. It did not. She would do well to remember not only that he wanted her gone from his life, but also that he was capable of a fierce vengeance.

What of the man he had gone to see in Kensington? She would try to write her questions during the meal.

As Millie helped her put on her shoes, someone knocked at the door. Millie opened it to a sprightly maid who stood with a tray of food in her hands.

"Lord Drayton sends her ladyship's meal."

Katherine stared at the tray in confusion.

"Her ladyship is going to the dining room," Millie told the girl. She turned questioningly toward Katherine.

"But he ordered supper brought to her room," the younger servant said.

Why? To make her stay in her bedchamber until her departure? Katherine's cheeks flushed hotly and her heart drummed like the hooves of a runaway mare.

Oh, no. The scoundrel might think he could dictate every aspect of her life and frighten her with his seething male anger, but he was truly mistaken. Hot wrath rushed through her as she looked at Millie and pointed to her slate.

She strode past both servants out of her room.

Chapter Nine

When Katherine stood in the doorway of the dining room, Alex knew that his calm dinner, attended by Elizabeth, Robert, and two woman-chasing merchants from London, was at an end. But with her eyes ablaze and cheeks flaming color, Katherine's fury only made her more beautiful.

"Good evening, Lady Katherine," Robert said in a mild tone. Brows raised, his gaze lowered to her hands, then back to her face. "How are you?"

She acknowledged Robert with a curt nod and then resumed glaring at Alex, who, despite his decision to exclude her from this meal to keep her away from the lewd stares of the merchants, rose to help her into a chair next to Elizabeth. He drew in breath as he took in the graceful curve of her neck. Were he only able to lean down and touch his lips to her creamy, scented skin.

He crushed his thoughts and returned to his chair, giving an inward growl at the merchants licking their lips over her low bodice. Elizabeth, thankfully, had dressed with her customary modesty. "Your meal was sent to your room," he said to Katherine, gesturing to a servant to bring writing supplies to the table. "Did you not receive it?"

Sitting on Alex's left, Elizabeth flitted him a bird-like glance.

Katherine reached for the quill. Mouth set and brow furrowed in concentration, she brushed her hand over the pen until she could grasp it, then maneuvered it within the cotton bandages of her hand until it was upright.

His guests' eyes, Alex noticed, followed her hands as she maneuvered the tip into the opening of the inkwell, held it over the bottle to catch any drips, and then wrote on the paper in slow, meticulous strokes. Too many times during the process she re-inked her quill.

They all waited in silence for her to finish. Even the servants at the sideboard seemed to hold their breaths.

Alex wished to God she could just voice her reply to his question. How any man would be able to put up with her lack of speech, he had no idea.

Katherine finally set down the pen and held out her paper to him. Without taking it, he leaned toward Elizabeth and read her words.

I wish to eat at your table.

"I disagree," he replied with a surreptitious glance at the merchants. "'Tis better for you to—"

Katherine smacked her left hand on the table, cringed, and then stretched her right arm over Elizabeth's plate, thrusting out the paper until it hovered inches from Alex face.

Elizabeth made a small, shocked sound and leaned back.

Alex snatched the paper from her hand, balled it up, and flung it onto the floor. Despite his effort to stay composed, his voice gained volume. "The answer is *no*. Millie," he ordered the maid standing near the other servants, "Escort Lady Katherine back to her room."

Katherine flashed a scathing look at him and stayed seated, and for a moment Alex felt an unexpected approval of her courage. He waited.

Her fingers inched toward the pen.

"I have given you my answer." Ignoring the curious stares of the merchants, who clearly expected him to control his lovely but disobedient ward, Alex picked up his pewter wine goblet and took a slow sip. He watched the intelligent sparkle of challenge in her eyes and hid the delight that trickled through him. If she could only speak, what glittering discourse they would have!

He'd much rather see her furious like this than sad. No. What he would rather see was her naked and writhing with pleasure in his arms.

His goblet almost toppled in his hand at the thought.

But she narrowed her eyes. Pure insolence gleamed from them as, instead of picking up the pen, she held out her hands for the slate and chalk that Millie held.

Keeping her eyes lowered, Millie plucked the chalk from its holder and set it into Katherine's hand.

Katherine clutched the chalk, sent a warning glance toward Alex, and battered it over the slate with long, hard strokes.

Each drawn out screech gouged reverberating ice into Alex's ears and straight down to his feet. He gripped the edge of the table.

On his right, Robert breathed, "God Almighty."

On his left, Elizabeth gave a small whimper. The merchants were rendered slack-jawed.

Katherine raised her chin and turned the slate toward Alex.

NO.

The word took up the entire surface.

Alex bristled and shot to his feet, his approval of her vivacity pooling like melting wax. She knew he hated the chalk's sound. Why else did she think he had set up paper and pens all over the house? "By God, Katherine, you *will* do as I say," he said through clenched teeth.

"Indeed," Robert said under his breath.

She merely regarded both of them as one would two pesky flies.

How in hell could this stubborn female continue her impertinence? "Leave this table *now*."

In answer, Katherine gave him a smug smile and, grasping her fork clumsily between her thumb and index finger, she took a narrow sliver of meat from the tray in front of her. She kept her eyes glued to his as she skated the morsel once over her pink tongue, and then delicately sucked it into her mouth.

Alex saw the triumphant gleam in her eyes. Even as the sensuality of her action caused heat to rush to his groin, he reacted to the molten steel that surged through his veins.

In one fluid movement, he was at her side with his hand like a talon on her shoulder. Something primal and hot spiraled through him at the feel of her silky skin under his fingers, but he ignored it. "Rise," he commanded harshly, "or feel the cut of my whip on your bare back."

She gasped. Under his hand she stiffened and trembled, and he felt like a louse. Her lavender scent caressed his senses and he fought the urge to gentle his grip on her soft shoulder and tell her he meant nothing by his threat.

Useless now, his fingers slid off her shoulder when she stood.

Her face was frozen in a pleasant expression, but guarded uncertainty filled her eyes. Without looking at him, she left the room with Millie following close behind.

He wanted to follow and quietly explain the reasons behind his decision. With great effort, he returned to his seat.

"Interesting woman," one of the merchants remarked as he lifted his goblet to his thin lips. "A bit too active for my tastes."

The second man straightened his ill-fitting black wig. "I wonder if she's that much of a wildcat in bed," he mused with a chuckle.

Robert asked, "Do you think she'll ever understand your rules?"

"She understands that she will not dine at my table," Alex answered. His two reasons were sitting at his table right now, discussing her body and behavior. Alex wanted to shield her without her thinking that he cared a whit about her, which he did not.

Elizabeth spoke in her hesitant murmur, "Pray do not be unkind to her."

"I have made my decision, Elizabeth," Alex warned with a smoldering look. "Do not question me further." His cousin didn't understand his intentions, and he saw no cause to explain them.

Elizabeth quaked under his gaze and murmured her assent.

As Alex led his guests toward the parlor after dinner, he was surprised to see Katherine, tight-lipped and pale, descending the stairs. He strolled over and waited until she had reached the bottom step. "Did you enjoy your solitude?"

The question was not meant to mock her, yet she apparently took it as such. Engaged by the fire flashing in her eyes, Alex almost missed the hand that shot up to slap him. He caught her wrist and noticed that she had removed her bandages. For the first time, he saw a pink scar that extended in a thick line across her palm.

Another injury! But this one was not new. "What—" he began, and then she stunned him by swinging around her other hand and cuffing his chin. Her face, set in determined resolve, nonetheless revealed the pain it must have taken to ball up her fist and strike the hard bone of his jaw. Behind him, he heard Robert's guffaw and Elizabeth's shocked intake of breath.

"What did I tell you?" one of the merchants muttered to the other with a smug nod. "Hellcat."

Alex wanted to throw back his head and laugh—an odd sensation, since he had not truly laughed for at least four years—but instead, he adopted a frosty expression and spoke to Katherine with threatening calm. "You would take care not to give me grounds to put you out of this house, my lady."

To his dismay, her eyes filled with tears. He took a quick breath and stepped back. He hadn't meant to make her cry.

She swiped at the moisture with the back of her hand, thrust out her chin, and nodded.

Perplexity replaced his concern. "What?"

She pointed at the front door with a quick flick of her hand.

"You *want* to leave?"

He read her vehement nod just as clearly as if she had shouted the words. Yes. She wanted to leave. And *right now.*

Was she serious? Alex stared at her, then moved so close that his breath stirred the darling curls along her forehead. "You really are a dolt," he said quietly so his guests wouldn't hear. "Don't you know that if you walk out of here, you'll be in danger? Don't you know what's out there in the night? The things you'll be made to do by men who don't care that you're a lady of high status?"

She was listening, but her eyes told him she wasn't convinced.

He lowered his voice to a heated whisper. "You'll become a filthy, begging whore within days. You'll have to lie with many men in order to survive. And within weeks, you will die of starvation or disease. Now just give the signal, *Lady* Katherine, and I'll have my servant open the door."

Her features now rigid, she shook her head in small, jerky movements.

Alex ran his gaze over her attentive face, the fast moving pulse point on her soft throat, the lovely tops of her breasts that swelled from her lacy bodice. She needed to stay here, under his protection.

Under him.

The unbidden thought made a sudden, powerful heat shoot through his loins and all at once, his arms itched to lock her within them. He felt his body calling to hers with a passion that rocked him to the core.

She was chipping away at his barriers. He would not allow it. "No," he whispered savagely through tight lips. "You can't do this."

Wide-eyed, Katherine shook her head again. She thought he referred to her leaving, and he didn't correct her.

"Still a burden, is she?" came a low, amused voice in his right ear. Alex glanced at Robert and then turned his attention back to Katherine, who, with irritation sparking in her eyes, ran that pink tongue over her lips.

The sight nearly undid him.

He had to turn away lest she see the physical proof of his attraction for her. He beckoned to the merchants and strolled toward the parlor, leaving her standing alone. To his guests, it seemed he had bypassed honoring her request without appearing like he gave a damn.

"She'll be leaving soon," he said to Robert. "I've procured a husband for her." He looked back and saw her glaring after them with her hands on her hips.

"Ah. Will you bed her before you send her off? Or was virginity part of your contract—if she is a virgin?"

"It wasn't mentioned," Alex said, thinking that if she were willing, she'd be in his bed this very night, "but I doubt Wiltshire cares. His days of fornication are long over." He absently rubbed his sore jaw.

Robert chuckled. "You might wish to gain her affection before she pummels you black and blue. Or give her the whip, as you warned."

Distaste filled him. Had she been sent to Robert to do with as he pleased, Robert would have gladly dispensed punishment. "I won't beat her. And I'm not interested in gaining her affection. Or any woman's, for that matter."

Robert hesitated at the door to the parlor. "Which

brings me to the purpose of my visit, Alex. Your wife has been dead over a year now. Perhaps 'tis time to reconcile your grief."

Alex steeled himself. "And I know you want your daughter to help me do that."

Chapter Ten

In her bedchamber, Katherine studied her tender fingertips for a moment before lifting the quill with a loose grip.

The letter was succinct, albeit in a sloppy scrawl.

Lord Drayton,

I must relate to you my feelings. Your treatment of me is offensive and intolerable. I wish to be placed with another guardian, one who will not frighten me with punishment nor ban me to my bedchamber to eat.

I also wish to have a say in the matter of choosing my husband. You have been most rude in keeping me uninformed.

Signed, Katherine Seymour

There. After sprinkling fine sand over the ink to dry it, she folded the letter and sealed it with wax.

She waited for Millie to come and tell her that Lord Drayton summoned her. She would give him her letter and would not leave his study until he'd given her an answer.

To pass the time until he called for her, she read one of the books she had pilfered from Ellis' collection. He would never miss them since he rarely read; the books were ornaments in his parlor to impress his wealthy guests.

Memories of her last parties in London surfaced in her mind and overtook her concentration of the pages. Memories of condescending looks and whispers behind fans. Averted eyes and exasperated brows. Ellis' rigid smile signifying his embarrassed impatience over her clumsy efforts to keep up with conversation through her slate.

Lord Drayton, too, must be uncomfortable by her silent presence. Why else would he keep her from his table? He might have used the valid excuse of the presence of the soldiers this morning, but in the dining room sat two rather bland-looking men with several chins and wide bodies. No danger there. She was used to being ogled during parties, and had ignored their stares at her breasts.

The light gradually faded from the edges of the curtains, and no summons came. Her stomach rumbling with hunger, Katherine closed the book. She would go to the kitchen and get some bread and cheese from the pantry.

Someone knocked on the door.

At last. Katherine rose and picked up her letter.

But there stood only Elizabeth with folded hands and an uncertain gaze. "I wanted to see if you were all right."

Katherine exhaled in exasperation and stepped back to allow Elizabeth access. How to respond? Yes, she was all right, and frustrated, and anxious.

And smarting with the realization that Lord Drayton didn't care to see her again this night.

Elizabeth touched Katherine's arm and her head lowered. "I'm so sorry for my cousin's actions."

Katherine shrugged. It was all she could do.

Elizabeth cleared her throat and spoke in hushed tones, as if afraid of someone overhearing. "Please don't take offense at what I say. I know you are from London and perhaps things are different there. But out here—" she raised a slim hand and gestured around her—"ladies must do exactly as their guardians decree."

And then literally cease to exist except to please the men who claimed them. The familiar rebellion rose in Katherine's heart. She waved Elizabeth to a chair and then took a seat at the writing table.

Could there never be a loving meeting of the heart and mind of two people? Would she always have to yield to the whims of whatever man had power over her, of having the vitality crushed from her being?

It wasn't London that was so different from the country; it was she who was different from many women who, seemingly without struggle, accepted their fate as property. She herself would be given to a stranger in a matter of weeks or even days, and would have no say in the matter.

Elizabeth sighed, shifted on the brown brocade seat, and looked around the room. "'Tis so sad in here. The colors...." She was quiet for a moment, then said, "He has changed over the last four years. He became a different person during Mary's...infirmities." She shrugged her delicate shoulders and looked at Katherine with apology in her gray eyes.

Katherine penned a note while she tapped one foot on the floor and prayed for patience. Although Elizabeth seemed to be more comfortable around her, she still maintained a maddeningly hesitant manner of speaking. And her penchant for taking blame for everything made Katherine want to shake her.

What was he like before?

Elizabeth read, and then studied a knothole embedded in the thick wood planks of the floor. "Happy," she said. "Smiling and laughing. As he almost did downstairs, right after you—you struck him. Life comes into his eyes when he looks at you."

Of course life came into his eyes—flashing fire at Katherine. Well, he'd had his chance to throw her out, but when she'd agreed, he had backed down. She leaned one elbow on the writing table and placed her chin on the heel of her hand.

Elizabeth continued. "He went through a terrible time during his marriage. He believes he caused his wife's death and refuses even to discuss it."

Katherine raised her chin off her hand. What did Elizabeth mean, caused his wife's death? She picked up the quill. *How did she die? What happened?*

Elizabeth flinched at the question. "Many things happened. Mary wasn't well. She-she said things about Alex that I did not believe. But I've only been living here since my mother died three months ago, so I don't know the truth. All I can tell you is that he's not the same man." Elizabeth touched her bodice. "'Tis as if he died inside, in his heart. He shows little emotion except...except sometimes, he seems so sad."

Katherine ridiculed the sympathetic tug in her heart. Why should she waste compassion on him? Yet she nodded her understanding. She knew sadness.

"Please have patience with him," Elizabeth said. "I think by his actions that he means only to protect you."

I will try. But I dislike him so! It was not the absolute

truth, but Elizabeth didn't need to know otherwise.

As Katherine capped the inkwell, a ghost of a smile played on Elizabeth's lips. "There are times that I dislike him, too."

It gladdened Katherine that Elizabeth had at least a spark of pluck within her.

The next morning, after a lone breakfast in the dining room—Lord Drayton, wisely, had not sent the maid with another tray—Millie informed Katherine that he and Elizabeth were not home. Katherine decided to leave the letter in his study.

Millie stood fidgeting by the study door and spoke up in muted tones. "If I may be so bold, m'lady. Lord Drayton does not like anyone goin' in there."

Katherine looked pointedly at Millie and then at the door handle.

"M'lady, Lord Drayton—"

Katherine set her lips and opened the door herself.

She stepped inside, breathing in his masculine scent...warm and spicy with a hint of sandalwood, and none of the body stink that clung to some men.

The slanted top of the oak desk had been left open, and her gaze roved over the papers and ledgers that littered the surface. How was he ever able to get any work done? Her letter would be lost among this mess. She turned to the small table nearby. Its surface was not quite as cluttered.

Carefully, she stacked papers to leave room for her letter so he'd see it. Then, she couldn't resist turning back to his desk and sliding into his chair, watching Millie slap a hand over her mouth in shock.

Engulfed by the oversized leather chair, Katherine caressed its smooth arms, closed her eyes, and inhaled deeply. His essence surrounded her, a comforting, cocooning sensation.

She opened her eyes and shoved away the feeling. He'd only tried to make her life miserable.

Pursing her lips in thought, she regarded his papers. Then, curiously, she leaned forward and spread open one of his ledgers.

"Oh, Lady Katherine! Oh, my!" Millie muffled through her hand.

Katherine stood and waved Millie toward the door.

She asked with wide eyes, “D’ye wish me t’leave?”

At Katherine’s nod, Millie, with a wounded glance, went out.

Now, Katherine would see how Lord Drayton kept his books.

Sliding her finger along the poorly written numbers, she stopped in consternation about halfway down. The subtraction was wrong. He’d forgotten to add a zero back in and his total was off by at least three hundred pounds.

She closed this book and selected another, titled Estate—Sheep Count. This one should be accurate. How difficult could it be to count the smelly things, anyway? But it, too, was off by fifty-seven sheep. He’d skipped two lines and continued down the column.

Could the man not add and subtract?

Thoroughly engrossed, she examined two other ledgers, one on crops and the other on household goods—candles and rushlights were listed regularly—and both contained errors that were costing him a great deal of money.

And his correspondence! She tossed the ledgers aside and picked up one of his letters, and squinted as she held the paper near her face. How could anyone make sense of his terrible handwriting?

He needed help. Taking care of her father’s estate books had honed her lightning-quick addition and subtraction.

Pulling a ledger back toward her, she uncapped the inkwell and set to work.

Minutes later, her quill scratching rapidly down the column, Katherine vaguely heard a door open and then shut. When she heard voices speaking—one older and feminine, the other childlike—she jerked up her head and slammed the ledger closed. Someone had entered from the hall to the withdrawing room next to the study.

She shot to her feet, cursing her forgetfulness when the chair scraped on the wood floor.

Holding her hands to her skirts to keep them from swishing, she trotted to the door leading to the corridor, and opened it. As she stepped from the room, however, a large, shadowy form entered the corridor from the Hall and headed her way.

Lord Drayton!

Katherine ducked back into the room. The people in the withdrawing room would see her if she went out through the connecting door. Where would she go from there?

There was no place to hide. And he would see the neat stacks she'd made on his table, and then turn and see her....

She dashed to the table and swept the papers to and fro in an attempt to make the surface look undisturbed. Then, as the booted footsteps echoed closer, she raced to the wall beside the door hinges and pressed herself against it.

The door flew open, almost hitting her. Heart pounding so hard she feared it would burst, she watched Lord Drayton stride in. His presence filled the room.

An intense, ragged cough threatened to burst forth. She clamped both hands to her mouth and fought the spasms in her chest and throat.

He strode across the room and paused at his desk. Oh, mercy. Would he sit?

He did not, but rather lifted the candle on his desk—the candle she'd brought with her—and then opened the door to his withdrawing room. He stepped through, pulling the door closed behind him. But it didn't latch.

"Come here," she heard him say. "No need to cower in the corner."

Now was her chance to escape. Yet she listened, the cough feeling finally subsiding. Someone was in the next room, cowering from him in the corner. What had happened?

Alex studied the skinny, shivering boy—not yet nine years old, and clearly frightened. He looked like he hadn't eaten a decent meal in days.

The child drew near, his lower lip trembling. Tears stood on the brink of spilling down his filthy face. He wrapped his thin arms around himself.

"What has befallen you, Pace?"

"I've stolen a cloak from town, m'lord." The child fixed his gaze to the floor. "I been hidin' in your keep to get away from the merchants, but Mama needed my help on the farm."

From the looks of him, he badly needed a cloak. But his family should have money to buy needed items. Why had he stolen it?

"What should I do with you?" Alex asked, towering over him with his hands on his hips. It would not do to show warmth toward his serfs. "Do you suppose a thrashing would cure your stealing tendencies?"

"Y-yes sir," the boy faltered. "As you wish, m'lord." Tears escaped his eyes and made cleansing tracks through the dirt on his bony cheeks.

Alex kept his expression pitiless. He knew Pace's father had died recently, but had no idea the widow and her son had fallen to such despair. His mind raced. Hadn't he set aside a penance for them? Was it something his former steward had overlooked? "Your mother, does she know of your crime?"

He heard a sound near the door that led to the hall. A woman tottered up from a chair in the dark corner and waddled toward him, hair matted and skin dark with dirt. From the looks of her swollen belly, her babe would come forth very soon.

"M'lord, I beg yer kindness," she said. "Please, if y'would but take the rod to my back and spare his. He's a sickly lad, and a whippin' such as ye'd give might be the death of him."

"No, Mama!" the boy cried in horror as he spun toward her. "No. 'Twas my wrong and I'll pay for it." He swung to Alex and raised himself to his full, small height. "I am ready." He knelt.

After a moment of gazing at the mop of dull, tangled black curls crowning Pace's head, Alex thought of his little used rod hanging from the hook in his study. He could flog the child and perhaps the mother—simply dole out justice as Robert did so freely with his whip—and send them both on their way, bruised and bleeding, with a severe warning.

"Stand," he ordered the boy.

Immediately Pace did so, and his emaciated body tensed. He shut his eyes, bowed his head, and pressed his lips together to stifle a moan as he waited, clearly expecting Alex to strike him. A tear splashed onto the worn planks of the floor.

Although a part of Alex yearned to draw back into his comforting waters of detachment, he pulled several coins from his waistcoat pocket. Lifting the boy's filthy hand, he placed them onto his palm. Pace opened his eyes at his mother's gasp and stared at the coins.

"This money will buy you food and clothing," Alex said as he turned to the mother. "Why have you not asked me for help, Clara?"

Clara bowed her head. "My husband died o' the pox. 'Twas after I became great with child. He went to Patsy's brothel."

It was widely considered a man's right to satisfy his needs in any way he wished, but Alex didn't share this view. Nor did he voice it to Clara. "You have no cause for shame," he said. "'Tis not your fault he caught the disease."

"I'm a God-fearin' woman, m'lord," Clara said with a sob. "I must have sinned greatly for such terrible judgment. Me and Pace, we're bein' punished for some wrongdoin', I know."

Pace approached Clara and wrapped his arms as far around her girth as he could. "Don't cry, Mama," he murmured, his cheek pressed to her rounded belly. "Pray don't cry."

Alex attributed the tightening in his throat to impatience with the woman and child. He had no time for this emotional blather. "You may leave now. Pace can let me know when the babe's time comes, and I will send for a midwife. In the meantime, do not hesitate to ask me for help." He walked to the door leading to the corridor and opened it. "No one on my land should suffer cold and hunger. You will be fed and clothed as long as you remain."

The woman gave a cry and clutched her lower belly, and Alex had a moment of terror that she would give birth right there in his withdrawing room.

But she was crying for joy, and he wanted them gone. As the boy passed him on his way out the door, Alex ruffled his hair. Pace looked up at him with shining dark eyes full of hope and admiration.

This was too much. Alex cleared his throat and wheeled toward his study. And stopped abruptly.

One bright eye stared at him through the partly open door. The eye widened, then vanished.

"What the bloody hell," he muttered. He strode to the door and shoved it open with a thump of his hand.

The room was empty. But the door that led to the hall was wide open. Running footsteps—and the sound of a familiar cough—receded down the dim corridor, drowned out by Clara's heavy tread and Pace's excited chatter.

Katherine. What cause would she have to invade his study?

Unless she had looked for the marriage contract, which he had drawn up and planned to take to Wiltshire in Chiswick before nightfall. He started after her, and then turned back to his desk.

Dropping into his chair he searched for it—sweeping, flipping, tossing, until he was sure he'd seen every document on his desk. Scratching his chin, he'd set his attention to his table when he saw Sam in the open doorway.

"Do you need assistance, m'lord?"

"I must take the marriage contract to town for Wiltshire to look over," Alex said. "I can't find the blasted thing, and I think I know why." The contract wasn't her concern, wasn't hers to look over and change. She had no cause to take it unless she wanted to stay here, and he couldn't imagine why she would want that.

"Would you like me to help you?"

"Yes. He's waiting for me. At this rate I'll not get back out there until dark."

"Where is he?"

"Lobb's Inn."

"Do you really want to go so late in the day? I can send a servant to let him know you'll be there tomorrow."

"I need to," Alex said. "He's waiting."

"Yes, you've told me that."

Alex straightened and fixed a glower on Sam. "What are you getting at, old man?"

"I rarely see you rush at anything. You must be in a hurry to get her from your life."

"Yes? So?"

Sam's craggy face lit up in a smile. "You're smitten with her."

Alex stared at him a moment, then flipped through the papers on his table. "I don't have time for your love-lorn tittle-tattle," he growled. "Be useful and help me."

As he rummaged, the faintest scent of lavender reached his nose, and abruptly Alex stilled his hands over the documents. In his mind flashed an image of Katherine lying naked upon his own bed, her loose hair spread over the pillow.

Alex felt his jaw grow slack.

Yes. Her eyes would be half closed in desire, her lips parted in her charming smile. Her arms, folded leisurely above her head, would lift and reach out for him.

The image of the rest of her supple curves fogged his mind, and he swallowed twice and rubbed damp hands on his hips.

What was he looking for?

"Alex?"

"The marriage contract." Alex gave up on the table and turned back to his desk. He hadn't checked the drawers. "'Tisn't as if she possesses a complicated dowry," he muttered, yanking open the first one. "The old toad probably just can't remember the details."

Sam moved each document methodically from one side of the table to the other. "What were you thinking just now?"

"Nothing." Only her smile, her ability to say so much with her eyes and hands. Her loveliness and grace. Even that endearing, defiant way she raised her chin. "He will be fortunate to have her," he murmured.

"As would you, lad."

Alex scoffed. "Not me."

"What's this?" Sam lifted a folded piece of paper to his nose. "Smells like a woman."

"Let me see it." Alex took the paper, unfolded it, and read it silently. A sinking sensation weighted his heart. "'Tis from Katherine," he said, keeping his voice casual. This was the reason she had been in his study. "She wishes for another guardian."

"Oh. Does she say why?"

"She says my treatment of her is intolerable. It seems I've frightened her with punishment and banned her to her bedchamber to eat."

"Well, that you have," Sam said with a frown. "You say you want to keep her safe, and then you threaten to whip her. No wonder she's frightened of you."

Alex shrugged. "I never meant anything by it. And you saw those two merchants. They were trying to stare through her gown."

"Then you need to tell her you meant nothing. What else did she write?"

Alex glanced over the last words and gave a derisive snort. "She wants to choose her own husband. Now *that* will not happen. She'll want to wait until she falls in love with one of them, and I'll never be rid of her."

"Since you'll be honoring her request for a new guardian, you won't have to worry about being rid of her," Sam said.

Alex folded the note with clenched jaw. Sam always had a way of bringing the point home. On the night Roundheads attacked and took the castle, Sam had hidden him deep among the maze of passageways under the fortress. Alex had cried out for his parents and tried to run back outside to where their bodies lay. *They're dead, lad*, Sam had whispered fiercely, his hand clamped over Alex's mouth. *Dead. Now be quiet, or you'll be dead, too.*

Feeling a bit sobered by Sam's statement, Alex opened the third drawer, and there it was. The contract faced him with its written proof of his declaration to Katherine on the day she'd arrived.

He sat back, pushing aside the strange reluctance that crept over him. "I found it."

"You're sure of your intentions?"

Alex snatched up the contract and stood. "I said I'd find her a husband, and I have. No more to be said." He trudged out, ignoring Sam's skepticism.

Chapter Eleven

Katherine held her hand to her chest in an attempt to calm her racing heart. Lord Drayton had seen her. Any second now, he'd pound on her door. But the minutes ticked by and he didn't appear.

She parted the curtains a little and opened the window, relishing the warm breeze wafting into her bedchamber.

His kindness toward the boy and his mother entranced her. No one, not even her own father, would have treated his workers with such generosity. How could this compassionate man have assisted his deranged wife out the window to her death?

"Greetings, m'lady!"

The source of the high, thin voice belonged to the dark-eyed boy who'd cried and trembled in Lord Drayton's study. Now he looked up at Katherine with a wide grin on his dirty face. He stood with his thin right arm stretched taut, his small hands clutching the reins of a calm but mighty gray stallion.

Charmed, Katherine smiled and waved to the child. With a bath and a haircut, he could be quite a handsome boy.

Then, Lord Drayton strode into her line of vision. He pivoted, seemingly immobilized, and stared up at her with eyes transformed to sapphires in the slanting late afternoon sun.

The look of horror on his face made her own eyes widen.

"Get away from the window, Katherine!"

She cocked her head and turned up her palms at the strange request.

He spoke with controlled calm, yet it seemed his entire body, tense and hard, lambasted her. "Now."

Shaken, she drew back and watched him visibly relax. But of course he would be nervous seeing her in the window from where his wife had fallen—assuming he'd had no hand in the matter. Otherwise, it was guilt that haunted him.

She peeked back out and saw him tuck a folded document into his front breast pocket. Her letter, perhaps? Yes, he'd found it, and in his impatience to get her out of his house, was rushing off to make the necessary arrangements with a new guardian.

Katherine clutched the damask drapes. She hadn't thought he would act so promptly on her request.

Truly, she had assumed he wouldn't act on it at all.

Long after dark, the drum of hooves reached Katherine's ears. Heart in her throat, she leaped out of bed to peek from her window. Lord Drayton came into view and then rode on around the corner of the castle. Would she be gone by morning?

He said nothing to her at breakfast—didn't even look at her, in fact. Elizabeth, also quiet, darted occasional anxious glances toward him.

At one point, Katherine scribbled a short note on the paper near her and then slid it over to him. He seemed blind to it as he sat hunched over his plate wolfing down bread slathered with almond butter.

Lips pressed together in irritation, Katherine picked up her pewter spoon and struck her plate with it three times, in rapid succession.

It worked. She had his attention. Lord Drayton froze in the act of gulping down a cup of watered ale. His gaze slid to her, and his brows rose as if he considered her no better than a speck of dust. "Yes?"

She let out a long impatient breath and pointed to the note.

He ran his eyes over her two questions. "Yes. I read your letter. No. I will not procure a new guardian for you."

He must have seen her relief because something changed in his eyes, something subtle and melting. In the next instant, derision replaced the softer look. "You don't need a guardian," he said. "You need a husband, and I have chosen one for you."

Katherine waved her hands in short, jerky movements. She took up her quill and wrote, *Who is he?*

"A baron," Lord Drayton answered. "Thomas Bliss, Lord Wiltshire. Your future will be secure, and I can go on with my life." He slid back his chair. "Who knows, mayhap you'll fall in love with his lordship."

Katherine, her temper flaring, glared at him, then scribbled two words on another sheet of paper.

"But Lord Wiltshire is..." began Elizabeth, then stopped as bright color rose to her cheeks.

Lord Drayton apparently picked up on her meaning. "Yes, he is. But he desires—"

Katherine thrust her paper toward him. *Pompous ass!*

A slight flaring of Lord Drayton's nostrils gave evidence of his growing irritation. "To whom are you referring, my lady? Lord Wiltshire or myself?"

She'd leave that up to him.

He returned his attention to Elizabeth. "Lord Wiltshire desires a wife, and has agreed to marry Katherine—if he approves of her. I've assured him that although she cannot speak, she is not dimwitted as first thought."

Katherine crossed her arms in exasperation at having no say in the matter. Instead of relief at knowing what her future held, her stomach clenched with tension. The marriage arrangement had taken place so quickly.

Gnawing at her top lip, she glanced at Elizabeth, who sat studying the contents of her coffee cup as if there were something fascinating floating in it. Lord Wiltshire was...what? Thick? Pockmarked? Covered with warts? She grimaced, unsure she even wanted to speculate.

And what good was meeting him if it was just to see if he wanted her? What if she didn't want *him*?

"Katherine."

She met Lord Drayton' icy stare.

"When he arrives, you *will* be courteous." He jabbed a finger on her words. "And if you show any defiance, or offend him as you have just insulted me...." He drew in breath between tight lips.

Beneath his glower, she detected a gleam of frustration in his eyes. He was clearly anxious to be rid of her.

She swallowed the sudden thickness in her throat and wondered at the ache in her chest. She looked away from him and nodded.

"What are your plans today, Elizabeth?" Lord Drayton asked briskly as he rose and walked toward the door. "I can accompany you to town if you wish to go."

Elizabeth said, "I do need to go to market with the cook. And Alex, I—I would like to show Katherine the keep later today. If that will be all right."

Lord Drayton was already through the door. "I'll be leaving shortly," he called back.

Katherine raised her head. Enthusiasm trickled through her at the prospect of touring the ancient keep.

Unexpectedly, Lord Drayton reappeared in the doorway.

"You say you're taking Katherine to the keep?"

"Well...yes, I would like to." Elizabeth replied.

"No. I don't want you to do that."

"As you wish," Elizabeth said without hesitation. Her chin trembled.

Katherine closed her eyes and shook her head. Would he allow her no amusement? Or was he implying that since she would be leaving, there was no use in exploring the castle? She slanted a narrowed glance at him and picked up the quill, but his next words, although gruff, stayed her hand.

"Elizabeth, you know better. Those stones are loose and some of the stairs are treacherous. You could easily fall."

He studied Katherine. The concern in his eyes startled her.

"I can imagine something happening to Elizabeth, and your becoming lost and unable to voice your distress." He shook his head. "I cannot allow the two of you to go."

"That is well," Elizabeth said. "I'm sorry, Lady Katherine, to disappoint you."

He was right, Katherine thought, but then realized his true intentions. If something happened, she'd be unable to present herself at her best for her prospective suitor, and Lord Drayton would have to house her for a longer period. This was the main reason he wanted her kept safe.

"I know you wish to see the keep," he continued, and the blue of his eyes seemed to darken as he gazed at her. "When I return from town, I'll take you through it myself.

But you'll need to don a simpler gown. That one looks too cumbersome." He hesitated then, seeming to grope for words. "Although...'tis becoming on you."

Katherine took a quick breath of astonishment, and then wondered at her foolishness in feeling so gratified at his small compliment. He had implied only that he wanted her to look pretty so the baron would approve of her. He himself cared not at all.

Later in the morning, dressed simply in a loose yellow morning gown, Katherine waited for Lord Drayton in the dim parlor. She sat bent forward over her needlework, peering closely at the linen to get the stitches straight.

When her neck began to ache and she couldn't keep the threads from twisting, she flung the linen to the floor, stood, and turned to the window. Lord Drayton wasn't here. What was the harm in opening the drapes for just a while so she would not go blind or permanently bent? His rule was so very ridiculous!

She glanced behind her at Millie sitting in a chair against the wall bowed over some mending, and then stole to the windows and grasped the panels of the dark drapes. She ignored the memory of fear in Elizabeth's eyes, and flung the drapes open one by one until light spilled through all three tall windows. She spun to survey the room as Millie sprang up.

The maid clutched her mending. "You mustn't" she said, her voice high and tense. "Lord Drayton, he...." She trailed off as she looked around the room.

Yes—the room! Katherine's heart soared with sudden gladness. In the radiant light, the parlor gleamed.

Beams of sun glistened on ivory-cream tiles that surrounded the ornate fireplace and mantel hearth. It twinkled off the glass of the cabinet above the mantel and brought to life the blue and white china showcased within. Two tapestries woven, embroidered in once colorless shapes now came alive with reds, golds, and greens of an autumn hunting scene. Oak tables on either side of the sea-blue velvet couch shone, and the lyre and flute near the corner showcased their fine blond wood.

Tiny dust motes floated above the glistening wool threads on the thick blue and green carpet covering the polished wood floor.

And finally, Katherine was able to see in its glorious detail the exquisitely carved oak paneled wall that enclosed the room.

"M'lady," Millie said, and then sat heavily in the chair. "Oh, m'lady...."

Katherine, smiling, retrieved her tree-of-life embroidery and sat back on the couch, perusing the room once more. She would close the drapes the instant his horse passed by on the drive. At a snuffle from Millie, however, she looked over at her with concern.

"If I may speak?" Millie asked, her voice thick with emotion.

Katherine sighed and nodded, fully expecting another reminder of the silly rule.

"Lord Drayton hasn't had the curtains opened since Lady Drayton died."

Katherine dropped her needlework onto her lap. Surely he grieved the loss of his wife, but his quality of mourning seemed to stretch into unreasonable actions. Still, she waited for further explanation.

Millie spoke hurriedly. "She fell from her window, like I told ye. The night she died, Lord Drayton told us he didn't want t'see a window in his house ever again. He shouted at the servants, said he'd take his rod to us if we ever opened them. And then he went around and tore her portraits off the wall." Millie lowered her eyes and added, "I don't know if his threat of whippin' ye was real or not. But if it is true, ye won't be able to call for help. Please, m'lady. Ye *must* do what he says."

Fear invaded Katherine's self-assurance. She hadn't taken his threat seriously. Now she wondered if she'd been wrong, again, about the type of man he was.

Millie gasped as the trotting of hooves sounded outside. Katherine spun toward the windows.

And locked eyes with Lord Drayton as he rode by on his gray horse.

She gulped in alarm at the sight of his eyes narrowing into twin blue glaciers, and then she doubled over with one hand on her stomach and the other over her mouth in a bout of frantic coughing.

Millie dashed to each window. Seconds later, dimness once again encased the parlor and shrouded everything in muted colors.

The echoing slam of a door sounded. Booted footsteps rang closer. Katherine straightened and stared at the open entrance of the parlor.

In he strode, glancing at the drapes before returning his gaze to her. His chest rose and fell with a deep breath, and he stood for a moment as if making a decision. Then, his eyes swept over her. "I see you're ready to explore the keep."

Would he not he reprimand her for opening his drapes? His caginess kept her from knowing his thoughts. She clasped her hands together so he wouldn't see their shaking. Forcing her mouth into a smile that felt wooden and false, she nodded.

"Then we will do so now. 'Tis best to go in bright daylight. Are you ready?" With no expression save the coolness of his gaze, he turned and offered his elbow.

Katherine shot a desperate look at Millie.

"Millie may accompany you." A bare twinkle, gone before she had time to examine its implications, flickered in his eyes. But he did not smile. "It would be the proper thing, I suppose. Millie may bring your slate along since paper and pen won't be feasible."

Katherine hesitated. She'd hit him, called him names. Fool!

"Come," he said. His eyes bore into hers.

With lead feet, she walked to him and, with trembling hand, took his proffered arm.

Chapter Twelve

Panic swept over Katherine's features. She trembled visibly as if yearning to dash far away from Alex. That was nothing new to him, her alarm acutely reminiscent of Mary during her feral-like spells of clawing terror.

He would say nothing of Katherine breaking his rule, and focused on the tour in an attempt to allay her fear. As they walked through the Hall, he gave her a reassuring smile and said, "There are several entrances, but the one I'm taking you to is the safest. Do you enjoy exploring new places?"

She nodded and sent him a furtive glance.

Perhaps he might venture a question, and said casually, "You seem to have a keen inquisitiveness. You went into the closet to see my wife's portrait, did you not? I noticed it had been moved."

Again she nodded, this time staring straight ahead.

They'd arrived at the back corridor and turned right. "I'm curious. Did something frighten you so much that you fainted?"

Katherine frowned and shook her head.

"What happened to you, then? The closet door handle was not broken."

She glanced at the slate Millie held.

"Please do." Relieved to finally know, Alex stopped and, taking the slate from Millie, handed it to Katherine. He tried to hide his grimace in anticipation of the chalk's squeak.

It is my concern only, she wrote.

The unseen wall of distrust thickened between them. Annoyance made him retort, "Was your eavesdropping in my study yesterday also only your concern?"

Katherine lowered her eyes and bit her lip, then wrote, *No*. She hesitated and added, *You were kind to them*.

"Clara is a good person," he said with a shrug. "Pace helps in the barn. He's a fine lad."

They walked on.

Taking her to the keep was a bad idea. He should turn around now and escort her back to the parlor, and then leave her there until Wiltshire arrived. But the battlements were special, a connection to his past that he felt compelled to share with her.

The battlements held no ghosts from his past.

Katherine could, perhaps, see him as a man wishing only to live a solitary life instead of the indifferent rogue she surely regarded him as now.

And he could give her over to the baron tonight with no further thought that he could have done more to ease her mind.

****

At the end of the long, dark corridor, another wing extended to the left. It seemed they were walking toward the back of the house.

To break the silence, and to gauge Lord Drayton's temperament, Katherine paused to venture a question on her slate. *Is this your family home?*

He brightened as he read her words. "Yes. Built two centuries ago in front of the keep. Cromwell's men took possession of it during the king's exile, but Charles reclaimed it for me after he came into power."

He loved his home, she noted as she felt the old floor boards echo beneath her heeled shoes. She no longer trembled, but instead looked forward to the tour.

The passage began to narrow and descend. They stopped at a heavy oak wooden door at the end. When Lord Drayton grasped the handle and pulled it open, the ponderous creak of its old hinges seemed overly loud in the quiet.

He led Katherine and Millie through the door and down two dozen or so stone steps that were smoothed and dipped from centuries of the feet that had trod them. "The original steps of the keep," he told them, "built in the thirteenth century during Henry III's reign."

The air cooled as they descended.

At the bottom of the stairway, he opened another door that led to a long straight tunnel of rough gray stone walls and floors.

"Stay close, Katherine. You as well, Millie. 'Tis dark, and there are rats about." Without hesitation he stepped forward, holding out his lantern. His footsteps rang hollowly.

Katherine peered ahead and saw...nothing.

Dear God. All was swallowed up in blackness. Then the air grew stale and dank and the tunnel shrank all around her. She wanted to keep her distance from Lord Drayton and fought against the roiling panic, but the old terror tumbled her closer to him. The toe of her shoe almost touched his booted heel and it was all she could do not to clutch at his waistcoat.

Maybe she could turn and find her way back. Millie had procured a lantern for her and the tunnel was a straight path back to the door. But she couldn't retreat.

Unaware of her paralyzing emotion, Lord Drayton abruptly turned down one twisting passage, then another, and another until Katherine had no idea where she was. Perhaps her confusion was exactly what he'd intended.

The passage grew more constricted and airless with every step, and ragged breaths tore from her pounding chest.

Up ahead, skittering sounds warned of the rats.

Lord Drayton glanced over his shoulder. "Can you see why we worried for you on the night we couldn't find you? I thought you might have gone exploring. No one would hear you if you became lost or hurt among these twisting paths."

His words took on a sinister meaning, and Katherine glanced behind her at Millie. The maid's face was obscured in the shadows thrown by the lanterns.

Hideous fear knotted Katherine's belly as the passage further narrowed and Lord Drayton had to duck his head. She dabbed trembling fingers at the beads of perspiration on her upper lip. Her legs shook and she could barely move them. One more moment and it would be impossible to conceal her utter disintegration.

"M'lord, Lady Katherine—she's feeling poorly," Millie called out in alarm.

Katherine sagged against the wall, gasping with short breaths. Both lantern and slate slipped from her numb hands and made echoing clatters as they hit the damp stone floor.

"What is it, Katherine?"

Lord Drayton touched her arm, and she reached out to him like a lifeline. His features wavered and blurred. Her gaze slid from him to Millie, but darkness invaded her vision. The rough stone wall tearing at her back was her only sensation as she slid toward the floor.

Struggling for breath, she was vaguely aware of something sturdy and gentle wrapping around her waist. Her head lolled against solid warmth, and the rhythmic beating of a heart sounded in her ear.

A faraway voice gurgled as if speaking through water. "We're almost there."

Distantly, she heard the working of a latch and a deep groaning of hinges.

A soothing voice murmured in her ear. "'Tis all right now, Katherine. We've arrived at the keep."

She was lowered to a sitting position on cold stone, and then felt herself enveloped in the warmth and strength of his arms.

After several minutes, her racing heart and panting slowed. She remained motionless, unwilling to be free of the captivating heat that surrounded her.

His heat, his strength. So natural to be held by him. Unabashed and unafraid, she turned her face into his chest and breathed him in. Her heart again quickened, but for a different reason altogether.

She felt languid and warm and never wanted to break away, loving the way he cuddled her against his body, the way his hand caressed her cheek.

"How do you feel?"

His words broke her bizarre state of mind. The man holding her like a lover was the turbulent and obstinate Lord Drayton. The desire, the sensation of sheltering protection—no, it was all wrong and quite improper. And yet...she couldn't let go.

She disliked him, she reminded herself, feared him, needed to be gone from his home so that she would no longer have these ridiculous feelings.

Summoning all her will, she pushed at his chest and felt his body stiffen under her hands.

Abruptly he released her and stood. "Tend to her, Millie." His voice held a rough edge.

Stark emptiness filled her where the warmth had been.

The maid came forward, her kindly round features creased with worry. She knelt and dabbed at Katherine's forehead with the corner of her apron.

Katherine waved her away. She was more in control of herself now and there was no need to fuss.

Lord Drayton held out his hand. Obligated to take it, she let him help her up. He didn't release his hold on her hand and remained close, his face hard scrutiny. "I want the truth. What happened in the closet?"

The closet? She shook her head, confused.

"I found you in there curled up like a babe, with your fingertips torn to bits. The wall in the back of the closet is embedded with the scratches you made." He released her hand and took the slate from Millie, and thrust it toward her. "What happened? Answer me."

It was none of his business, really, but she supposed he deserved an explanation. Frowning, she took the slate, shrugged, and wrote, *Afraid of small spaces.*

He shoved out a breath. "As I thought. Why did you go in there?"

Curious.

"And your meddling mind got the better of your fear."

Brows creasing in irritation, she looked into his eyes. *Yes,* she mouthed with stiff lips.

"Had I known what your reaction would be in these tunnels, I would not have brought you. 'Tis good that Elizabeth told me of her plans with you this morning."

Had Katherine known what it would take to come to the keep, she wouldn't have come at all. Yet she didn't write the retort. Instead, she turned her attention to the cavernous room before her. They were here. She may as well try to enjoy it.

"In any case, we will return another way. We'll have to climb over some rocks, but there are no small spaces." He walked with her, apparently finished with his reprimand, and gestured with a broad sweep of his hand. "This is the main hall of the keep. Since you're a curious sort, I'll take you through what I can, but some of the sections have become treacherous. Especially when Cromwell's men destroyed part of it when I was a boy."

Katherine looked up at him and caught the pain in his expression, but just as quickly the aloofness returned. Perhaps if circumstances were different, she might ask him to tell her about his childhood, his life. It wasn't necessary to know, however, and she chided herself for possessing even a remote interest.

She perused the two huge hearths on opposite stone walls, then craned her head back and peered up at the narrow windows high above. Part of the roof was gone and the afternoon sun shone down on them. The vast room was empty of furniture, but she imagined a time centuries ago when tables and chairs and rugs would have filled it. The crackling fires in the hearths would have both warmed the fortress and sustained the bellies of the occupants who cooked food over its roaring flames.

"This was the family bedchamber," Lord Drayton said, leading her over the uneven floor to an arched doorway tucked under narrow stone steps. Through the entrance lay an identical empty room, only much smaller. "Everyone slept here. I imagine some of my ancestors were conceived and born in this room until my great-great grandfather built the castle in front of it."

He seemed far more relaxed, the transformation remarkable, as they traversed the main room to the steps built against one wall. He looked over at Millie hugging the door that led back through the passages. "You do not wish to accompany us to the battlement?"

She shook her head and brought her hands up over her chest. "If ye please, m'lord, I'll stay here. I'm not partial to climbin' up t'high places."

Lord Drayton dismissed the maid with a wave, his attention on Katherine. "Careful here," he said as he began to climb the steps. "Take my arm, please. I'll carry your slate for you."

She did so with flutters of apprehension. They would be alone upstairs.

While part of her marveled once again at the muscular arm beneath her fingers, she cautioned herself against the seething temper that might simmer beneath Lord Drayton's concern for her safety.

They reached the top of the steps and walked through a short passage. This led to another set of stairs winding up through a circular tower that could hold fifty men. He gazed down at her with a pleasing upward curve of his mouth and an appreciative glint in his eyes, and Katherine couldn't help thinking that he was unspeakably handsome when he looked at her like this.

"Would you like to proceed to the battlements?" he asked. "They afford a fine view of my lands."

Was his pleasant voice and smile intended to put her off guard? Her traitorous body denied that he might harm her while her mind rationalized that very the possibility.

"Are you also afraid of heights? We can return downstairs and go back to the house if you'd like."

He had misread her hesitation. She forced herself to smile and shake her head. With her free hand, she motioned him on.

A foolish act, perhaps. She'd always been much too curious, but it was imperative—she knew not why—that she know whether she could trust him.

The steps were steep and numerous, and as they ascended, Lord Drayton released her hand from his arm and took her elbow. He stayed by her side and matched his pace with hers, saying nothing. But it was a comfortable silence, and when she glanced up at him, he still maintained his agreeable expression.

At the top, she stood for a moment catching her breath while looking out on a sun-washed open walkway that circled the inside perimeter of a wide circular tower. Rectangular openings in the outer wall afforded views of the green fields.

"Stay close to me," he said, pointing to where most of the stone balustrade on the inner side of the walkway was missing. "'Tis a long fall to the bottom of the tower."

They stayed near the wall as they walked. Partway around, Lord Drayton paused to look out through one of the openings and swept his hand at the vast countryside. "Here the men guarding the keep could see for miles."

Katherine stood beside him and absorbed the hills dotted with white sheep and small cottages. She pointed to the vast forest beyond, then to him, and raised her brows in question.

"Yes, the forest is mine," he said, as if perfectly understanding her inquiry. "There's a shortcut to Chiswick through it, but a highwayman is said to be lurking there. My men and I have yet to flush him out." He took a breath and said, "I once considered living in Chiswick, but I prefer to remain out here in my ancestral home."

She held out her hand for her slate, and when he gave it to her she wrote, *Alone?*

The wind lifted his loose golden hair. "Yes. Alone. The way I prefer to live. No interruptions, arguing, finding fault...nothing at all. Just quiet. Peace and solitude. And when Elizabeth is married to that turtle, Edward—if he ever moves along in his courting—I'll have what I desire."

As he spoke, his expression darkened with some unvoiced suffering, and one hand gripped the stone sill of the fortress. Once again, he seemed to withdraw inside himself.

Katherine watched his head lower, and her heart sank with him. Why would he want to be alone? What devils crawled within and pained him so?

After a moment he raised his head and stared at the blue sky, his gaze seeming to follow the smooth flight of a solitary bird. "That hawk is like you, Katherine. It drifts through the air on silent wings, yet 'tis strong and spirited."

She didn't consider herself strong and spirited. Despite her suspicions of him, however, he made her feel that way.

He turned to her and took her hand, tracing with his thumb the scar running across her palm. "We've both endured almost more than we can take. Yet you are undaunted. My hands are not scarred, but they could do nothing to save the ones I loved."

Lord Drayton's gentle words and unexpected tenderness shattered whatever mistrust she'd had of him. As if in a dream, she watched his hands close over hers, and then looked into his eyes.

Haunted sorrow filled them. Katherine took in his grief, his want, and with crystal clarity she understood. His shattered heart, masked by cold indifference, longed for salvation.

Lord Drayton didn't want to be alone. And he'd never hurt anyone. He wanted, needed to be loved.

With trembling legs, Katherine felt herself succumbing to the alarming charm of this unpredictable man. *The same man who'd arranged for her to marry another*. What was she doing?

He didn't want her. She'd been a fool to come up here. He had no intention of wedding her himself, only wished to torment her with the rough silk of his voice and a glimpse of vulnerability within his tower of male strength.

And soon he would give her over to a stranger.

With a silent sob, she pulled her hand from his and backed away from him.

"Katherine?" The question in his eyes quickly changed to wariness. His mouth drew into a tight line, his hands twin blocks of clenched intensity. "I know not your sudden change in mood, but if you wish to leave by this ledge, you will have quite a descent." Deadly calm gave his words a cold fatality. He advanced toward her.

She must escape his compelling enticement, flee to her room, and await her fate. She turned. The heel of her shoe caught a piece of crumbled balustrade. She fought to keep her balance but toppled to the left—toward the edge of the walkway. Frantically she flailed her arms as she felt herself careening over the edge.

In the last second before she fell to her death, her eyes locked onto Lord Drayton's. In their blue depths was panic.

And anguish.

Chapter Thirteen

"No!" Lord Drayton roared, and lunged for Katherine. His arms clamped around her body and it seemed he, too, would fall. But he wrenched himself to the right. Clutching her to him, he fell onto his back on the rough gray stone of the walkway with her on top of him.

With a ragged breath, he held her. His gentle fingers slipped through her hair and stroked her head until she had quieted.

"Katherine." His hand, warm and tender, moved in a caress. "I almost lost you." His voice sounded broken, as if reaching to her from the depths of murky water.

She forgot all her doubts and despair in the hard warmth of his body against hers. She felt his heart pounding as he pressed her against him. Willing his sensuous mouth to hers, she slid her hands over his chest.

His lips met hers, passionate yet with a warm, gentle strength, and for the first time in her life, a lush heaviness deep within burst forth and blazed with white hot intensity.

He rolled her onto her back and kept her wrapped in his arms to cradle her from the stone beneath her. She reveled in the sensation of his hard body lying over hers, his silky hair, his mouth on hers.

When the tip of his tongue teased her lips, a primitive, heated desire shot straight to her core. She opened her mouth to gasp, and his tongue thrust in.

And suddenly there was nothing else in the world but this man.

To simply surrender, to yield to whatever he wanted to do with her, overrode all else. She clutched him to her.

He was so close. But she wanted more.

His kiss held a deep, profound need. She met his passion, and intuitively knew that this sort of comfort was just what Alexander Fletcher needed to sweeten his bitter soul.

Wanting him, all of him, she met his tongue with her own and heard his deep growl of pleasure.

Soft breezes hummed through the openings along the battlement wall and tempered the warmth of the bright sun shining on her face. Katherine slid her hands over the delicious, sunbathed heat of his shoulders and back. At last she could touch him. At last. All time ended, all pretense vanished.

His thigh moved over her leg and brushed the very center of her and she silently begged for more, more.

Alex.

He broke the kiss, murmured as he nuzzled her neck, roved down over the tops of her breasts, then returned to her lips and plundered her mouth once again.

Her entire body sang. She turned her hips and wrapped one leg around his, pulling him against her in desperate need. He groaned, and she knew that he was hard and ready.

His hand slid to her shoulder and began to pull down her dress, his trailing lips leaving exquisite hot tingles along her chest. Arching her neck, Katherine could only respond with fast, hard breaths. Her body went liquid in his arms when he slid his hand into her bodice and cupped her breast.

But warning bells rang deep within, distantly at first and then louder, telling her to stop this. Ignoring them, she kissed his neck and the small white scar on his jaw, and gave a silent whimper when he played his fingers over her nipple. She gave in to his mouth when it demanded hers, and clutched at his shoulders. Oh, God, how she wanted him.

The warning grew as reality snaked through her being. Slowly the luscious sensations subsided as Katherine grew cold with the knowledge that she was giving herself to this man like a wanton whore.

She stiffened and shoved at him, and with clear surprise he moved off her. Quickly she scooted back and then got to her feet, pulling her bodice back into place with short, shaky jerks.

He remained on his side, propped on one elbow, his gaze roaming over her face. A battle of expressions—

perplexity, frustration, and finally the familiar coldness—crossed his features.

They stared at each other. Strands of loosened hair blew into her face and she brushed them aside. His eyes left hers and followed the impatient movements of her hands.

She detested the betrayal of her body, hated that she reacted so strongly to him. But even with the knowledge that he would soon give her to another, the urge to lower herself to him and let him resume his lovemaking made her tremble.

Finally Alex stood, but did not approach. His throat moved as he swallowed. Several times he seemed about to speak, and then finally declared, "I was only being flippant with my suggestion to leave by the ledge. You seemed fool enough to try."

She was more of a fool for allowing him to seduce her. She looked around for her slate to write a terse message concerning her intention to never again let him near her.

"Gone," he said, shrugging. "Fallen over the ledge, as you almost did."

Realization dawned on her, and with it confusion. He had held and kissed her like a lover. She needed to know, right now, his feelings.

Carefully, she edged to a spot on the ledge that still held a bit of stone balustrade, and peered down. Somewhere far below her slate lay, most likely in pieces among the crumbled gray stones.

She felt him at her shoulder, and the urge to lean back into his arms was disconcerting. She hastened back toward the winding stone staircase, feeling the wind lift her loosened hair and toss it about her shoulders.

"Since you do not find my presence pleasing, I'll be sure to remain distant from you whenever I can," he said from behind her. "I wouldn't want you to suffer more than necessary until you leave here."

She stopped and wheeled toward him, greatly wishing to give him the quarrel of his life, to tell him exactly what she thought of him, how she wanted him—no, *didn't* want him—and demand an explanation of the past.

Unexpectedly, he was very near. His white cravat had come loosened, and blonde curls peeked from the open neck of his shirt. If she leaned forward and stood on her toes, her lips would meet the beckoning hollow of his throat.

Then, she looked into his eyes and saw the desperate need beneath the mockery. Flustered, she dropped her gaze to the stone floor.

Alex—Lord Drayton—placed a finger under her chin and lifted her face. His touch lit another warm flush inside her, and as his eyes dropped to her lips and lingered there, she thought for a dazed second that he would kiss her again.

To her mortification, she knew she would welcome him.

But he took a deep, ragged breath, and seemed once again to battle for his words. "Listen to me," he finally said in a voice gruff with emotion. "If your suitor refuses you, nothing will happen between us. You will make no requests of me or think of me as anything but your guardian. You may eat at my table and sleep in my house. Beyond that, my deepest wish is to find you a husband and get you out of my life."

Oh, such vile words, and from lips that had kissed her so fervently only moments ago.

Katherine jerked away before he could see her tears.

****

Alex took Katherine back to the main house by a different route to avoid the narrow labyrinth they'd traveled before. With Millie following—she evidently knew something had happened between them because she looked from him to Katherine with curious, cautious eyes—they picked their way through treacherous stones to reach the massive jagged opening where once a mighty door had stood. Four times Katherine almost stumbled. Although touching her would dissolve his determination like rain on salt, Alex held her close to keep her steady.

He gritted his teeth at the delicate firmness of her body, her lavender scent, the remembered sweetness of her mouth. As he helped her over a piece of the fallen archway, he glanced at her beautiful face and knew he wanted her.

Dear God, he wanted her.

No, damnation. Mute baggage she was, nothing

more. Keeping her would only fuel reminders of Cromwell's spies, like her traitorous father, who'd destroyed his life. Caring for her only generated emotion that he wanted left dead. He must crush the hope and happiness that bloomed within him—useless feelings that would only lead to more sorrow.

The sooner Thomas Bliss carted her off, the better.

"'Tis just a walk down this path now," he said gruffly as he led her past tangled vines and tall weeds.

She didn't acknowledge his words. He waited for a gesture of her hands, the charming tilt of her head or the raising of her brow, something—anything—that would give him an idea what she was thinking. But her body and expression revealed nothing, save for the set line of her mouth. She stared straight ahead when they reached the weed-choked pebbled path, and quickened her stride.

He almost wished she'd just clout him.

As they reached the front of the house, a carriage rolled up the drive and stopped. "Agnes," he muttered in irritation. "Has she no other friends?"

Katherine slanted a glance toward him.

"Good day, Agnes," Alex said with an obligatory smile. "I believe Elizabeth should have returned from the market by now." He glanced over at his stable, and yes, his carriage sat empty in front of it.

"Good day to you, Lord Drayton," Agnes said. "And how are you, Lady Katherine? My, you're out of breath. And your cheeks are bright with color."

Katherine nodded awkwardly and then stared at the door as if willing it to open by itself.

"I've just shown Lady Katherine the keep," Alex explained. "We went up to one of the battlements."

"Ah. Do you remember when you took me up there?" Agnes asked. "I *so* enjoyed myself." She smiled and cocked her head, which made her springy curls bounce.

Katherine turned to him. Her eyes, had they been daggers, would have cut him to bloody bits. He knew what she was thinking—that he'd taken Agnes up there and shared such a kiss of passion with her as to forget that everything existed but the taste and feel of her—but said simply, "Indeed, I have taken many guests up there."

Katherine misconstrued his meaning. Her eyes widened, then narrowed in fury. She turned once more to the door and gestured sharply for Millie to open it.

Agnes's gaze swung from Alex to Katherine with a suspicious glint, but she said nothing.

"I will show you to the parlor and inform Elizabeth that you're here to visit," he said to Agnes as they entered. "Perhaps you can meet Lady Katherine's suitor before you return home."

Agnes brightened. "Suitor? How nice, Lady Katherine! Oh, I do wish you the best of luck. Who is he, my lord?"

As if she didn't know. Alex had informed Robert, who had surely told his inquisitive wife and daughter. "Thomas Bliss, Lord Wiltshire, from London. He recently settled into his summer home nearby. Mayhap you've met him."

Agnes wrinkled her nose. "I have. He is positively ancient, and smells of onions."

Ahead of them, Alex saw Katherine's shoulders droop.

"But he dresses nicely," Agnes added. "And he is *quite* rich."

Sam stood quietly near the parlor door. With quick eyes he took in Alex and Katherine's disheveled appearance, cleared his throat, and bowed deeply.

Alex stiffened at the slight smirk Sam attempted to mask. Stepping closer, he hissed, "If you've nothing better to do than guard the door, go scrape up shit in the barn."

"Yes, my lord," Sam said, casting his gaze to the floor in seeming repentance. "Whatever you wish."

Alex swore under his breath. "Well, out with it. Why are you standing there?"

"Lord Wiltshire has been here for the past half hour, my lord," Sam whispered.

Alex stifled unreasonable anger. "He wasn't to arrive so soon."

"Oh, may I join him, Lord Drayton?" Agnes asked, her eyes sparkling.

Alex glanced at Katherine. Face pinched, she stood with arms crossed and foot tapping the floor.

"I'm sure you'd be welcomed, Agnes. We shall join you all shortly. I imagine Lady Katherine would like to change into a finer dress to meet her suitor." Alex gestured Katherine to walk ahead of him, then turned to Sam. "Come upstairs with me."

As Katherine slowly ascended the stairs, Alex noted the stiff set of her back.

In his bedchamber, Sam handed him a towel to dry his face and hands after he washed them. "I'm sorry," Sam said. "This must be difficult for you."

"No. She wishes to leave. 'Tis best."

"For whom?" Sam asked. "You or her?"

Alex tossed the towel onto the washstand and ran a hand through his hair. "We had...an event on the battlement. She almost fell off the edge of the walkway, and I caught her. I lost my self-control."

"Wait," Sam said, looking confused. "She almost fell, and you caught her. How did you lose control?"

"I kissed her. Touched her." His calloused fingers tingled at the memory of her nipple hardening under them.

"Ah." Sam busied himself with retrieving a fresh shirt from the cabinet.

"If she had fallen..." Alex's voice hitched, and he swallowed to bring it under control. Roughly he took the shirt, pulled it over his head, and thrust his hands through the sleeves.

"Do you want her to go?"

"I want her to be happy."

"Do you want her to go, Alex?"

"Don't test me, Sam." Alex spoke more harshly than he'd intended.

Clearly unimpressed, Sam turned his back and tidied up the washstand.

"I've been thinking of a way to bring back her voice." The words left Alex's lips before he could stop them.

Sam paused in the act of drying the bowl. "A woman that spirited must find her condition so very frustrating."

"It doesn't frustrate Wiltshire. He doesn't seem to care. But he doesn't know what a contrary woman Katherine is."

Sam sighed. "If she ever regains her voice, Lord Wiltshire will find her an unusually assertive mate."

Alex stilled as he tied his cravat, one hand fingering a length of snowy cloth. "Likely, Wiltshire would take a stiff rod to her back." And after a few months, Katherine would become a motionless, submissive shell—as good as dead.

Sudden, unbidden tears blurred his vision. He coughed, placed his hand on the back of the armchair, and lowered his head, taking deep, gulping breaths. It seemed that a dozen powerful fingers had taken hold of his throat.

Sam dropped the bowl with a thud and rushed to Alex, laying a bony hand on his shoulder. "Are you all right, lad?"

"Leave, please. I can finish dressing alone." Alex passed a hand over his eyes.

"Alex?"

"Go."

Sam left quietly.

Alex snatched up his boots, flung himself into his chair, and pulled the boots on with swift, jerky movements. Then, he sat back, staring into the fire.

This would not do, this strange sorrow. There was no reason for it. Katherine would be treated as any woman who displeased her husband. All men had a right to discipline their wives.

Even though Alex secretly welcomed her strength of mind, he was satisfied with being alone. He wanted no mate with whom to share the rest of his days.

There would be nothing in his life to cause him grief as long as he kept his emotions intact.

There would be nothing at all.

Chapter Fourteen

Crimson skirts beribboned with satin bows rustled about Katherine as she trudged down the steps. She nervously smoothed the rich scarlet and gold embroidery worked through her waistcoat. No one could complain that she hadn't dressed well, but this was all happening so quickly. Why hadn't her suitor waited until later to arrive? Would it have made much difference in her readiness?

Her aching spirit and tormented body were forever stamped with the sensual feel of Lord Drayton—she would never, ever refer to him as Alex—kissing her with such intense desire. But just as quickly, the image flashed to him telling her that he wanted her gone from his life.

She was in no mood to meet her suitor and wished to God she'd never gone to the keep.

Would she retch when she looked upon the ancient baron? Did he really smell like onions?

No matter what kind of person Lord Wiltshire was, she knew that no man would ever make her feel the way Lord Drayton had at the top of the sun-soaked battlement.

Millie shot her a sympathetic glance and led her to Lord Drayton's withdrawing room off his study to await his escort to the parlor. Katherine paced the room for a few minutes before dropping onto a carved oak bench, her voluminous skirts settling about her. Her hands felt empty without her slate, and she folded them in her lap, then unfolded them and removed her perfumed, gold-bordered crimson gloves. She brought her fingers close to the light of the candle on a nearby table to study them.

So ugly. The nails were rough and stubby from her embarrassing incident in the closet, and the tips of her fingers were pink with tender new skin. She turned her hands over and studied the revolting scar on one palm.

The old feeling rose within her once again. She could have saved the two small children if only she'd been able to grasp the scorching handle of the door inside their house...perhaps even reached her father in time, and preserved her voice. Life would be normal.

But they'd all died because of her failure. And now she waited, vulnerable and afraid, and unable to crack the hard exterior of the man who held her future in the palm of his own large hand.

Lord Drayton should have let her fall.

The door opened and closed with a bang. Startled, Katherine looked up through a blur of tears to see him striding to her with swift, sure steps.

He pulled up short, however, and concern replaced his hard expression before settling into amused boredom.

"Surely you aren't so troubled from the prospect of meeting your suitor that you would shed tears."

He held out a lacy white mouchoir. When she snatched it from him, he stood waiting with his arms folded across his broad chest.

Scowling at his crass comment, she wiped her tears and stared ahead of her, but her gaze was taken up by his firm thighs accentuated by snug black breeches. Which of his legs had she wrapped hers around to pull him closer? And the hardness of him...he had settled now, but she could still see his shape....

Mortified at her lewd thoughts, she lowered her eyes to his boots and pulled her gloves onto her hands.

He turned away abruptly with an impatient grunt and walked to the door. "Keep the mouchoir. 'Tis best that we go on to the parlor."

She stood with heavy reluctance and followed him like a woman in a nightmare unable to stop her feet. The man waiting in the parlor might as well be her captor instead of her future husband. Lord Drayton opened the door and stood aside for her to leave first. She stopped and searched his eyes.

He must be an accomplished actor, for he gazed back at her with the same impassivity he'd shown on the day of her arrival.

Out in the passage that led to the Hall, Katherine lay her hand lightly on the forearm he held out for her. Immediately, the sensations she'd felt on the high battlement flooded back to her as the firm, corded warmth of his arm tingled her hand.

"Your hand is shaking," he said as he glanced down at it. "No need to be anxious. I've found Lord Wiltshire to be quite pleasant."

Oh, she wanted to slap him. Why was he acting as if he hadn't kissed her and held her like a lover just an hour before? Didn't he know what he'd done to her? The desire he'd unleashed in the midst of her trepidation?

She slowed in the dim passage, to turn with him back to his study so she could write down her feelings. And he owed her the truth about his past, an insight to his heart.

But he misread her hesitation. "If you're concerned that I'll mention our error to Lord Wiltshire, rest assured that I will not," he said with airy assurance.

Error! Katherine halted and looked him full in the face. Were there no feelings in the man? Did he habitually take women up to the heights of the battlement and kiss them into a stupor? Had he done the same with Agnes? With other women? Tears stung her eyes afresh.

His façade of indifference broke. His voice became gruff, his face tight. "Yes, our kiss was a mistake. What I felt—feel—has no bearing on the present." His throat moved as he swallowed.

She reached for him then, took his hand in both of hers. Her lips moved. *Talk to me.*

His gaze locked on her mouth. He raised one of her hands to his lips, pressing them to her palm and sending a tingle straight to her toes. Then, he lowered her hand and shook his head. "I cannot. 'Tis a pact I made."

Determined, Katherine reached up and brushed her thumb over the scar on his jaw and then across his lips, lips that were so soft for a man whose heart had grown so hardened.

His head lowered toward hers. "My lady...what are you doing to me?"

Their lips met again, hungry and determined. His tongue found hers and played it in passionate thrusts. She clung to his shoulders as her legs went weak.

He clutched her to him, almost lifting her off the floor with his strength of desire, nuzzling her neck and breasts.

His hands moved over her back in slow, sensual strokes. "Katherine," he moaned.

She gasped with hot desire and tangled her hands in his hair, pulling him closer, wanting for nothing else in the world but the feel of his mouth, his body, on hers.

He pulled back and his eyes held both hope and uncertainty. Gradually, though, regret filled them. "I'm sorry. Once again I've lost control." He drew his hands from her tense, heated body and placed them on her shoulders. "'Tis best that you leave here. You mustn't care for me. I would only bring you sorrow."

Katherine stiffened and pulled away, left cold from her own confusion and embarrassment that she had again flung herself at a man who was about to marry her off to another.

His expression resolute, he held out his arm once more and led her silently through the Hall to the parlor.

As he opened the door, she heard him speak under his breath. "And so it ends."

She wasn't ready for this. Her emotions hung upside down and every rational thought had been shaken out. Wanting nothing more than to turn and flee to her bedchamber, she stepped slowly to the door and heard feminine laughter followed by a deeper voice.

"...looked quite grand," the voice said. The entire—ah, Lord Drayton."

"Lord Wiltshire," Alex answered in greeting, and both his voice and slight bow held a grim intensity. He stepped aside and Katherine had full view of the man who approached them.

Smallish brown eyes encased within laugh lines twinkled warmly at her over round, apple-red cheeks. Not ancient as Agnes had declared, the baron nonetheless had seen a good many years. His body seemed to creak as he bowed while sweeping off a wide-brimmed black hat sporting a vivid maroon feather. A fluffy black wig, the top of which raised his height by several inches, curled past his shoulders and framed his powdered face.

He wore a waist-length purple satin jacket edged with gold trim to accentuate the white shirt that puffed out below. His matching petticoat breeches, fashionably distended, ended at his knees amidst a flurry of vivid green, white and purple ribbons that matched those fluttering at his wrists. Gold-buckled black leather shoes completed the ensemble. Clearly, the baron enjoyed keeping abreast of the king's fondness for extravagant fashion.

He could be Katherine's own grandfather, only he was to become her husband—if she accepted him. And this she would not do.

She noted a startling contrast between tall, grim Lord Drayton in his plain black breeches with black jacket and white shirt, and the diminutive Lord Wiltshire, smiling in all his fine, colorful attire. They resembled a magnificent stag looming over a ridiculous little rooster.

Katherine forced her face into a pleasant smile and steeled herself for what was to come.

"May I present the Lady Katherine Seymour, daughter of Lord and Lady Thomas Seymour," Alex said, trying not to growl out the words. "Lady Katherine, allow me to introduce you to The Right Honorable Lord Wiltshire, Thomas Bliss." He noticed that Elizabeth had joined Agnes. "I apologize for keeping you waiting, Lord Wiltshire. I trust my neighbor and cousin are entertaining you." He adopted an affable smile as he watched Katherine compare him to the clownish fop before him, but he felt strangely inadequate. From the way her lips curved up at Lord Wiltshire's appearance, it was clear that she preferred his manner of dress. Perhaps he himself should have worn loose breeches to hide his throbbing desire.

Her lips looked swollen from his rough kiss in the Hall. He shut out his sudden craving to carry her upstairs and run his tongue and hands over the rest of her.

"We've had a grand hour!" Lord Wiltshire declared, unabashedly exploring Katherine. He paid particular attention to the smooth mounds pushing up out of her bodice.

"Indeed we have, Lord Drayton," Agnes said from the couch. "I do believe Lord Wiltshire has caused my stays to loosen from all the laughing I've done."

"Agnes!" Elizabeth said with a giggle. "My goodness!"

Alex studied his cousin with surprise. He'd never seen her so animated.

Thankfully, the baron had concluded his scrutiny of Katherine. Alex hadn't expected this lustful behavior from the old man. Gads, it was as if she were a side of beef hanging at the market. His roving eyes annoyed Alex almost beyond endurance.

When Wiltshire took her right hand and meandered his lips over the back of it in a lingering kiss, something ferocious stirred within Alex. If the baron dared turn it over and kiss her palm, as Alex himself had done—

"Shall we sit?" he asked through gritted teeth.

Wiltshire straightened, his wrinkled hand still clutching Katherine's fingers in his old man grip.

Pulling back her hand, she sucked in a quick breath between her teeth. Pain bloomed on her face.

"Take heed," Alex said quickly. "Her fingers are healing from an injury."

"Injured!" Wiltshire fired an accusatory glance toward Alex.

Alex replied coolly, "I will explain what happened later so as to save her embarrassment."

"Yes, you will," Wiltshire said, chin held high as he held out his arm for Katherine.

Alex noted the ease and trust with which Katherine placed her hand on the baron's arm. A pain ripped through his gut that he himself hadn't been able to earn her trust.

But he had none to give her. Madness and bitter sorrow had prevailed in this house for years, and lingered on after Mary's death. Hope and trust would never reach these walls, nor his heart.

"Good day, Lady Katherine," Elizabeth said as she stood and indicated a chair for her.

The baron reclaimed his seat nearest the fire in the hearth. Alex waited until both Katherine and Elizabeth were seated before heading toward an empty chair.

Agnes, reclined on the couch, cocked her head and placed her left hand beside her, giving the blue brocade cushion a subtle pat. Alex summoned a smile, the sort a gladiator might level at his opponent, and lowered his frame into the chair. The woman had become outrageous in her attempts at persuasion. Apparently Robert had not relayed Alex's candid assertion of disinterest. If Agnes declined the hint now, she was a dolt as well as a flagrant flirt.

"My dear lady," Lord Wiltshire, exposing even yellow teeth, said to Katherine, "I realize you're without a voice, but 'tisn't important. I will always speak for you. And of course, I'll fill your ears with lively chatter."

Alex crossed an ankle over his knee. "I believe Lady Katherine would like to regain her voice. 'Tis quite important to her."

Katherine's grimace disappeared as she swung her startled gaze to Alex.

"Ah, but silence is a virtue among our fair sex," Wiltshire countered. "She should consider it a gift." He sat back and sipped his wine, either ignoring or oblivious to the disgust that now crossed Katherine's face.

"Lord Wiltshire, do tell your story about Charles' restoration to the throne," Agnes said.

"Ah, yes," the baron said, and a smile lit his face. "The day the king rode into the city, with hundreds of flowers in his path, was the day of London's rebirth."

"I was there!" Elizabeth exclaimed, startling Alex with her uncharacteristic vibrancy. Was she drunk? She turned to him with bright eyes. "Alex, do you remember that day in London? The king's restoration? I was only fifteen, but 'tis still all so clear. Oh, the king looked so handsome, and he smiled at me as he passed." She fluttered a hand to her heart.

"I remember," Alex replied flatly. The purpose of the trip was to meet his bride. How optimistic he had been!

"I was too young to go," Agnes said. "Were you there, Lady Katherine?"

Alex looked over to see her reply, thinking he would need to get her a new slate before she left—one on which the chalk wouldn't squeak so badly. She had been toying with a ribbon on her dress and jerked up her head at Agnes's question. She blinked as if she hadn't heard.

Agnes rolled her eyes. "I asked you—oh, never mind. Go on, please, Lord Wiltshire. I would like to hear all about Court."

Wiltshire's small eyes peered at Katherine. "Are you well, my lady?"

"Perhaps she is tired," Alex said. "We toured the keep today." That wasn't it, though, he knew. The searing knowledge was evident under his breech laces.

"I see," the baron replied. He droned on with his witty reflections, closing his eyes at times as if he were standing in Whitehall all over again.

Katherine slanted her eyes toward Alex, and then she straightened in her chair and held her head erect. She wore a quite pleasant and utterly false expression. Alex noted the slow tapping of her thumb on her folded hands.

What was she thinking right now? Could she be worried about the marriage arrangement? Surely she'd know that he wouldn't pass her off to the first man who would have her, although it seemed he'd done just that.

Or, her mood could stem from her lingering disgust over his actions on the battlement, which she had spurned with disdain. Why had she suddenly broken away from him?

And why, just a few minutes ago, had she gone limp in his arms, her hands in his hair roving with sensuous languor, her mouth opening to his? She had returned his kiss with such enthusiasm. For a moment, he'd known of her passion for him. Or was it simple loneliness?

Regardless of the reason for her response, he knew it was temporary. His slip of self-control would not happen again.

The servants announced the meal, and as Agnes was still in attendance, Elizabeth invited her to dine. Alex thought Agnes's display of hesitation to be almost believable.

During the meal, Elizabeth's eyes widened in fascination as Wiltshire continued his colorful story of Court life. For the first time since Alex could remember, her shyness vanished. She laughed with recklessness and seemed to come alive under the baron's twinkling eyes.

She never behaved this way with Edward. Alex had the feeling that Robert's son, so cautious and slow in his courtship, would be wise to liven his pace if he wanted to keep her attentions.

Agnes also seemed enthralled, for once apparently forgetting herself and reacting with delight at the baron's lively anecdotes.

Only Katherine seemed unmoved. She had surely attended regular parties at the palace and witnessed the courtiers' tendency for frivolous wantonness. Perhaps she had engaged in affairs herself, but from her uncultivated response atop the battlement, Alex had the feeling that her purity was intact.

The thought of another man possessing her body made something deep in his gut twist into a jealous knot.

"And then that obnoxious Duke of Lauderdale," Wiltshire was saying with a laugh, "invited himself to a small dining party given for King Charles. To get rid of him, Charles, after conferring secretly with his host, ordered a double syllabub as refreshment, and offered one to the duke. The duke drank it down, praising that no person had such good taste in drink as His Majesty. Well, in due time, the king cried out, 'My lord, Lauderdale is sick!' and they carried him out. And the king was no longer troubled with the duke inviting himself to private parties." With a twinkle in his eyes, the baron grinned at each of them in turn.

"What?" Elizabeth asked with a wide smile. "What was in the drink?"

"Syllabub, of course," Lord Wiltshire replied, "with an ample quantity of horse urine."

Elizabeth and Agnes giggled freely into their hands, and Alex, chuckling in spite of himself at the story, glanced over at Katherine. Normally ramrod straight when she sat, she was now casually resting against the back of the chair and regarding him with a thoughtful expression. As she gazed at him, a slow smile lit her features. A rusted joy surged through Alex.

Oh, if he could only keep her here with him to harness that joy. If only he could love her, protect her, and hope that she wouldn't learn to hate him.

As Mary had.

Chapter Fifteen

"Katherine, I'm so happy for you," Elizabeth said as they sat in the parlor after the meal. "Lord Wiltshire seems like a good man."

Indeed he did. But she didn't want him.

"Oh, I do agree. Don't you, Katherine?" Agnes prodded.

Katherine sighed her agreement. What else could she do? The prison doors were fast closing on her

"My goodness, but doesn't Alexander make him seem a withered old goat?" Agnes asked with a giggle. Then, she held up her nails to examine them. "I suppose Alexander can court me now that his year of mourning is over."

"How nice, Agnes," Elizabeth said with surprise in her voice. "I wasn't aware that he wished to. Alex often hides his feelings."

Katherine feigned disinterest, but she grew heated by the memory of being held in his arms. He hadn't hid his feelings on the battlement, nor in the corridor outside his study. His mouth had been warm and tender and demanding, his hands gentle yet ardent.

Would he kiss Agnes like that? Would he hold her and make her feel that she was the only woman on earth? A sudden, hot flash of jealousy made Katherine close her eyes to wipe out the image.

"Katherine? Are you ill?" Elizabeth asked.

"Your face is flushed," added Agnes.

Gads! It was no use. She couldn't conceal her emotions. And Agnes had read her mind, as was apparent by the narrow-eyed look the woman was bestowing upon her.

Katherine forced herself to relax, and returned Agnes's scowl with a fierce smile, as wicked as any glare.

"You must be swooning over your baron," Agnes said. "I'm truly sorry you're leaving. I hardly got the chance to know you. Someday, I hope we shall be friends. When I am Lady Drayton and you're Lady Wiltshire, we can hold lovely parties and visit one another. Alexander can take me to London whenever I wish, and perhaps I'll dance with King Charles." She held her fan over her mouth. Her voice lowered. "Perhaps, if the king wishes it, I'll become his mistress. I've heard that he has a large—"

Appalled, Katherine shot up a hand to stop her.

Elizabeth stood, pink and flustered. "Katherine, you are quiet flushed. I'll get a damp towel for your face." She hobbled out quickly as if grabbing at any excuse to be away from Agnes.

Despite Katherine's sparring with Agnes, she had a rare opportunity to question her about Lord Drayton's past. She was almost certain now that he was kind and gentle behind the walls of his brusque exterior, but Millie had said that Mary and Agnes had been friends. Agnes would know the details of Mary's death, and Katherine's heart would be settled.

She went to the writing table and wrote her question.

"Oh, what is it?" Agnes asked crossly. She took the note. A strange look crossed her face as she read the words. "Whatever makes you curious about how his wife died? She fell from her window, 'tis all." Agnes raised and lowered her bare shoulder and then fanned herself with rapid strokes.

Relief filled Katherine like a soothing tonic, and she relaxed in her chair. She would refuse Lord Wiltshire's offer of marriage, if he made one. There was time to get to know Alex, to cut through the armor surrounding his heart.

A glance at Agnes, however, gave her pause. A measuring glint had lit the woman's eyes. "Just what do you know? Did Alexander say anything? Elizabeth?"

Katherine shook her head.

The paper disappeared into a pocket of Agnes's dress. "Well, I don't know what you've heard, so I will tell you what you need to know." She bent forward and Katherine became locked into her emerald green eyes. "You know that he was married to a madwoman. She was my best friend. I tried to help her, truly I did. She—"

"Here we are." Elizabeth limped in with a towel in

her hand. "There was still a water pitcher in the dining room."

Katherine dismissed Agnes's words, only giving heed to the fact that the woman had tried to help Lady Drayton in her condition. Perhaps Agnes possessed a smidgeon of compassion.

She didn't need the towel now, but rose and took it from Elizabeth with a nod of thanks. Smiling, she fetched a candle from a table near the door and headed toward Alex's study to tell the baron he could go home.

She reached the study door and knocked, but there was no answer. Voices sounded, though, from the withdrawing room off the study, and she crept closer.

"...take care of her."

"Why would I not? She is a lovely woman. Truly, I don't understand your sudden reluctance. Are you wanting her for yourself, Drayton?"

There was no answer from Lord Drayton. Katherine's hand was suddenly leaden, and she dropped it to her side. Would he not champion her?

"I suppose your silence means no. I will take her off your hands tomorrow, then."

The scrape of a chair made Katherine falter backwards until her shoulders touched the opposite wall. Quickly she turned and fled.

The meeting had ended and the details worked out. Now, she needed the cool dampness of the towel on her brow.

Soon she would be far from this dark, anguished castle.

And far from the man who made it so.

****

"Wait, Wiltshire," Alex said. "Sit back down."

"What now? I've told you that I'll be kind to her, that she'll want for nothing. You've informed me of her fear of small spaces. What else do you want? Gadzoks, Drayton, you'd think the woman was your own daughter!" Wiltshire plunked his body back onto the plush, high-backed wing chair that flanked the round table.

What did he want? Alex knew Katherine dearly wanted to leave. What woman wouldn't who had been kissed and held and then told that it all meant nothing?

But it meant a great deal to him, especially when, on the battlement, he realized that he no longer held her from worry over her near demise, but for another reason altogether. When a year's worth of stout refusal to let go of his emotions had culminated in a blazing kiss.

But had she not pushed him away in disgust, he might have taken her right there on the windswept stone.

The marriage contract lay on the table between them, awaiting his signature. For some reason, he could not make his hand pick up the quill. He groped for words to delay the moment.

Wiltshire glowered. "Well? Did you bring me from Kensington just to give me excuses?"

"A doctor," Alex declared suddenly. "Yes. I have a doctor coming to look at her throat. He will be here within a fortnight."

Wiltshire shrugged. "Fine. Send him on over to my home to look at her. But I rather enjoy her silence."

Alex wanted to wrap his hands around the man's plump throat. "I cannot."

Wiltshire raised thick graying brows. "Because?"

"He is coming in secrecy. No one can know."

Wiltshire rolled his eyes and puckered his lips in impatience. "What are you talking about?"

Alex lifted his tankard of ale, grasping at thoughts while he gulped the cool, pungent liquid. Then, he set the mug down. "He is a Jew."

A stunned silence ensued, marked only by the crackling of oak logs in the fireplace. At length, Wiltshire cried out, "Are you daft? Those people are the devil's spawn!"

"They are healthy. They rarely have the diseases we have. And I have heard that their doctors are among the most learned in the world."

"They are not part of us, Drayton," Wiltshire sputtered, his face reddening. He pounded the chair's carved arm with his fist. "They've been sneaking into England for years. I don't care if the king protects them. By God, I will not let one defile my wife with his filthy hands!"

Alex glanced at the blank signature line on the contract. "She is not your wife, Wiltshire. You have no hold on her."

"Did you not tell me that the king's own physician

examined her throat and proclaimed that she would never speak again? Why are you asking an inferior doctor to look at her?"

For Alex to admit his belief that Jewish doctors might be more knowledgeable that those of the king would be treasonous. "I shall search out all cures before giving up on her voice."

"Bah! Piss on her voice!" Wiltshire's face bulged with rage. "I'll enjoy her body and teach her to pleasure me. That is *all* that matters."

Alex shot to his feet, as did Wiltshire, who thrust out his wobbling chins and stared up at him. He could snap the baron's neck in a single twist, or shake him like a rag doll.

Instead, with deliberate calm, Alex picked up the contract and held it in front of Wiltshire's indignant face.

"No," he said. "That is not all that matters. And I have changed my mind." He flung the contract into the fire. "Lady Katherine shall not become your wife."

Chapter Sixteen

No light filled the room when Katherine ran her hands down her naked body. Powerful, sizzling desire made her gasp and tremble.

She waited for him, her nipples hard and tingling, her inner thighs hot and slick with wetness. She touched herself and writhed in pleasure.

Hurry. Please, hurry.

At last, the creak of her bedchamber door was a welcome sound, his footsteps toward her bed even more so. She turned eagerly toward him. He lifted the covers and slid down beside her, his naked body warm and hard.

He drew her within his arms. She sighed in contentment and curled into the broad expanse of his chest.

He nuzzled her neck and then kissed her for many minutes. She held his face tenderly, slid her arms over his powerful shoulders, stroked his smooth back.

Wanting engulfed her as his hands caressed her hot skin and his lips whispered endearments. Now. It must be *now*.

Finally, he poised above her. Instinctively she parted her legs for him, knowing what she needed to free the coiled spring inside her—exactly what he had to give.

Take me...take me, Alex.

Her long sighs of pleasure woke her.

She explored her hot, damp body, entwined with her nightgown. And knew she was alone.

For a time she lay still, staring at the dark shape of the canopy overhead.

The strength of the dream and her reaction to it paled in her baffling disappointment that it wasn't real.

****

Lord Wiltshire's presence at breakfast caused Elizabeth to display more of her unusual behavior of the evening before. She laughed heartily at the baron's witticisms, and Katherine was certain the woman had gone completely daft.

He spoke with much less enthusiasm than he had last night, but he really hadn't been funny then, either. Katherine had heard the stories before; Ellis himself had witnessed the Duke of Lauderdale's unfortunate acquaintance with horse urine. The only thing she'd enjoyed about the baron's version was Lord Drayton's resulting smile. It had lit up his face.

This morning, though, his lordship glowered down at his plate and speared his hot mutton pie with harsh stabs of his three-pronged fork, and made the barest attempt to join the conversation.

Katherine sipped her coffee and studied his face. In her betraying dream, she knew he'd had no crease between his brows, no grim downward turn of his lips.

Might his shoulders and back be as smooth as her mind had imagined? And his hips, would they fit perfectly between her thighs as if he were made for her body?

Unbidden desire shook her. Her coffee sloshed over the cup and onto the white-clothed table. She gasped, but not at any pain.

Lord Drayton raised his head, and his startled gaze met hers before darting to her hand still holding the cup.

"Oh! Have you burned yourself?" Elizabeth stood too quickly and, hip twisting, lost her balance. She lurched to her right. With a small scream, she fell against Lord Wiltshire, turning his wig askew so that it covered one half of his face.

"Damnation!" the baron exclaimed as he shot up a hand to catch her.

Alex rushed to Katherine's side as Lord Wiltshire helped Elizabeth back into her chair. "Is everyone all right?" Alex asked, but his eyes never left Katherine.

"I am. Thank you," Lord Wiltshire said with a haughty air. He lifted his hands to his wig and gave it a jerk to the left.

Elizabeth sat, red-faced and blinking tears.

It was an appropriate farce to end her stay here, Katherine thought, although as far as she knew, her trunks still hadn't been packed. She slid back her chair as a servant approached with a cloth to lay over the coffee puddled on the table.

"Is your hand injured?" Lord Drayton asked her.

What did he care? He wanted her gone. Katherine shook her head and coolly held up her hand to show him that the coffee hadn't touched it. Nonetheless, he took her fingers and peered closely at them. At his tender touch, Katherine's breath caught in her throat.

"'Twould be one more wound," he muttered, and released her hand. "I'll have to keep you protected in a room full of cushions before long."

Katherine looked sharply at him. What did he mean, before long? She was leaving, wasn't she?

"The baron will be departing, but I believe he would like to speak to you first," Lord Drayton said.

The awareness that he had answered her unspoken question was overshadowed by the implication of his words.

"I most certainly would," the baron replied in a flat tone. "I shall converse with her directly after breakfast."

Katherine gasped. She might stay. With Lord Drayton. *Alex.*

They locked eyes as he resumed his seat. This time, something in his expression—could it be hope?—betrayed his usual aloof countenance. Ignoring her nervousness, she inclined her head and pegged him with a direct thought.

Before the day ended, she was certain he would tell her the truth about himself.

Chapter Seventeen

Rain pummeled the coach with relentless fury. Deep ruts in the muddy road jostled them so badly that several times Millie was thrown against Katherine, who clutched the leather loop over the window with both hands. Alex sat across from them struggling to remain still, feet flat on the floorboard, hands pressed to the seat. A day later and he still hadn't explained his intentions to Katherine. He'd said nothing of marriage, or of finding her a Jewish physician. Silence was familiar ground. Although he possessed a voice, he wasn't accustomed to using it in heartfelt disclosures and had only issued instructions to pack for London.

After Millie's third whimper of pain and Katherine's futile attempts to shield herself, he said, "Katherine, move across to sit beside me."

She appeared decidedly uncertain and not a little annoyed, and he could hardly blame her. He'd hurried her into the coach with the barest explanation. Justifying his actions was also an alien state.

To try and allay her fears, he smiled. "I'm not bouncing around like Millie. Come to this side before you're covered with bruises."

As she half-stood to move across the coach, it lurched to the right, and she raised her hands to catch herself.

"Steady now." Alex caught her around her waist and pulled her down beside him, noting her stiffness. He did not immediately release her.

She pulled away from him and leaned forward, and drew a folded piece of paper from her small satchel. Watching him, she held it out.

"You have questions," he said, taking the note with a pang of guilt. He should have told her why he was taking her on this journey.

The carriage lurched again and she was thrown to

the side, and would have bumped her head had he not grabbed her again. He tucked her arm into his to keep her secure. Millie now held the strap with both hands.

"We'll discuss my plans in a moment," Alex said. He kept his voice firm. "For now, I'll tell you that this morning, I discovered your prying in one of my ledgers."

Her eyes widened, but she didn't flinch from his steady gaze.

Alex couldn't help smiling. "'Twasn't I who made all the mistakes. You met my dishonest steward in that book. He died several months ago, in town." Watching the trickling shadows on her face created by the rain through the windows, he continued. "The first errors began around the date when my wife first showed signs of madness. Apparently, he took advantage of my distraction and trust, and pocketed much of my profits for the next few months. I've not the patience to go back and correct all my books."

Katherine might be willing to offer her help in correcting his ledgers, but right now she wanted answers. She pointed to Alex's waistcoat pocket.

"Yes. Your letter." He took it out—almost tearing it in half in another lurch from the coach wheels—and read, "'As you know, my inability to speak leaves me unable to fully express my thoughts'—I know this, Katherine. You compensate by knocking me about." With a wry glance at her heating cheeks, he continued. "'I know not your intentions. Lord Wiltshire warned me that the doctor you are seeking is inept and dangerous to my well-being.'"

Alex stopped. Pain passed over his features and his eyes swept across the page as if reading the lines again. The light faded from his eyes and his mouth resumed its tightness. He didn't argue or explain himself, but instead read the rest of her letter in silence.

There was little else she had written—only that she hoped his intentions were honorable as she had done nothing to deserve his malice. The unwritten words, those that stayed hidden in her heart, spoke of her draw toward him, the perplexing mix of longing and uncertainty.

Now he raised his face, his expression naked and open, and Katherine's heart went out to the dejected man beneath the aloof exterior.

"I have none but honorable intentions, Katherine. Do

you truly think me a man of malice?" His eyes searched hers.

Her mouth moved. *No.*

His relief showed in the relaxing of his jaw. "Such lovely lips," he said, gazing at her mouth. "How I long to hear you speak." He was silent for a moment, and then said so quietly that she had to strain to hear him over the pounding rain, "I seek the most talented doctor that I can find to heal you. This is the reason we travel to London."

Katherine's hand rose slowly to her throat, where a lump had formed. Alex had no obligation to the king save providing her food and shelter, yet he would try to help her speak again.

Was there any way to express her gratitude?

There was. Taking his face in both her hands, she pulled him down to her and pressed a soft kiss to his lips.

Chapter Eighteen

When the bleak gray sky began to fade to black, Alex directed the carriage to stop at Three Hooves Inn, a well-tended building but for the mud-spattered pebbled path that led to its planked door. He covered Katherine with his cloak and hastened her in from the rain.

Later, they entered the public eating room where he ordered a meat pasty for each of them and a pitcher of strong ale to share.

He waited until the serving girl left before he spoke. Discussing his feelings was a foreign experience, but he had to be honest with her. "I've done nothing to earn your trust. I thought it unnecessary when I received the king's letter explaining why you were coming to my home."

Katherine watched him steadily.

"My servant told me you listened at my study door the other night while I spoke with Lord Wiltshire. No, don't be embarrassed," he added when Katherine lowered her eyes. "I've grown quite used to your curious nature. But you heard only part of the conversation, apparently. Sam told me you left before the baron and I argued."

The ale arrived, and he drank. Katherine lifted her own cup with both hands and sipped the heady liquid. She kept an even expression, yet he saw the inquisitiveness in her eyes.

"Lord Wiltshire disagreed with me about the doctor. He desired your silence. 'Tis why I tore up the marriage contract." He shook his head and added, "I was wrong in thinking I could marry you off to someone like that." Or anyone, an insistent voice spoke up in his mind.

Eyes narrowed in speculation, Katherine wrapped her fingers around her tankard and slowly drummed it.

Alex licked his lips and took a breath. "The doctor I seek is Jewish. The king might think I doubted the skill of the royal physician who examined you. This is why I concealed my reason for our journey to London. I did not even tell Elizabeth."

He saw the slight shift of Katherine's head, the dawning of understanding in her eyes. Lifting a quill that she brought with her along with ink and paper, she dipped it and wrote, *The baron made it seem that you wish to harm me.*

"Harm you?" he exclaimed, frowning, when he read her words. "No. The baron simply distrusts Jews." He leaned toward her then, his voice low and tense. "I'll tell you why I want to help you, Katherine. My wife, Mary, went insane. She thought I wanted to kill her. She ran from me, jumped out her window. I found her broken and bleeding on the ground. I want to help you because—" He passed a hand over his face and took a choking breath. "—because I could not help *her*. I want to think I can make a difference. If we fail, if you never get your voice back...well then, at least we tried."

Gripping the quill as if frozen, Katherine stared at him.

"But hear me," Alex continued, keeping his words soft although they wanted to rip straight from his soul, "I made a pact with myself the night she died. No woman will ever shred me in two like she did. *No* woman will cause me pain. 'Tis why I wanted you married and gone from my life."

Unused to this emotion, Alex paused gratefully as the serving girl arrived with platters of food. The venison pasty, a seasoned meat concoction wrapped in dough, was hot and fresh from the oven. He stabbed into it with his three-pronged fork and spread around the meaty juice that bubbled up through the holes and sent a savory steam into the air.

But Katherine reached over and jabbed his hand hard with the point of her quill.

Alex dropped his fork in surprise. Clearly unsatisfied with his explanation, she flicked her paper across to him.

The words jolted him with their directness. "Why, you ask? Why not give love a chance?" He grunted his impatience. "That doesn't matter. You needn't be concerned with my feelings, Katherine. I wish only to help you regain your voice. 'Tis something I would do for anyone under my care. Do not take it as a token of affection."

Katherine's mouth tensed in frustration, and she spent the next few minutes cutting up her pasty with vicious strokes of her knife. Several times she looked at the quill as if she would respond, but didn't lift it.

Alex watched her. If only he could convince her that she wouldn't be happy with him. Mary had proven that.

Finally, she set down her fork and wrote while he refilled their tankards.

I would not cause you pain.

Startled, he studied her expression, warm and wanting. Did her feelings run so deep? Had Agnes, in her comments to Edward in the herbarium, been accurate?

"I know that you wish to settle into a loving marriage," he said softly. "I cannot provide that for you, Katherine. I will not."

The warmth vanished from her eyes. Setting her mouth into a thin line, she scribbled, *I did not ask.*

"Then you understand that you and I will never be together." As soon as the words left his lips, the familiar sorrow attacked him, chipping away at the ice that clung stubbornly his emotions. He gritted his teeth and crushed the feeling with all his might.

She waited, watching him, her eyes questioning.

He leaned toward her and his voice was a strangled whisper. "Listen to me. I want no one. I love *no one.* I want to remain *alone.*"

Katherine acquiesced his words with neither compassion nor indifference. Instead, her eyes narrowed in anger. *Your choice,* she wrote, and then jabbed a finger at her earlier words.

"No, you did not ask. And yes. 'Tis my choice." He took a deep breath and summoned his long-practiced pragmatism. Clearing his throat, he adopted a passive tone. "As I said, I made a mistake with the baron. He's an old man. I will choose someone younger who can give you children. And I promise that you'll have the final say in the matter. Mayhap you'll even fall in love."

She frowned and wrote, *I do not want children.*

Surprised, Alex was silent for a long moment, observing the stoic finality in her stiff posture. Her head was bent as she picked at the remains of her pasty.

"Look at me, Katherine."

When she did, he saw tears brimming on the edges of her eyes. The shame filling her face stunned him.

"What happened to you?" Then, the reason struck him. "Ah. The fire. It destroyed your womb."

Katherine shook her head. *Two children, neighbors*, she wrote. *Trapped. Died.* She held up her hand with the thick pink scar slashed across her palm. Then, she pulled the paper toward her again and added, *door handle.*

Alex made a sound under his breath. "How terrible. When you tried to open the door to get to them, the handle seared your palm."

She nodded.

"The children died because you couldn't get to them. And now you feel you don't deserve children. Is that it?"

Katherine didn't respond, and wouldn't meet his gaze.

He leaned in, wishing he could pull her into his arms to comfort her. "'Tis not your fault. You did what you could. Did no one else help you? The children's parents? Where was your father?"

All dead.

Yes, her traitorous father was dead, and that was why she was with him right now. He took her hand and watched it disappear in his. It was time to tell her what he knew about her past.

When she looked up at him, however, he found that the words, however gently he could say them, wouldn't come. Why add more suffering to what she had already been through? The information could wait.

He noticed then that her gaze slid from him to a point just off his right shoulder. Her hand within his clenched.

Alex turned. There at the door stood Ellis Potts, Earl of Rochester—Katherine's ex-betrothed.

"Why, there sits Lord Drayton with his prize," Rochester called out with a laugh. "Have you exacted your revenge?"

Chapter Nineteen

Katherine fell straight into a coughing fit. Ellis. What was he doing here? The shock of seeing the man who had broken their betrothal because of her injury was almost more than she could bear after hearing that Alex would never allow her into his life.

And what was this talk of revenge?

The earl curled his lips into an arrogant smile and sauntered to the table. "Do you travel to London or have you just been there?"

"Going," Alex snapped. He stood, rigid as a lion scenting prey, and turned to Katherine. "Would you like to leave, my lady?"

Taking calming breaths with her hand over her chest, Katherine nodded and rose, observing the fine silver embroidery that glistened on Ellis' blue satin jacket and petticoat breeches. By his side stood a woman with black hair, richly dressed in lime green with pink underskirt and pink ribbons on her full sleeves.

Both of them looked as if they should be making merry at Whitehall instead of visiting this humble inn.

"Then we have just missed you, I'm afraid," Ellis said. He turned to his companion and introduced her as Mrs. Rosemary Mallet. "Mrs. Mallet, these are acquaintances of mine, Lady Katherine Seymour and Lord Drayton, Alexander Fletcher."

"Your servant, Madam," Alex said, and bowed.

Acquaintance. In the weeks since he had put her in his carriage and walked into his house without a backward glance, Katherine had been reduced to an acquaintance. She returned his smirk with contempt.

Mrs. Mallet's eyes sparkled. "Lord Rochester has—"

Ellis placed a possessive hand on her arm. "We are traveling to an estate in the country."

Ellis' voice was coarse from too many nights of drinking and raucous yelling. And had he grown fat in the weeks since she had seen him? No. He hadn't changed. Katherine had simply grown used to seeing the tall, athletic build of the man beside her.

Ellis glanced at her hands and then down at the table before inclining his head toward Alex. "She doesn't have her slate, I see. Thank heaven. That squeaky chalk—why, my teeth rattled each time she used it. "Tell me, did it bother you so much that you banned her from it?"

Katherine leaned down and plucked up the quill. How she wished she had her slate and chalk. She would ensure that Ellis' teeth rattled right out of his mouth.

"Of course not," Alex said. "It fell and broke accidentally."

Ellis chuckled. "Accidentally. Good one, Drayton. Should have destroyed it myself."

"I didn't say I destroyed it." Heat laced Alex's voice.

Katherine straightened with her paper and waved her hand for attention.

Ellis gave her a familiar condescending glance, and sighed. "Oh, gads. I haven't missed this."

Poltroon! How she wished she could spit the word at him.

Alex read her words and locked eyes with her. "We'll talk later. Now is not the time."

Something in his eyes kept her from insisting on an immediate explanation about this revenge Ellis spoke of. With growing unease, she lowered the paper.

Ellis had also read it. "I'm surprised you've waited, Drayton. But why tell the mute now? What's the occasion?"

The mute? *The mute*? Appalled, Katherine glared at Ellis. He'd never referred to her thus. Not in her presence, anyway.

Ellis knew he'd caused a stir. He smiled and regarded Alex, who towered above him by a head or more, with mischievous challenge in his eyes.

Alex's hand moved with cool surety to his sword hilt. "If you wish to play, Rochester, the muddy ground outside will make for an amusing duel. Especially when I bury your face in the muck."

Ellis blanched. He was clearly unused to being called

on his words. "Dueling is illegal," he sputtered. "The king made it so just last year. 'Twould land us both in the Tower."

"If you please, sir, your table is ready," the serving girl said from behind him.

Ellis regained his poise by snarling at her. "I am talking to friends. You will wait."

Around them, people had stopped their conversations and began watching the exchange.

"We're not your friends, Rochester," Alex said. "And the next time you refer to my betrothed as 'the mute,' I will challenge you whether it is illegal or not."

Katherine heard only one word from that declaration.

"You will do no such thing. Do you know who I am?" Ellis' face was pale.

"Oh, yes," Alex said, placing his arm around Katherine's shoulders. "I know perfectly well who the bloody hell you are, and what you did to her."

Ellis was quiet for a moment, his eyes sliding from Alex to Katherine and back again. He smiled, and his voice became velvet. "Lord Drayton, would you care to have a drink with me later?"

Katherine shot the earl a look of suspicion. What was he doing?

"Certainly," Alex replied. "I will meet you here after our ladies have gone to sleep." He turned to Katherine. "Come, my lady. I'll see you to your room so you may rest."

"Surely resting is not what you have in mind, Lord Drayton," Ellis said. "Enjoy yourself. I already had my fill of her."

Katherine whirled back to Ellis, her hand raised to slap the lying words from his mouth. Alex caught her arm at the elbow and tucked it deftly under his.

"I will handle this," he murmured in her ear. He turned and gathered the papers, quill, and ink from the table, then paid for their meal and steered Katherine from the room. "A bumblebee in a cow turd thinks himself a king," he said to her as they ascended the steps. "What a pretentious ass."

Katherine could only shake her head. Ellis had always acted arrogant, but until he had cried off their engagement, she'd thought that under his glittering cravat brooch beat the heart of a kind man. Now she knew what a vile person he really was. Why had her father insisted on pursuing a marriage contract with him?

More on her mind, however, was Alex's reference to her as his betrothed. She stopped him in the hall by his door and raised her brows in expectation.

He knew what she asked, and waved his hands in agitation. "I don't know why I said it. 'Twas a protective gesture, nothing more."

But his eyes revealed his true feelings. She saw his need for companionship as clearly as she'd heard his declaration of solitude. As wrong as she had been about Ellis, she knew she was dead on in her instincts about Alex.

Wearily, she turned to walk to her room. Only when the words from his lips rang true to those in his heart would she gather up her scattered hope.

"Katherine."

Facing him once more, she waited. He stood for a moment, his eyes moving from her forehead to her lips in unhurried study. "He didn't deserve you," he said softly. "You are so beautiful. All of you. Body and soul."

His words sounded as if he had carefully wrapped them in silk and then spun them loose in slow, flowing cadence.

He grasped her hand and kissed her palm, then let it go and slid his hand around the back of her head.

Lowering his head, he kissed her amidst a clatter of the inkwell, pen, and papers he dropped.

She welcomed his mouth on hers, his arms enfolding her like a blanket. She pulled him closer, to deepen the kiss.

He did.

The warm, masculine scent and feel of him made a joyful, throbbing haze flow through her body.

He moaned deep in his throat as he reached behind her and opened his door. Backing her into the room, he closed the door and pressed her against it. "My love," he murmured into her neck, and then found her lips again as his hand slid up her waist and cupped her breast.

The words cut through her sensual fog.

His love. After telling her that he'd love no one, he

called her his love.

Why did he romp with her emotions like this? A surge of anger made her push at his shoulders. He owed her more than this hilly ride of insecurity. She deserved more.

He broke the kiss and stood looking down at her, his hands pressed to the door on either side of her head. He lowered his forehead until it met hers. His hair tickled her cheek.

"I'm sorry," he said, his voice gruff. "I did it again. I'm allowing my body to speak for me. It won't happen—"

Furious, Katherine ducked under his arm and went to his writing table. *I am no fool.* She thumped her hand on the paper in frustration.

He stood beside her. "No, you're not. You know I want you." His hands made fists. "I'm the fool, Katherine. I'm allowing the past to dictate everything I do." Gripping her arms, he brought her to her feet. "I want you. But I can't have you. I'll only cause you pain. Do you understand?"

He didn't give her time to answer. He kissed her, his mouth hard and possessive, and then abruptly let her go.

Reeling, Katherine dropped into the chair and stared at him, and then propped her elbows on the table and put her head in her hands.

The man was impossible.

She heard him pacing the room, his boot heels ringing on the bare floorboards. "I know two things. One is that you're making me crazy. You've got me tied up in knots that would put a sailor to shame."

Katherine raised her head and rested her chin in her hand. What was he getting at now?

His voice took on a trace of arrogance. "The other thing I know is that I want no other man to have you." His footfalls stopped. "We can marry, you know. You can give me heirs, and I can carry on my name."

Katherine jumped to her feet. Oh, to be able to tell the oaf exactly what she thought of him! Why could he not admit his feelings? She dashed across the room and jerked open the door to leave.

"Where are you going? I'm not finished discussing this matter."

Oh yes, he was. This bumbling attempt at a marriage proposal was as close as Alex would ever come to opening his heart to her. She headed toward her room.

She could tell by his voice that he had followed her into the hall. "I did not give you permission to leave."

She stopped and spun toward him, and flashed him such a look of disdain that he flinched, albeit every so slightly. Still, she was satisfied with his reaction, and continued on to her room.

The seconds passed as she neared her door. She placed her hand on the doorknob, knowing that entering her room and shutting the door would shut him off from her forever.

"Wait. Please."

Katherine stopped and turned to him, her chin raised, relief and want making her legs weak.

"Come back," he said softly, his expression contrite. "I'm doing this all wrong, I know."

Slowly Katherine returned to him, then moved past inside his room.

He took a deep breath, hesitated, and cupped her cheeks with gentle hands. For a moment he seemed about to kiss her. But he asked, "Do you want to be my wife or not?"

Gads! She knocked his hands away and went for the door.

Before she could open it, Alex grabbed her arm and swung her around to him. "Blast it, I'm no good at poetic drivel. I don't know how to say what I'm feeling. But I can show you."

Down came his mouth on hers. The kiss was at once sweet and forceful, loving and possessive. He thrust his tongue into her mouth with a tender fury that at once thrilled her and pushed aside all doubts of his sentiment.

A melting sensation overcame her and she was lost in him, sliding her hands down along his hips, marveling in his firm physique. She couldn't believe how quickly he could dissolve her anger and then solidify it right back into fierce need.

Breathless, she gasped when he ended the kiss. His lips trailed over her face and neck and his arms tightened around her in warmth and protection. Hot pulsations pounded through her and she was vaguely aware that he was backing her up.

Scandal warred with desire as he lowered her to the bed.

However, he slid his arms from her, leaving her alone on the bed while he took a chair a few feet away.

His steady gaze on hers, he spoke. "My head battles my body, and my heart does the same with my words. I am ill-suited to parry such consuming need and now it's pieced me through.."

His words, uttered slowly and with care, caused a deep yearning within Katherine's heart. She nodded for him to go on.

"I didn't have a happy marriage, Katherine. I don't know how much of it was my fault, how much harder I could have tried to save her." He leaned forward, resting his elbows on his knees and clasping his hands together. His voice dropped. "I'm afraid of doing this again. I'm afraid that I'll lose you, that you'll grow to hate me, as Mary did. I can't promise you love. I'm not ready for that. But I pledge to take care of you for the rest of your life. If you'll have me."

Alex moved off the chair and knelt in front of her. He took her hands in his.

She gazed back at him, taking in the open, vulnerable expression on his face, and wishing his heart could be the same.

"My dear lady," he asked, "Would you do me the honor of becoming my wife?"

Chapter Twenty

Late that night, at a table in the corner of the mostly empty eating room, Rochester poked an unsteady finger under his peruke and scratched at his head. "Lemmee think. When I broke the betrothal, I tol' her it was because I wanted the gold her father promised, but then my men found nothin' in the ruins of her house." His powdered face, of which most of the white had been rubbed off from lovemaking with Mrs. Mallet and drinking three pitchers of ale with Alex, even now expressed his indignation.

Alex set his mouth in a grin and leaned his arms on the scratched table. "Oh ho! Her father had gold! How much?"

"Eighty thousand pounds. Traitor's money, Charles said. He wouldn't lemmee have it." Rochester gave a dramatic sigh, and Alex fought not to rear back from the earl's ale-drenched breath. "So she had no dowry after Charles took the gold. But she did have the necessary at—at—attributes befitting a man o' my status. An' she would have made for good breedin', o' course."

Alex smiled with congenial warmth. He wanted the full details of her father's treason. "I'd like to tumble with her myself."

"I never did. Tried. She wouldn't lemmee. Wouldn't let anyone. Wanted t'wait for marriage." He shook his head in disgust.

Alex was glad to hear it. "What else did you tell her?"

"Hmmm. I tol' her that as a man o' dis—distinction, I couldn't take a mute to wife."

"So you cried off." Alex held up his cup in a friendly toast. "Good riddance, say you."

"I mos' certainly didn't cry off," Rochester sniffed in contempt. "The decision was 'ers." He put back his head and drained the last of his ale, then leaned forward and slammed the cup onto the table.

"I'm sure," Alex said, refilling the earl's cup as steadily as he could, yet splashing some of the dark yellow liquid onto the table. He wanted to pound the man with the pewter pitcher. Holding it up, he signaled to the tired-looking serving girl for another.

"Kate seems well," Rochester said. "Not at all what I would've expected by now." He stared into his cup, and the ends of his brown wig curled in the puddle of ale on the table.

"I was not in agreement with Lady Castlemaine's plan to have her punished," Alex said. "She's in good health, although she became trapped in her closet and injured her fingers trying to get out. She has an affliction with small spaces."

"Since the fire," Rochester said with a nod. "She went into a house t'save two children. They died anyway, an' she lost her voice." He shrugged.

"And you tried to help her? You had doctors look at her?"

"Two. An' the king sent his own doctor. All agreed she won't speak again. But we wouldn't 'ave bothered if we knew the truth." His head began to lower slowly toward his cup. When his nose touched it, he snapped up his head. "Got to sleep," he muttered. "Long day."

"Ah, but we have one more pitcher coming," Alex said. "Let us drink like old friends. I enjoy your company." He smiled. "Why had no one told Katherine what her father did?"

Rochester straightened in his chair and cocked his head. "Oh, she knew. I'm sure someone tol' her. I guess she chose t'be silent about it. Not too hard for her to do, be silent." He chortled at his own joke, then turned his head and emitted a long, wet belch.

Alex raised his brows. "She knows nothing. And you obviously didn't tell her. How much did Lady Castlemaine pay you?" He sat back as the server set the pitcher on the table.

"Enough." Ellis' face was red and puffy with drunkenness, and his words were slurred and slow. "It goes back to last year. Lord Seymour wanted Kate to be Charles' mistress. Lady Castlemaine paid me to offer her marriage to get her away from the king. So I courted her. Even after the fire." He took a long swig of his ale, set the cup down, and ran the back of his hand across his mouth. "And then, last month when they found 'er father's papers outlining plans to have Kate spy on the king's dealings, the agreement ended. So I tol' everyone she cried off, and Lady Castlemaine came up with her plan to send Kate to you." Ellis rubbed his eyes. "You're goin' t'London, right? You'll see Charles?

Alex nodded.

"Here." Ellis pulled out his pouch and shook out its contents.

Across the empty room, the server perked up at the sound of coins jingling onto the table.

"If the king asks, you never saw me."

The man carried around an extraordinary amount of money. "I don't want it," Alex said. He placed his hands on the table and pushed himself up, knowing he would get no more information from the earl.

Ellis hesitated, then gathered up the coins and put them back in their leather bag. The serving girl slumped back in her chair. "One more thing, Drayton," he said, his lip curled in a drunken sneer. "You say Kate knows nothing. When you go see the king, take her with you. Let her be standin' there when he tells you about her pigeon-livered father."

****

Rolling toward London the following morning, Alex wouldn't reveal the details of his conversation with Ellis. By the time the familiar oily, fecal stench of the city hit them that afternoon, Katherine was frazzled with curiosity over what the two men had discussed.

Even more than that, however, was the knowledge that this very day, she would marry Alexander Fletcher. So cold he had been upon their first meeting, and how aloof during her first weeks in his home.

Now she watched as he turned from the coach window to her, smiled, and took her hand.

"We have a busy day ahead of us," he said, and his blue eyes held warmth and promise.

Could this be the same man who had declared that he wanted nothing more than to get her married and out of his house as quickly as possible? What had changed him, even since last night when he'd declared his intention of wishing to remain alone?

She didn't know. But she reveled in the peace that filled his eyes.

"I don't understand how the nobles here consider country life so dull," Alex said, looking past her out the window as the coach crossed noisy London Bridge. "I could not live in London with its crowds and stench. And I can still smell burnt wood."

As they turned left down Fleet Street, Katherine saw that in the weeks she had been gone, the king had made more progress with rebuilding the city. Wider streets that had previously been narrow and sunless from the overhanging roofs of houses now boasted buildings under construction with straight walls built of masonry instead of wood.

She thought Alex's generalization to be unfair. The smell of London seemed simply part of the life of the city. For her, seeing the din of activity from the coach window brought a strange homesickness, one never to be rectified as she had no home to return to.

Perhaps, someday, she could voice her view of the city to Alex.

Millie stared from the window. "Will ye look at all the people!" she exclaimed. "They walk in the street among the horses and carts like they wish t'be killed!"

"They probably *are* killed," Alex said, although his mind was not at all on the bustling street. He knew that Katherine wondered at his change of heart, and he himself wondered why he would invite turmoil and misery back into his house by taking another wife.

Yet the woman sitting beside him was neither chaotic nor miserable. Her calm demeanor—calm unless he riled her, that was—caused a tranquility within him that had replaced his almost constant tension.

The prospect of spending the rest of his life with Katherine pleased him. He could be sure she remained well and happy.

He would care for her and protect her, yes. But love her? The prospect of opening his heart again to love made sweat bead on his upper lip.

****

Katherine wore a white satin dress with silver lace underskirt that she and Millie had procured from a merchant who sold ready-made clothing. It didn't fit as well as would one made for her, but it would have to do.

The wedding was not what she had imagined her nuptials would entail, but she had little time to reflect on that. Her mind was on Alex. He may as well have been a block of wood bathed in reds and blues from the sun glittering through stained glass windows. Although he didn't hesitate as he said his vows, neither did he put any sentiment into his words.

She experienced a sinking uncertainty as she became Lady Drayton, afraid she'd made a terrible mistake marrying a man who had made it clear he'd never love her.

Chapter Twenty-one

Alex studied his wife's anxious face that evening in their bedroom at the London inn as they lingered over artichoke pie and boiled mallard.

They'd kept the conversation light and avoided any talk of their own concerns. During the course of the meal, Katherine had filled two pages of their discussion of London's rebuilding, the plans for the new cathedral designed by Inigo Jones, and the current play in the theater.

'Twould be a pleasure to see a play again, if you'd like to go tomorrow," Alex said with a smile as he poured the last of the wine into their goblets.

Katherine nodded her assent and then searched his face for an answer to some question she'd not asked.

Their wedding night might be what she wished to discuss, but Alex doubted it. After declaring that he would never again marry, he'd asked for her hand. What, she surely wanted to know, had changed his mind?

"Rochester," he said.

Katherine stopped with her goblet midway to her mouth and raised baffled brows.

"I'm usually not a man of indecision," Alex said, "but in case you're wondering, 'twas Ellis Potts who changed my mind about marrying again. He hurt you. I want to make you happy, to give you a good life."

Katherine picked up her pen. As always, her response was direct. *But not love.*

He could love her so easily. But he shook his head. "Please don't ask that of me."

****

Katherine tried to maintain interest on her dessert of apple cream sweetened with sugar. The wedding night loomed ahead, and her husband didn't love her. Did all marriages begin like this? Would they consummate their union with a physical act that would mean nothing to him? Would he claim her body only to beget his heirs?

The cream no longer tasted good. Katherine put down her spoon.

Alex, apparently seeing her action as an end to the meal, reached past the wine bottle between them. His big hands were warm and comforting on hers. "Let us not think about anything but each other tonight," he said. "I want to pleasure you."

Katherine swallowed and made desperate attempts to remember her mother's lecture. Something about duty, and lying perfectly still during the act, and feeling unclean afterwards, but also the satisfaction of knowing she wouldn't be touched during her monthly time of evil blood. There hadn't been mention of pleasure. But then again, her mother hadn't loved her father at all.

"Lady Drayton," he said as if testing the words. His brow creased slightly as he turned her palms up. "Your hands are damp."

Katherine gazed at her husband and smiled, unwilling to allow her tension to show. Whatever happened, she would do her wifely part.

"Are you nervous about tonight?"

She was nervous about the rest of her life with this man. His cool statement that he couldn't love her warred with his hot kisses, but which could she ever believe?

She smiled a little shyly, and nodded. As she thought about his mouth on hers, however, a restlessness stirred within. Her dreams came back to her in full force and she shivered with anticipation and ran her tongue across her lips.

Watching her, Alex's eyes grew intense. His long fingers played over hers across the table. "Have you a chill?" His voice was teasing, for he knew exactly what she was thinking, could surely see it in her eyes.

She smiled, wider this time, as did he.

Alex rose and stood next to her chair. "Perhaps I can help to warm you, my lady. If you please, I shall accompany you to our bed."

Oh, mercy. Here it was. She nibbled at her bottom lip.

He pulled her up to him and wrapped her in his arms. She could feel a low sound in his chest, perhaps a chuckle. "Your heart is pounding. 'Tis all right. I'll be gentle."

She was surrounded by him, his scent, his warmth. He simply stood and held her for a time, caressing her back and head, until her heart began to pound not with nerves, but with desire. A sensation grew deep within her that made her mouth open slightly and her breath quicken.

He cradled her head. "My wife." He met her mouth with a long, slow kiss that tasted of wine, his tongue moving in languorous strokes in her mouth.

He kept his mouth sealed on hers as he lifted her and carried her to the bed, and lowered her to it. For long moments he lay beside her, teasing her lips and tongue with his, and then kissed her cheeks, her eyes, her forehead.

Sitting up, he removed his boots, an intimate act to her because of what it would lead to. And she wanted it, wanted to be with him. Her hand caressed the smooth velvet of his black waistcoat as he half tossed the boots toward the wall and then turned to her.

As they had dismissed Millie for the night two hours before, Katherine still had on her wedding dress, and the full, billowing monteau skirt spread over the bed. The numerous bunches and points down the waist and skirt along with the minipuffed sleeves gave Alex pause.

"You're wearing armor," he mused, running his gaze over the yards and layers of white beribboned material and the hard, flat stomacher over her middle. "They don't make this easy on a man, do they?"

Laughing silently, Katherine began unfastening the stomacher. Alex joined in, and soon they had removed it.

"There went your shield," he said, tossing it over his shoulder. He fingered the tiny satin buttons that fastened her bodice together. "Now for the breastplate."

A moment later, her bodice loosened, Katherine's lacy petticoat was revealed. Feeling suddenly shy, she closed her eyes as Alex moved his lips over her breasts.

"So sweet," he sighed, and then kissed her mouth again.

He helped her to her feet, and she stood on trembling legs as the dress puddled to the floor. Kneeling, he reached under her petticoat and slid his hands up her legs, then removed each white silk stocking. The erotic pressure of his fingers on her thighs nearly made her knees buckle, but she anchored her hands on his broad shoulders until she had lifted each foot for him to slide the stockings off.

He rose then, his hands moving leisurely up her legs and hips and waist. Kissing her neck and shoulders, he skimmed his fingers over the sleeves of the petticoat until it joined the clothing on the floor.

Alex stepped back. At his slow, encompassing gaze up her body, she almost spun toward the opposite wall to hide herself. But then, she looked into his eyes, sultry and dark blue with want, and all at once, every bit of her anxiety vanished.

"You are more beautiful than I ever imagined," he breathed.

She felt beautiful under his gaze. And bold, now. Approaching him, she placed her hands on his black velvet vest and spread it until it fell from his shoulders. Then, she tugged his long linen shirt from his breeches.

Moving faster now, his breath quickening, Alex tore at the broad folds of his cravat until it floated to the floor in a heap of rich lace. He dragged his long white shirt over his head.

Katherine had never been naked in front of a man before, but right now, watching how the candlelight shone golden on his naked torso, she had no sense of awkwardness. Enjoying watching him, she lay down on the bed and stretched her arms lazily behind her head.

Alex froze, mouth open, his fingers tangled in the fabric laces of his black petticoat breeches, bought just this afternoon for the wedding. "Oh." The word was a bare sound. He swallowed, then licked his lips. "I pictured you like this. The day I couldn't find the marriage contract."

She arched one brow.

"Pay no mind." Without another word, he jerked the laces free. The voluminous breeches fell to his feet.

Katherine's breath left her. He was magnificent. Her gaze meandered down his chest and flat stomach until it stopped at his hips. With a dismayed gasp, she jerked to a sitting position.

He couldn't be serious.

"When you can speak, you'll have to tell me why you look so taken aback," Alex said, concern filling his face. "Have you never seen a man, Katherine?"

Katherine nibbled at her lip and nodded her head. She had accidentally walked in on a couple at Whitehall one evening, and none other than the Duke of Buckingham had leaped up from the red velvet couch, his stiff penis bobbing like an actor taking a bow. Katherine had fled the room in appall, barely registering the Marchioness of Mansfield tugging down her skirt.

She had seen a man, but never did she consider that they could vary so greatly in size.

Alex sat down beside her and brushed a warm, moist feather of a kiss on her cheek. "There's no need to be afraid. There will be some pain, but it will pass."

She was still for a moment, regarding him doubtfully. Then, she lifted the thin coverlet that was folded at the foot of the bed. Shaking it loose, she wrapped it around herself and rose.

"Katherine?" Alex stood with her, questioning, but she put up a hand for him to wait.

She walked to the table where sat paper and pen, and stood for a moment, tapping the end of the quill on her lips. How to broach the subject? Finally, she dipped the quill into the ink.

With somber expression she handed him the paper.

Alex looked at it and shook his head. "What's this?" He read her words again. "'You need a larger wife.'" Understanding dawned on his face. His lips spread, then widened into a grin.

All at once, he threw back his head and roared with laughter.

He thought she was joking. Katherine folded her arms and drummed her bare foot on the floor. All the same, she was aware that this was the first time she had heard him laugh like this, a deep, thunderous sound that filled the room and in no time had her smiling. Still, the whole idea of this coupling seemed impossible.

"Need a larger...oh, now there's a good one, Katherine," he said, and fell back onto the bed holding his stomach.

Katherine began to sit on the bed to await his composure, but Alex, still chortling, pulled her down against him.

She buried her face in the soft part of his neck and tried to plan a way out of this. How could she convince him it wouldn't work? While she thought about it, she noted how clean and smooth was his neck, how carefully he had shaved for her. She tasted him with the tip of her tongue. Slightly salty, fragrant, and very pleasant. She squirmed against him.

His laughter tapered off to a breathy moan as he rolled her onto her back and pulled the coverlet from her body.

Her eyes widened and her thighs clenched. Too late.

"Wait and see," he whispered, caressing her cheek. "'Twill fit, love. Wait and see."

She gave a dubious nod and opened her legs a bit, squeezed her eyes shut, and waited for him to mount her. Perhaps it would be over soon.

When nothing happened, she opened her eyes long enough to see what he was doing. Most likely preparing himself with his hand, as she had caught her father's stable boy doing one day in the corner of a stall.

Alex was doing nothing but watching her, and the amused smirk on his lips irritated her to the point that she grasped his head and pulled his mouth down onto hers.

He groaned softly and parted her lips with his tongue, exploring her mouth with slow, sure strokes. One of his hands found her breasts, and he tweaked and pulled at her nipple until she writhed in pleasure. After a while he moved to take her other nipple into his mouth, lapping at it with quick flicks of his tongue. It was then that his fingers slid down her stomach and found her hot center.

Katherine gasped, and turned to jelly. Every bit of doubt and anxiety vanished under his deft hands.

No one had ever told her what it was like to be loved by a man, how he could do things to her that made her quiver and sigh in ecstasy. How his very nearness and warmth, the slide of his naked skin on hers, could bring her to paradise.

There was more, though, something wild inside her that cried out for release. She clutched him, her entire body alive with the all-consuming sensation of his mouth moving over the most intimate and sensitive parts of her. His hands caressed her like feathers, then gently squeezed her flesh until she didn't even know where she was anymore.

Sweet heaven, how could he know exactly where to stroke her with his tongue and hands until she thought she would faint away?

Emboldened, she explored him, touching, tasting his golden skin, nuzzling the tickling hair on his chest. She listened to his soft sighs and whispers of endearment, kissed the rippling, candle-shadowed muscles of his arms and back. Her hand lowering, she glided her fingers along his hard shaft.

She found her power there, her ability to make him gasp and moan and call out her name, to render him unable to move.

She delighted in him.

That deep aching within her longed for release, and instinctively she pulled at his shoulders until he moved on top of her. His body was a warm heavy blanket over her, delightfully weighing her down onto the feather mattress.

"My beloved," Alex whispered, and spread her legs with his.

Beloved. The word burned through her intense pleasure. He might not love her with his heart, but he adored her with his body.

He pushed himself into her.

Katherine stiffened with the sudden, sharp pain. *Stop*, she cried out in her mind, and tried to move out from beneath him.

He had frozen, was watching her. "There, love, there, 'tis all right. The pain will leave you. Shhh, now, 'tis all right."

He kissed the tears from her eyes, then remained poised above her, waiting, his face a mask of concentrated control.

After a moment the pain did subside, and Katherine relaxed. He shifted within her. She gasped at the sensation.

He began to move slowly, rhythmically, watching her all the while until he closed his eyes, and Katherine marveled that her body could cause him such pleasure.

At the same time she noticed that his hips did indeed fit between her thighs perfectly, and that he filled her without hurting her. She lifted her legs and wrapped them around him.

Alex drew in a ragged breath, and grunted his pleasure.

Now that the pain had subsided, Katherine found that he was reaching a pleasurable spot deep within her that she never knew existed.

Until now. And he was moving much too slowly. She squirmed to lift her hips.

"Yes." It was a guttural sound. He drove in deeper, his thrusts becoming more rapid and powerful, his muscular body hard and hot and tense.

Katherine spiraled upwards. Her breath came shallower, faster. After a time her entire body began to stiffen as if she approached the brink of learning some wondrous secret.

She reached it, gasping, arching her neck. What on earth was happening?

And then, that damnable cough broke through her throat and severed whatever pleasure might lay beyond the edge.

A second later, Alex's body stiffened. With a primal cry, he throbbed his release deep within her womb.

Katherine turned her head and covered her face with her hand. She didn't know whether to cry in humiliation or pound on Alex's back with frustrated whacks.

He lay still for a time, breathing hard, and then raised his head and gave her gentle kisses on her cheek while he smoothed her tangled hair. "I'm sorry. I should have waited." He slid off her and pulled her into his arms. "But I couldn't. Katherine, 'twas the strangest feeling. You coughed, and you just...gripped and pulled at me somehow." He smiled sheepishly. "Not that I want you coughing every time I make love to you, but I tell you that it sent me straight over the top."

Katherine gave a silent, sardonic laugh and closed her eyes. At least she had found a use for her affliction.

"How do you feel?" he asked.

Good. Wonderful. But incomplete. She opened her eyes, wondering how to put in written words the not-quite-there frustration that screamed within her right now, but she didn't understand it enough to describe it. So she simply shrugged and nodded.

"Hmmm." He slid his hand between her legs and touched her on her sensitive little nub.

Katherine arched her back and sucked in breath in sudden, hot pleasure. She felt him against her leg, hardening again, and she wanted him inside her.

"I thought so. I've not satisfied you," he murmured, stroking her gently and kissing her neck. "I shall remedy that right away, my lovely wife."

And he did. Oh, yes, he did.

****

Deep into the night, Alex raised himself on one elbow and gazed upon his slumbering beauty. She lay on her side facing him, hair loose and tousled, her face peaceful, her lips well-kissed. His wife.

Bless her, Alex thought. Bless the fates—her father's treachery, the fire, Rochester's bootlicking deeds—for bringing Katherine into his arms. He searched deep within himself and found absolutely no regrets.

"Thank you, dear Katherine," he whispered, and gave her a gentle kiss on one smooth shoulder. "Thank you."

Chapter Twenty-two

That afternoon, her heart pounding with hope and anxiety, Katherine paced the inn room while Millie stood watch at the window. Alex had gone for the doctor.

Katherine paused every so often with tiny, shivering gasps, recalling last night and early this morning. Ah, what wonderful things Alex had done to her with the most virile part of him that she had at first feared would tear her up inside.

But oh, even though her body ached in her most tender, secretive places, she wanted him again, right now. He'd done something to her that second time, and again a third, something that made her explode in hot pleasure and lose all sense of the world.

"They're here!" Millie turned from the window with a wide smile that showed all three gaps between her front teeth.

A moment later, Alex and a tall, thin man wearing all black entered the room.

When Alex came to stand by her side, his eyes hungry and possessive, Katherine's tender nipples burned.

Alex made introductions, and Katherine lowered a curtsy on her wobbly legs. He placed a hand on her elbow and, with a knowing sparkle and warmth that lit his eyes, helped her back up.

The doctor set a large brown leather bag on the floor, then regarded her with kindly features and intelligent gaze. "You lost your voice by breathing in heated smoke, is that correct?"

Katherine nodded.

"And you have tried to speak since then?"

Of course she had. She nodded again as impatience nipped at her.

"The king's physician pronounced her permanently mute," Alex said. "And the Earl of Rochester had two other doctors examine her."

The doctor nodded slowly, his eyes on Katherine. "Yes. And they also found nothing?"

Katherine hesitated, sensing hope seep away. Three doctors had concluded her condition as permanent, and one was the king's own physician. Who would question an authority such as he?

"No, nothing," Alex answered for her.

"Did they give recommendations despite their findings?" the doctor asked.

At the table Katherine wrote, *Said try to sing. Shout. They used leeches. Arsenic and bismuth. King's touch.* Disgust curled her lips at this last as she recalled His Majesty first stroking her throat like a lover, then slipping his hand into her bodice to squeeze her breast. Over her shoulder, she heard Alex's grunt of displeasure.

"Fools. How could they want you to sing and shout if you couldn't even speak?" he asked.

"And you mentioned a cough, Lord Drayton," the doctor said.

"She coughed a great deal when she arrived at my home, but it seems to have subsided somewhat." Alex paused. "Except for last night."

Her head lowered, Katherine tried to hide the blush that burned her cheeks.

"The clean country air has helped, I presume," said the doctor, either ignoring or unaware of the implication of that statement. "And this cough began when?"

The fire—smoke.

"Ah. Do you see blood when you cough?"

Katherine frowned and shook her head.

"Good." The doctor leaned down and snapped opened his bag. "I shall now examine you. Please take a seat."

Millie's eyes shone as she looked from Alex to Katherine. "Come, m'lady, let's get ye seated here," she said. She pulled up a chair near the window.

While Katherine sat, the doctor removed a strange contraption from his brown leather bag. It resembled a lantern, yet was attached with a long brass tube with a curved end. The tube narrowed until it was no more than the width of Katherine's pinkie.

"Interesting," Alex said, standing beside Katherine's

chair. "What is it?" His fingers brushed the back of her neck, and she gave a little shiver of pleasure.

The doctor smiled and held it toward him. "An illuminator. My brother and I created it. Look here, into this eyepiece."

Alex peered into the top of the lantern. "Mirrors!" he exclaimed, his face boyish in his excitement. "Katherine, see inside!"

Fighting the urge to slide her hand up Alex's inner thigh, Katherine looked into the eyepiece, and gasped in wonder. Within the tube, dozens of tiny, angled mirrors reflected upon each other in sparkling splendor. Even at its thinnest point, the mirrors extended around the narrow curve.

"I will insert the tube into your mouth," the doctor said, "and slide it back as far as possible. The light will shine down the tube and allow me to see deep into your throat."

Katherine nodded, and renewed hope warmed her. This man would see what had happened more clearly than the other doctors, who had only taken her out into the sunshine to peer into her mouth.

The doctor lit the candle inside the lantern. The wick blazed with a brilliant white light, and Katherine heard Alex's quick intake of breath. She found herself mesmerized by the fire's radiance.

"There is a powder in the wax that makes the flame more intense," Doctor Whittleby explained, "but it burns quickly. Do not stare at the light." He brought the lantern near Katherine's face.

Despite his warning, Katherine riveted her gaze on the radiant beam until she had to close her eyes. Behind her lids, white dots danced as if she'd stared too long at the sun.

"Open, now, please. Relax your jaw. Stay perfectly still."

Slowly he inserted the cold, hard brass tube into Katherine's mouth.

The other doctors had, with importance and finality, determined that her voice was completely gone. Now, as she closed her eyes and felt the tube slide along her tongue, she knew exactly what this doctor would say. 'I have determined, after much study and on account of my vast experience, that you shall never speak again.'

She almost halted the procedure, unwilling to face more disappointment. Instead, she reached for Alex's hand.

More than anything he had ever wished for, more than life itself, Alex yearned to hear Katherine's voice.

He enclosed her cold hand in both of his and willed her all the courage he possessed.

"Now tilt back your head a bit," the doctor said. "I'll stop if you begin to gag, to give you time to become used to it."

Alex wanted to help her as no one else had. He needed to prove that everything he touched was not destroyed. And she deserved to be helped even if her father had been a traitor to the king.

But another reason to help her regain her voice fought its way to the front of his mind, and no matter how much he denied it, this one took precedence over all the others.

If she could speak, she could tell him she loved him.

The thought jolted him. He considered the thought as he watched her take in the tube. Her eyes were squeezed shut.

Would she ever love him? Or did their marriage mean only that she would have the security she had so desperately sought?

The tube slid deeper into her mouth. Her hand in his became stiff and clammy.

"Calm yourself," he said quietly, stroking her hand. "Doctor, do you see anything yet?"

"Too soon," the doctor said, his brows creased in concentration. "Wait." He moved the tube forward very slowly. "You may feel it deep in your throat now. I'll move it down as far as I can. Just relax."

Katherine's hand went limp. Alex traced his fingers across the scar on her palm, and kept his eyes glued to the tube.

He desperately needed her to love him. Perhaps then he could let go of the doubt that plagued him.

The contraption had disappeared an impossible distance into Katherine's mouth. How far would the doctor insert it?

Finally, the doctor paused. He peered into the lantern.

Time froze. Alex didn't breathe. His fingers went still on Katherine's damp palm.

The doctor's eyes squinted. "Ah."

Katherine's fingers curled over Alex's and clamped down.

"Ah. Yes. I see now." The doctor slowly raised his head, his expression placid. "I will remove the tube now, Lady Drayton. You have remained most admirably calm."

The tube came out much faster than it had gone in. Katherine gasped, swallowed, and then looked at the doctor with wide, moist eyes.

Millie, standing a few feet away, wrung her hands.

"Well?" Alex demanded, ready to slam his fist through the wall.

The doctor carefully set the lantern on the writing table and then placed an iron cup over the candle to snuff it out. Somberly, he faced Katherine.

"You shall speak again, my lady."

Chapter Twenty-three

Alex bowed before the king, who sat on a lush red velvet chair on a dais in an elaborate room with white columns and hundreds of candles. The queen was not with him; mayhap she was in her chamber suffering from foul humors.

Charles was surrounded by courtiers dressed in so many dazzling colors and sparkling jewelry that Alex thought he might go blind with the unaccustomed brilliance.

Uncharacteristically self-conscious, Alex reconsidered his plain brown jacket, breeches, and boots. Perhaps he should have worn his fashionable wedding attire, which had looked too much like a dress but was more acceptable here.

The king's court, with its colorfully dressed, painted nobles who had ulterior motives for everything they did, wasn't his life. He couldn't wait to get back home with Katherine.

Katherine. Oh, how his wife's beautiful face had shown with happiness at the doctor's declaration that she would speak! For once, Alex didn't crush the joy that welled within him.

"Lord Drayton!" Charles cried merrily. "How do you do!"

"Majesty," Alex replied with a smile as he straightened.

"What brings you to London?" The king's smile was wide and friendly under his thin dark moustache, yet his eyes held a measured glint.

"I have business in town, Majesty," Alex answered, hoping the king would be satisfied with that. "I wished to pay my respects to you while I am here."

"Ah. Do you plan to stay long? We would enjoy your company this evening." He glanced at a few of the women who milled about. “The ladies do love an unfamiliar face.”

Several of them were already scrutinizing Alex, boldly sliding their gazes over his body. “I regret that I will leave when my dealings are concluded,” he said, nodding his apologies.

“Unfortunate. And not even Rochester here to flirt with them.”

Alex’s hands stiffened, yet he kept his expression bland. “Is Lord Rochester away?”

The king swung his head to the left as if to spit in contempt, but apparently thought better of it and returned his gaze to Alex. “Business? Ha! He left here three days past to go after Mrs. Mallet. He had his footmen forcibly take her from her grandfather, Lord Haly, at Charing Cross. Rochester put her into a coach with six horses and we haven’t seen the two of them since. It’s the Tower for him when we catch him.”

“And you wish to reclaim Mrs. Mallet?” Alex asked.

“We most certainly do. We had an...arrangement.”

Several of the courtiers glanced around, most likely for Lady Castlemaine, whose jealousy seemed at times to control England. Alex had always avoided the stunning yet forceful woman.

“Enough talk of the earl.” Charles’ mouthed widened, genial yet reserved. “Tell me, how is Thomas Seymour’s daughter faring?”

“She still cannot speak.” It was the truth, at least. “I inquired of eligible men for marriage, and she met a possible suitor.”

Charles’ brows rose. “When shall she marry?”

Candor would serve best with his monarch. “I married her, Majesty. ‘Tis an honor to have her as my wife.” Pride laced his voice.

“An honor?” A strong, feminine voice carried through the room, and the crowd swept aside. “An *honor*?”

Wishing he could say a quick farewell and escape, Alex smiled as Barbara Villiers Palmer, Countess of Castlemaine, sauntered toward him with a confident pout on her red lips.

Light on her feet despite having given birth to five children—the youngest only two years old—she was the most sensuous woman Alex had ever seen. Her deep brown eyes sparkled with intelligence and her shapely breasts bulged from the low bodice of her dress.

Alex utterly disliked the king's mistress. Holding his tight smile with effort, he bowed to her. "'Tis good to see you, my Lady Castlemaine."

Raising painted brows, she raked her gaze over him, giving a weighted pause at his thighs. "Your clothing leaves little to the imagination, my lord."

The tittering from the other courtiers caused further embarrassment for Alex. He stood still, and waited.

Lady Castlemaine turned toward the king with a smile. "Lord Drayton believes to honor himself by marrying a traitor's daughter."

"So he said." Charles scrutinized Alex, his face unreadable.

Slanting her eyes back toward Alex, Lady Castlemaine's pretty lips turn downward in a scowl. "You surprise me, Lord Drayton. After what her father did, I would think that you'd grind her until you tired of her, and then bring her back to London and leave her on the street to beg and whore until she starved to death."

Alex's jaw clenched. If the countess were a man, he would run her through with his sword. "Majesty, Katherine knows nothing of her father's deeds. No one told her why she was sent to me. She thinks only that you were kind enough to provide for her."

"You are aware that her father wanted her to spy for him?" Charles asked.

"Yes," Alex said, "but I don't believe she knew it."

Charles regarded him for a moment, then rose to his feet. Every man and woman present turned to him and bowed or curtsied.

"Walk with me," he ordered. Leaving Lady Castlemaine behind, he led Alex through the vast room, between two massive marble columns, and outside to a sumptuous walled garden.

They were alone save for two guards who stood at alert attention a few yards away near a bronze sundial. In the warmth of the sun, Alex faced King Charles—his equal in stature.

"I did hate to make the decision to give her over to you. She's a lovely young woman." His voice hardened.

"But we demand loyalty, Drayton. Someone has to pay for Seymour's crimes, and she is the only one left of her family. Her two brothers and mother died of the Plague. When we found his trunk full of the proof of his treason, we decided to allow *you* the satisfaction of exacting payment."

"Yes, Majesty, I understand that," Alex said, and his throat tightened with distress. The wrong words could jeopardize Katherine's safety. "But I have no doubt of her innocence. She knows nothing. Please, don't command me to hurt her."

Charles' dark eyes shone with a surprisingly amused glint. "I would never command that a woman be hurt. 'Twas not my intention that you punish her at all, Drayton. Of course, my Lady Castlemaine wondered why I went along so easily with her plans."

Relief welled within Alex, but the discussion wasn't finished. "Yet she's to pay, somehow, for her father's crimes."

"Therein lies my dilemma. I cannot simply forget it happened."

Alex, sensing a solution, didn't flinch from his sovereign's gaze. "Perhaps knowing the whereabouts of Mrs. Mallet would help to settle the score."

Charles' expression remained unchanged. Yet Alex, knowing Ellis Potts had run off with a woman the king wanted in his bed, noted a slight forward movement of his head and an increased intensity in his stance. Between the king's legs hung England's masculine pride.

"That may help," Charles quipped. He turned and commenced a leisurely, long-legged stroll through the pebbled garden path. "And what of our exquisite Katherine? Shall I trust you to rectify Lord Seymour's treachery?

Alex, keeping stride with ease, said, "You shall, Majesty. Katherine's misery will be punishment enough for her when she learns the truth. She believes her father was a staunch Royalist."

"And you?" Charles asked, sliding his long fingers along a tree's tender white blossom. "What of your own recompense?"

"If you are speaking of my parents' murder," Alex replied with a shrug, "'tis long past."

"Is it now?" Charles halted once more and faced Alex, his gaze both kind and forceful. "Drayton, there is a specific reason we sent the woman to you. A personal reason."

His next words turned Alex's blood to ice.

****

"Herbs, heat, lozenges." Millie bustled about the bedroom of the inn with no apparent purpose, almost chanting the words as Katherine sat cross-legged on her bed sipping from a cup of foul-tasting broth heavy with chili powder and salt.

She worked to swallow the vile concoction as she fingered the cloth pouch beside her containing lozenges made up of angelica root, myrrh, and cinnamon.

The doctor had wasted no time gathering his prescribed herbs and spices and giving specific instructions. Tomorrow Katherine and Alex would leave London, and in two days return to Drayton Castle as husband and wife.

Wouldn't Elizabeth be surprised! And Agnes would have quite a shock. Katherine couldn't help the glee coursing through her.

"Newly laid eggs. Cabbage broth with fat an' honey an' the finest wheat. An' garlic. Garlic with everything." Millie stopped and turned to Katherine. "But ye must eat lightly, m'lady. And nothing cold. Only warm white maguey wine for ye."

The doctor had written other instructions, and Katherine lifted the paper to read the long list. Juice of cinquefoil. Flowers of the Mallow plant boiled in oil, mixed with honey and alum, to be gargled daily. Sage and Rosemary were also listed, as was mustard seed—which, the doctor had warned her in grave tones, could stir up bodily lust. He had given her a small bag of each and advised planting more as soon as they returned home.

Home. Her home. Drayton Castle would see some changes, the first being the restoration of the dilapidated gardens. Then, the bedchamber she'd been using would be redecorated for guests.

Perhaps she could convince Alex to open the drapes.

Millie approached and checked Katherine's right arm

where the doctor had bled her with leeches. "Already healing," she declared, replacing the bandage.

Katherine was surprised to feel a deep calm that, she knew, wasn't a result of the contents of her drink. She forced a swallow of her broth while Millie turned and muttered her way around the room once more.

Alex. He'd astounded her with tears in his eyes at the doctor's announcement. More than relief, however, had passed between them, and more than their mutual bodily lust that needed no help from mustard seed. As he held her hand in his, she'd found a newfound trust, a warm, deep stirring within her that spoke of security and companionship. And love.

Yes, by the heavens, could it be? She loved him. He didn't feel the same—he'd made that clear although he certainly loved her with his body—she would speak, for him, because of him.

He wanted her voice back as much as she. And her first words after seven months of silence? *I love you, Alex.*

If only he could say them, too.

Chapter Twenty-four

Where was he?

The moon's pale light washed the rough planks of the inn floor and guided Katherine as she paced about on restless feet. He'd not returned since paying his respects to the king.

Would he have remained at Whitehall Palace to join the nightly frolics? It didn't seem like him—although if he were looking for entertainment, the palace provided an abundance of activity.

No. A man like Alex wouldn't seek to dance and play Court games. Would he? Katherine paused at the window, pensively nibbling at her tender lower lip.

She really didn't know him at all.

But after kissing her senseless this afternoon before leaving, he'd promised her that he would return before dark. From the loving warmth in his eyes, she knew he spoke the truth.

Was he safe? Katherine resumed her walking, envisioning him lost in London and unaware of the dangers of the city. She pressed a hand to her trembling mouth. Perhaps he'd been attacked and even now lay bleeding in a stinking gutter!

But this was silly. He was a big man, he carried a sword, and he certainly knew more about London than she gave him credit for.

But by the heavens, where was he?

Finally, the moon high and the hour late, she fell upon her bed in exhaustion.

Dawn's pink light colored the window when Millie woke her. "Somethin's wrong!" she whispered. "Lord Drayton just came back. He wants us to leave now. Without *him*."

Blinking herself awake, Katherine slid from the bed in confusion. Millie moved aside, and Katherine saw Alex slouched in the doorway, watching her with haunted eyes—as if she were a complete stranger.

Alarm twisted in Katherine's belly as she ran to him. The hand he shot up may as well have been a sword, for it stopped her cold.

"Go home," he said in a voice so emotionless it could have come from a dead man.

She reached for him, but he stepped back.

"No. Please. I just...need some time."

He turned from the door and left her standing there.

****

Alex warned his footmen to guard Katherine with their lives or they would answer to his blade.

He remained at the inn for a week, loath to go home and discuss this with her. He had to think. To grapple with the truth.

Finally, he chartered a horse and left London. Katherine was his wife. He owed her the knowledge of their tied past.

The mount, used to walking short distances along London's streets, had not Neos' spirit nor stamina and tired easily. Alex was forced to halt many times during the day. At night, he lay wrapped in his cloak in a field or the woods. He stared blankly at the sky or listened to the soft rustle of leaves on the trees, and tried to sort out what he had to do.

****

Fifteen days, and Alex still hadn't come home.

Sam had dispatched servants to look for him along the roads—and, because of rumors that the highwayman still lurked in the woods, had notified the sheriff that he was missing.

Was he still alive? Was he broken alongside the road, bleeding, dying, too weak to call for help while travelers passed by him unawares?

Worried to distraction, Katherine tried to work on her embroidery, giving up when the needle only pricked her trembling fingers. She drank the vile-tasting concoctions for her throat, and wandered the dim corridors. She sat in Alex's big chair in his study and found comfort there, closing her eyes and breathing deeply of his scent.

After a few days she consulted with Elizabeth, made

a list of things in the castle that needed attention, and set to work. The boxwood maze was trimmed and cleaned up under her supervision, as was the pretty knot garden. Outside the kitchen, she oversaw the planting of the herbs required for the healing of her throat.

She directed improvements to rooms of the castle. Upon discovering undesirable conditions in the kitchen, she promptly fired the head cook and hired a more efficient one through Elizabeth.

Only Alex's bedchamber did she leave alone.

Her things were still in her old chamber at the front of the house. She wouldn't move into her husband's chamber. Not until he came home to willingly share his bed with her.

Unable to sleep at night, she trod wearily through the halls. Many times, Elizabeth limped along beside her.

"He'll come home," Elizabeth soothed. But she could give no reason for his absence.

And, although living in the constant dimness was oppressing, Katherine did not order all the drapes opened. Alex could do so when he was ready to look at a window in his house again without thinking of Mary.

During the second week of his absence, as Katherine stood in a dilapidated flower garden directing the gardener with points and gestures, the Cookes' carriage rolled up the drive. Katherine expected Edward, as he must have heard of the unexpected letter Elizabeth had received from Lord Wiltshire stating his desire to see her.

But it was Agnes who stepped from the carriage. Katherine sighed and then shaped her lips into a wan smile.

"Well. Hello, Lady...Drayton," Agnes said as if the words got caught on her tongue. "I wish to visit with Elizabeth."

Katherine shook her head and pointed down the road, gripping her smile, wanting the woman to leave.

"Ah. Elizabeth is in town. Well, I'll be returning home, then." She began to turn toward her carriage but then stopped, tapping her lips with one gloved finger. "Father says that Lord Drayton has not returned from London."

So she knew. Katherine shrugged and nodded, hoping Agnes wouldn't see the tightening of her shoulders. It wasn't necessary to let Agnes know how much she worried.

"Mayhap he regrets his decision to marry you." Agnes's red painted mouth turned up in an impudent smile.

As soon as the carriage had disappeared around the bend in the drive, Katherine ran into the house, willing her tears to hold back until she could get to her bedchamber and fling herself onto the bed. Tears wetted her pillow as hopelessness and despair washed through her.

Perhaps Agnes was right. Alex was disappointed in her as a wife. He didn't want to come home.

Chapter Twenty-five

Two days later, Alex crashed open his heavy front door. "Wine! And bloody quick!"

He stomped into the parlor with head down and shoulders slumped under his scuffed brown cloak. This he flung to the floor while he headed toward a chair and dropped into it. With a long sigh, he closed his eyes and lay back his head.

A sound near the bookcase made him open his eyes a moment later to see Edward sidling toward the parlor door. "What do you want?"

Edward stopped and faced him. "I, uh, I'm waiting for Elizabeth. I didn't wish to disturb you, so I was just leaving the room. You look—well, quite worn out." Edward sounded as if rocks filled his throat. "A servant went to see if she—."

"Enough," Alex said. He scraped a hand through his windswept hair. "My head is pounding. Where is the blasted sack?"

Sam entered then with a tray holding the wine. He glanced at Edward and gave a slight bow. "Mister Cooke, Lady Elizabeth is on her way down."

"Yes, thank you," Edward said. "Well, I'll just wait for her at the stairs." He slipped out.

"Set it there," Alex said.

"Lady Drayton returned two weeks ago," Sam said as he poured sack to the brim of a sizeable cup. "We've been worried for your safety. What happened?"

"I've something to tell you." Alex tipped back the cup and gulped the wine. The pungent liquid warmed his stomach, but didn't ease his heartbreak.

There was a smile in Sam's voice. "Yes. How fortunate that she may speak again!"

"I learned something else about her father. I want to find out what she knows."

"I thought she knew nothing about her father."

"God help her, Sam."

"Alex? What is it?" Sam's voice held a worried edge.

"Leave me now. I want to be alone."

He heard the door close, and in the quiet of the parlor the king's words resounded like axes in his head. Alex knew he would get no peace until he confronted his wife.

His wife. He'd married her, spilled his life's seed into her, explored every secret of her sweet body. Loved her.

If she had known all this time of her father's acts and not admitted it to him—ah, the knowledge was a blade ripping out his heart.

He would confront her. But first, he needed sleep. He got to his feet, and with heavy footsteps left the parlor. On a bench in the Hall sat Edward, and he was kissing Elizabeth on her mouth.

Astonishment slapped Alex to a halt. "About bloody time," he growled.

Elizabeth jerked away from Edward and gazed with startled eyes at Alex.

Hunched and brooding, Alex raised a dismissive hand as he continued past. "Carry on, Edward. Glad to see you're a man after all."

"Alex!" The word was almost a breath, yet Elizabeth's disapproval was clear.

Alex stopped. "What?"

"That—that was quite rude!"

Edward stared at Elizabeth in surprise.

Alex sighed and rubbed his eyes with his thumb and index finger. "I apologize. 'Tis good to see your spirit, Bethie. I've missed that part of you." Then, his voice broke. "I'll need your courage when I speak with you later."

Elizabeth began to stand, and Edward jumped up to help her. "What troubles you?" she asked. "And why are you just now returning from London? Katherine has been frantic with worry."

Alex shook his head. "Not now. I'm going to lie down for awhile. The devil's splitting open my head."

"Has something happened? Were you robbed?" Edward asked.

Alex snorted. "Robbed? Yes. You could say that." He turned toward the stairs. "Tell a servant to bring the sack to my bedchamber."

Elizabeth hobbled after him. "What of Katherine? Do you not wish to see her?"

Alex hesitated, then moved on. "Not yet."

****

He'd come home. Home!

Heart drumming with anger, excitement, and concern, Katherine rushed from her drab bedchamber past Elizabeth and down the corridor toward Alex's chambers.

"Katherine, wait," Elizabeth called to her. "You must not go to him yet."

Katherine halted and wheeled back toward Elizabeth. Still unable to voice her hurt thoughts, she stamped her foot on the floor.

Elizabeth stood twisting her hands, her gray eyes wide and worried. "He said he does not wish to see you."

He didn't wish to see her? After sending her home alone and then staying away for a fortnight? Her husband, the man who should have swept her into his arms, formally introduced her to his household as Lady Drayton, and made love to her in his bed, didn't want to see her?

Oh, he was going to see her whether he liked it or not. And the man had some explaining to do.

Lowering her head in fury, Katherine balled up her fists and stalked toward his room.

What bothered her more than anything, what made her throat ache and caused her to cough again after more than two weeks of healing, was that her husband didn't want her, didn't care enough about her to seek her presence when he returned. Agnes's words of his regret in marrying her took on fresh importance.

Anguish filled Katherine as she grasped the latch and pushed open his door.

"Leave me," Alex growled behind closed lids when he heard the creak of his door. "I don't want to be bothered."

Seconds later, something smashed the wall above his head and rained wet, shattered pieces onto his face. With a roar, Alex leaped from his bed.

There his beautiful wife stood in the door, hands on hips, eyes blazing. Her chest and face were flushed pink with fury, and Alex willed his feet to be nailed to the floorboards to resist running to her, holding her close, kissing her.

He would have, had he not touched his forehead and pulled away fingers wet with blood. "Is this how you would greet me, *wife*? By cutting me?"

Katherine narrowed her eyes and kicked the door closed with her heel.

Ah, but she was ready for a fight. And so was he, headache and all.

"I trusted you," he said savagely, intent and anger and need to be near her propelling him across the room. He grasped her arms and smelled the heady lavender fragrance of her hair. "I thought you knew nothing. Why didn't you tell me, Katherine? You owed me the truth."

She blinked up at him in confusion, and he had a moment of doubt as he searched her eyes. Did she truly not know? His hands relaxed on her arms.

She backed away then and looked around his bedchamber.

"Yes, I'll get you paper so you can write your lies," he said, hating himself for not trusting her. Unwilling to face his doubt, he walked to his writing table and pulled paper, pen and ink from the drawer and slammed them onto the table. "Better start explaining."

Katherine remained where she was, no longer furious but thoroughly bewildered, trying to fathom what was happening. She had expected him to apologize, to explain that he was feeling poorly, had gone falconing with friends, had unexpected business in London. Something. But not this anger, this pain and sorrow that filled his eyes. What was she supposed to have told him?

"Well?" he asked as he jerked a finger toward the writing table. "What say you?"

Shaking her head in puzzlement, Katherine walked toward him, sat and picked up the quill. He stood at her left shoulder as she dipped the pen, and she could feel the heat from his thighs.

Her hand shook. *Where have you been?*

He leaned down beside her, his big hands clenched into fists on the table. "Does it matter? Katherine, I want answers."

She took in his haggard face and reddened eyes, his

lips that had trailed soft kisses down her back. Something terrible had happened. God's blood, the man owed her an explanation. She turned back to her paper and dipped the quill again. *I have none to give you. Talk to me now.*

He let out a slow, ragged breath, and straightened. His face reflected relief. "You don't know."

Katherine stood. Her husband was hurting, and he had something to tell her. Her hands slid over his shoulders and squeezed the tense muscles there.

"How do I say this?" His hands slid up her arms.

She placed a palm on his unshaven cheek, and anxiety snaked through her body. Valiantly she tried to keep tears from filling her eyes. Would he now voice his regret at marrying her?

"My parents...I told you how they were killed."

What was this? Surprised at the unexpected statement, she nodded.

Alex's eyes became searching, his voice gentle. "Your father was a spy during the war. He worked for Cromwell."

Katherine's face grew slack. No. Her father had been a Royalist, true to the king. She stared at him, then leaned down and grabbed the quill. *NOT TRUE!* She backed away from him, clutching both pen and paper.

"Katherine, after the fire they found—"

Such a despicable lie! She threw the quill at him, barely noticing the blooming black dots on his white shirt before the room tilted. Mouth open and trembling, she thrust out her hands, grabbing at something, anything to hold her up.

Alex caught her and pulled her up to face him. "Listen to me."

She would not! Rage charged through her and saturated her dizziness. Her fists pelted his chest. "Lying caitiff!"

The words barely held sound, but she registered the vibration on her throat. She froze.

Alex gave no indication of hearing it. He cupped her face in his hands and raised her face so that she had no choice but to look at him. His face was a mask of torment. Tears spilled down his cheeks.

"Katherine," he choked. "You were sent to me as

payment for your father's treason. I didn't know exactly why until I visited the king." He hugged her to him, his arms desperate in their strength. "He killed them, Katherine. Your father murdered my parents and left me for dead."

No. God, no. Katherine kept her gaze locked onto Alex's, finding and hating the truth in his tortured blue eyes.

Papa, her papa. A murderer. The shock of it reverberated through her body.

So cold. Ice gripped her, made her unable to stop shuddering. She shook her head again and again. Finally, a deep well of sorrow made her slump against him.

Alex carried her to his chair until he could gather up the sheet holding the glass from the water pitcher and set it on the floor. Pulling the quarterpane over the mattress, he then lifted Katherine onto it. Lying next to her he rocked her gently, brushed his hands over her hair and face, soothed her with a voice gouged with misery. "'Tis all right, my love. All right. I'm so sorry."

Spiraling into desolation, Katherine clung to him.

Chapter Twenty-six

"My lord?"

The voice was soft and breathy, and coming from the private dining room. Alex, on his way to his study, paused at the door.

"Oh. How do you do, Agnes."

"I am well." She sauntered into the Hall. "You look tired. Have you slept much since your return from London yesterday?"

"A little." Alex ran a hand over his face. What was she doing here alone?

"And Lady Drayton? Is she well?"

"She's...had a shock."

Agnes's eyes grew wide. "Nothing grave, I hope."

"Where is Elizabeth?"

"Oh, I came over with Edward and suggested that they take a stroll. 'Tis such a lovely evening."

"Is it?" His eyes itched, and he rubbed them. When had Agnes's voice become so deep and soothing, like a balm?

"Yes. Perhaps we can do the same. Will you walk with me?"

"She's leaving." Alex said the words aloud, hoping the assertion would help to fortify that unfeeling part of him that was his only defense. But the knowledge was killing him. "She wants to leave."

Agnes looked surprised, then moved closer to him. "I'm so sorry to hear that."

He grunted a sigh and raked a hand through his hair. "I apologize for my inattention. I haven't slept properly in days. May I walk you to your carriage?"

Agnes blinked, smiled, and cocked her head. "No. You need your rest. I would be happy if you called on me, though, when you're feeling better."

"Yes. I'll pay a call to your family. Goodbye, Agnes."

He turned to walk toward the corridor that would take him to his study, then stopped. "I haven't told the coachman to ready the carriage for her."

Agnes was quickly at his side. "Would you like me to do it? You are so weary, my lord." She placed a hand on his arm.

"I would. Thank you, Agnes."

Agnes smiled and moved so that her large breasts brushed his arm. "What is her destination?"

"Lobb's Inn." He paused, noting her closeness, her wide blue eyes and full, pouty lips accentuated by the white powder on her face. She was overwhelming in her sensuality.

"I will tell the coachman."

"You've been a big help through the years," he said, taking a step back. "I never properly thanked you for befriending Mary. You always seemed to know when to arrive, just before she had one of her spells. I don't know what she would have done without you."

Agnes stepped foreword. Her breath was warm on his chin. "Mary was a good friend. And I wanted to help you, Alexander."

"Thank you," he said again. "Her death...I wish I'd been in the room to help you before she fell. I was too late to save her."

"You thought she was just having another fit," Agnes said with a small shrug. "'Twasn't your fault."

Taller than Katherine, Agnes had only to raise her face so that her lips were near his. This she did, and her eyes became sultry slits.

Alex moved away from her. "I'll go to my study now. I have some work to do."

Agnes's smile, wide and innocent, remained. "Of course. I'll speak to the coachman right now."

****

It had taken Millie less than an hour to fold Katherine's clothing into her large trunk. The maid shut the lid and sat on it, then leaned forward to pull down the brass and leather clasps and latch it. "That's everythin'," she said, running the back of her hand across her forehead.

Millie now knew about her father. So did Sam. The entire household had to know by now, judging from the way they averted their eyes when she looked at them.

"Oh, sad day it is. And ye beginning to talk now," Millie said. "Poor lady. Sam, he says Lord Drayton doesn't want ye to go."

"But I can't face him," Katherine said in her raw, guttural half-whisper.

The thrill that should have surged in hearing her own voice was crushed by the weight of her heartache and shame. Her own father was a traitor. A murderer! Nothing could have prepared her for Alex's revelation.

Leaving was her only option. He wouldn't want her here to remind him of his tragedy. What man would?

He didn't love her. And now, she couldn't hope that he ever would. Katherine closed her eyes as her heart's last fragment of hope squeezed itself gray and died.

"What will happen to me? What will I do?" She brought her hand to her throat and bent her head with coughing.

"No, no, ye mustn't overwork yer throat," Millie said, rushing to her. She fell to her knees and tentatively stroked Katherine's hair. "There'll be time enough t'heal."

"Yes," Katherine choked. "Time enough. To forget him."

****

She's not at fault, lad," Sam said softly. "Have mercy on her plight."

"Sam." The word was a breath, but warning enough.

"You need not do this."

"'Tis done. She's gone. And she wished it."

"But she's your wife now. Did you want her to go?"

Alex drained his ale and set it on his desk. "No. But this is best. Now that she knows."

Sam picked up the tankard and set it on a tray. "Alex?"

"I don't want to talk about it."

"Do you love her?"

The question caught Alex off guard. For a moment he sat quiet and still, watching the numbers blur on one of the ledgers she had corrected. "I love no one."

Sam didn't answer, and left the study with a hard click of the door. Alex knew what Sam was thinking.

But this was best. Hadn't he told her repeatedly that

he didn't want her here? Even though he'd married her, his distrust had only made her leave him. And living here would only remind her of her father's murderous act. It made perfect sense.

Yet the castle, only hours after her departure, seemed so forlorn, just as it had been before she came here.

"I *am* a lying caitiff," he muttered.

No. He trampled the warmth that tried to fill his heart. Loving someone only meant death and heartache.

"Lying caitiff," he repeated. He stared, unseeing, at the freshly sharpened quill in his hands.

Where had he heard those words?

"Her words." He drew in a quick breath and jerked up his head. "*Her* words! She talked. She *talked*! And I missed it! God's bones, I missed it!"

He leaped to his feet, knocking his knees into the massive desk and lifting its front legs off the floor. The stacks of papers and ledgers toppled. His ink bottle fell off and left a curved ribbon of glistening black along the planked floor.

Alex raced from the study, headed for the servant stairs since they were closer, and took the steps three at a time.

At his bedchamber door, however, he stopped. Why fetch his cloak? Why try to bring her back? She would only grow to hate him, or fear him for some reason.

He turned. As if on their own volition, his feet took him in another direction, toward her bedchamber. Mary's chamber.

He opened the door and stepped inside, then took in the colorless drab. Why had he put Katherine in this dreadful room? Simply because she would have a good view of the front of the house?

No. That wasn't it at all.

He'd had this room readied for Katherine because Mary had chosen it for its distance from his bedchamber. Mary had wanted to be as far from him as possible.

He hadn't even met Katherine when he'd chosen this room, but had wanted her away from him and assumed she would wish the same.

At the window, he flicked aside the drapes and stared

down at the empty carriage drive. “Katherine,” he whispered. “What have I done?”

Then, he looked down at his hands clutching the window sill, and yanked them away. This was the sill that had held Mary before she jumped. This window meant death. A finality to madness.

Horrified, he turned and saw the room as it had been the night she'd died, smelled the fear prevalent in the sour stench of her bruised, perspiring skin.

He couldn't bring Katherine home. He couldn't dare love her.

All at once, the sorrow slammed into him. Alex collapsed to his knees and clutched his nauseated stomach with both hands.

The agony was a thousand swords strong.

“Stop. Please.”

He fought the wretched heartache with gritted teeth, his eyes squeezed shut, warding off the blades that stabbed at his emotions again and again. He cursed the raw wounds that wouldn't heal without the love of the woman who had soared in and out of his life on silent wings.

Alex pressed his forehead to the floor, his voice gritty with intensity. “I had to let her go.”

And the blades tore into him with fresh strength, ever deeper, slashing until the pain wrenched his soul. He fell onto his side, his voice now a moan. “What do you want?”

From long ago, his father's eyes met his in tender love, even as death took him.

“Alex!” his mother's terrified voice echoed. “Run!”

“Don't hurt Mama. Please.” It was only the whisper of a boy, unable to look away, as the man slit her throat and then came at him.

The boy already knew that he'd find the murderous lecher, oh yes, and when he did, he'd first kill his family and then tear him to pieces.

And now Mary was here, Mary as she'd been at the beginning of their marriage. Carefree and loving. And then four years later. Suspicious. Hateful.

She'd crouched by her bed, snarling at him as he crept forward, hands outstretched. “Mary, please.”

"You're trying to kill me. Get away. Get away!"

"Better go," Agnes had said from one corner.

He'd left the room. And Mary jumped from the window.

"I couldn't save you," Alex whispered now as he curled his body on the floor. "Any of you."

Now the murderer's daughter shimmered before him—Katherine, her hand warm on his cheek, her eyes full of love and acceptance.

"Katherine," Alex whispered. "Come back. I love you so much."

In that instant, he surrendered the past. Finally, the blades pierced his iron heart and ripped open every buried hatred, every anguish, every shame he'd ever hidden away and obscured with a mask of indifference.

He grieved. Dear God, he grieved.

Alex clutched his face and wept.

Chapter Twenty-seven

Later, Alex left the bedchamber feeling lighter. Cleansed. Strong.

He would bring his wife home, where she belonged. With sure strides he headed down the upstairs corridor.

Elizabeth was almost at the top of the stairs. "I've been looking for you," she said. "Why did Katherine leave?"

He paused in his stride. "Her father was a spy. He murdered my parents."

Tears sprang to Elizabeth's eyes. "Oh, how terrible. And now you've sent her away?"

"No. 'Twas her decision."

"You—you don't hate her for what her father did, do you?"

"Of course not. I'm going to get her now." Alex started to turn but then noticed the card Elizabeth held. "What do you have?"

Elizabeth's smile brightened her face. "The baron is coming to call on me."

"The baron?" Alex frowned.

Elizabeth held out the card. "Lord Wiltshire. He wants to see me!"

"No."

"Alex—"

"I said no. We did not part on good terms. He only wanted Katherine as a wife because she couldn't talk. What would he want with you?"

Elizabeth went pale. "What are you saying?"

"I'm saying the baron likes women who have a disfigurement."

"That's not true! He was a perfect gentleman when he was here that night."

"He's a cruel fop who enjoys belittling women. Elizabeth, I won't give consent for a courtship—if that's what he has in mind." Alex crossed his arms in impatience, wanting to get to Katherine. "What of Edward? I saw him kissing you last night. Did he propose?"

Elizabeth hesitated. "No. Agnes said she doesn't think he will."

"I'll speak to him when I return. It's time he asked for your hand."

"But the baron may wish to court me. He—he excites me."

Alex grimaced. "You're not serious. That old stinkard?"

"I like him." Elizabeth lowered her head.

He didn't have time for this. "All right, Bethie. I'll let you choose for yourself."

Elizabeth threw her slender arms around him. "Thank you, Alex!"

His cousin had never hugged him before, and he hid his awkward surprise by saying, "I must leave."

Elizabeth released him. "Oh, I've sent for a midwife for Clara. She is ready to give birth."

"Send Pace to the barn if he doesn't want to stay there," Alex said as he escaped down the steps.

Minutes later he swung up on Neos and raced down the road toward Lobb's Inn in Chiswick.

Halfway there, he met his returning carriage. He stopped to tell the coachman to go back to the inn for Katherine's trunks, but his words were cut short when Millie, her face reddened with weeping, stumbled out.

"M'lord," Millie began.

"Where is Lady Drayton?" Alex demanded.

Millie began to sob. "She's in town, m'lord."

"You left her alone at the inn? Why?"

"The inn? I wasn't ordered to take her to an inn," the coachman said, his face creasing in confused worry.

Alex went rigid as he swung his gaze up to the coachman. "What are you talking about? Of course you were."

Millie sobbed, "Why did ye do this to her, m'lord? She's done nothin' to deserve it."

Alex's voice rose to a near shout. "Where is she?"

"Patsy Eberly's brothel," said the coachman, his voice shaking. "Lady Agnes said you asked her to give me Lady

Drayton's destination."

"Brothel?" Alex choked. "No! You were to take her to Lobb's Inn!" Without waiting for an answer from the maid and coachman, he kicked Neos into a gallop. Just up the road, he headed into the forest. The shortcut would buy time—perhaps a half hour.

Alex prayed that he wasn't already too late.

Chapter Twenty-eight

"Fly, Neos!"

Trees blurred as he raced through shafts of sunlight, through copses of fresh green growth. Birdsong and the skitter of startled woodland creatures were all but lost in the muted, rhythmic pounding of Neos' hooves on the wet decayed foliage of the forest floor.

He had to get to her.

Would she ever forgive him for this slipshod mistake? Likely not. She'd hate him.

"Agnes." Alex spat her name into the rushing wind.

Why had he let Katherine go? God's nails, she was his wife!

She was his, and he might not reach her before the men got their hands on her. Hot viral dominance filled him. He gritted his teeth and bowed low over Neos' neck to give the horse full rein down the woodland path.

"Fly!"

The crack of a gunshot registered in his mind even as he felt a searing pain in his shoulder.

Neos, shying at the sound, lurched to the left and threw him off the saddle.

Alex hit the ground and rolled until his chest slammed into a tree. He lay still for a moment and tried to force air into his crushed lungs.

He had no time to react before a man was on him; no time to pull his rapier from its scabbard before he felt a blade cutting his throat.

****

The room at the brothel stank of sex, sweat, and vomit. Katherine pushed open the filthy window and gulped in fresh air.

"Better not be tryin' anything," the skinny snake of a man yelled through the door.

Despite his sinewy strong arms, she would escape.

No one could stop her. Did they actually think she was a whore, come to make money for that horrid Patsy? The woman had actually slapped her when she'd tried to explain that it had all been a mistake, that she would reenter her carriage and be on her way to the inn.

But the coachman had insisted that his directions, given through Lord Drayton, had been to bring her here. That was good enough for Patsy, and her man had practically carried Katherine down the hall and dumped her in this room, then locked the door until Patsy came to give her instructions on how to treat the men who would visit her this night.

Katherine wiped away fresh hot tears and swung one leg over the sill. She had no time to cry over Alex, wouldn't waste time on him. Their marriage was finished.

Her feet hit the ground. Turning, she lifted her skirts and dashed toward the street.

At the corner of the house, she skidded to a stop. Outside the front of the brothel stood a throng of men. There was Patsy on the steps, hailing Katherine as her fresh whore—not young, but beautiful nonetheless.

Katherine backed away until she was out of sight, then turned and stifled a thin scream as she found herself face to face with her guard.

He backhanded her across her cheek, then shook her. "Where th' hell ye goin', slut?"

****

Alex gazed up at the rogue's face, almost hidden beneath a dirty tangle of thick brown hair and beard. A hand rummaged through the pocket of his waistcoat and closed on his leather money pouch.

Alex gripped the man's wrist. "I have to—" he choked, and with great effort sucked in breath.

The knife pressed harder and split the skin on his neck.

"Now, now, sir," the highwayman soothed, his smile and soft voice a contrast to his heinous act, "no need to die today, eh?"

Alex loosened his hold, and the knife eased. Blood trickled down his neck.

Where was the pistol? Certainly the thief hadn't time to reload. But he also had a sword, and the knife.

The man stood and pocketed the pouch, then glanced behind him at Neos, who stood nearby stamping and huffing. He turned back toward Alex. "G'day, to ye, sir," he said, ludicrously polite.

He ambled toward Neos.

With a pained groan, Alex sat up. The man's hand was inches away from the bridle. There was no way Alex would get to Katherine in time without the speed of his horse.

"Neos," he called gruffly. "Back!"

Neos snorted and backed away, then reared, kicking out his hooves at the thief,.

"Cur!" the man snarled as he turned back toward Alex and withdrew his sword. "Should 'ave cut yer throat."

Alex staggered to his feet and realized with a shock that the other man almost equaled him in size. He reached for his rapier but agonizing pain ringed his shoulder. His right arm was useless for wielding the sword.

He stumbled back as the thief came at him swinging both sword and dagger.

With his left hand Alex tugged his rapier free. He parried the thief's sword just before it reached his throat. The dagger followed, slashing an inch from his chest.

They parried and thrust, circling, lunging. Alex grew dizzy with pain. He fended off both blades left-handed, but saw his own desperation mirrored in the calculating gleam of the thief's eyes.

Dear God, how had this happened? Katherine needed him. He had to get to her.

This had to end.

"Stop this now and you may live to see another day," he panted as he fended off yet another drive of the thief's sword.

Pausing, equally winded, the thief took a step back. "Come now. Is yer gold so important that ye'd die for it? Look at ye." He gestured with his sword at Alex's shoulder. "I shot ye. Yer bleedin'. And now I gots ter kill ye."

"Keep the gold." Alex, gritting his teeth in pain, unclasped his cloak. "Allow me my horse. A woman needs me."

The highwayman showed his rotting teeth, clearly enjoying the banter. "Needs ye? Aye, needs yer cock, no doubt. Who is this wench ye fancy grindin'?"

Alex's voice went low with fury. "Get out of my way or I'll kill you!"

"Ye'll 'ave to kill me," the thief said, his lips curled in a sneer, "because I want yer horse, too." With a yell, he leaped forward and lunged at Alex with his sword.

Shouting with rage and pain, Alex twisted to one side as he wrenched his cloak from his shoulders. He hurled the cloak over the thief's head and drove his rapier through the cloth.

A sickening pressure slowed the sword. Jerking it out, Alex then yanked the cloak away to reveal blood spilling from the highwayman's eye.

With a cry, the thief fell to his knees, staring with his remaining eye in bizarre astonishment. He crumpled forward.

Alex dropped his sword and stumbled back. He drank air in gulps as he took in the highwayman's limp body, and then closed his eyes.

Blackness swam into him, made him unable to focus. He slumped to the ground.

Warm nose on his head. A nudge.

Neos stood over him. With shaking hand, Alex gave his velvet gray nose a weak rub. Then, grimacing, he crawled to the dead man and retrieved his coins.

"How long?" he asked the black clouds that were overtaking the sky. "Am I too late?"

A low rumble of thunder to the west answered him.

"Easy, boy," he whispered to Neos as he got one foot in the stirrup. Grunting against the pain of his wounds, he pulled himself into the saddle. His neck was no longer bleeding, but his shirt and waistcoat shoulder were crimson from the bullet wound. He pulled his soiled cloak around him.

With grim determination, he nudged Neos toward town.

One hour later, when he got close to the brothel, he turned the horse down a narrow alley two buildings up and slid off the saddle.

"You, boy." He held up a shilling to a narrowed-eyed

boy. "Hold the reigns of my horse until I return. You'll get two more."

"Yes, sir!" The boy ran to take the reigns from Alex. "Are you all right, sir?"

"Yes. Fine," Alex muttered. His shoulder throbbed. Gray rings danced in his vision as he trudged back to the main street and approached the front of the brothel. There, a crowd of boisterous men, some stumbling as if drunk, milled about. With effort he straightened, pulled his cloak closed around himself, and adopted an equal look of excitement.

"Lord Drayton, I see you've come to see how she fares!" came a booming female voice at the door. Patsy gestured toward him. "You have this man to thank for the doe-eyed whore."

The men cheered. Alex sucked in air through his teeth and fought the blackness threatening to overtake him as friendly hands slapped his back and shoulders in good natured camaraderie.

The wide grimace he held must have been taken for a grin because no one seemed to notice his pain. He walked through the crowd to Patsy and held out two gold guineas. "I want her first."

"Oh ho!" Patsy threw back her head and laughed, then greedily licked her lips as she dropped the coins between her cleavage. "Sometimes the needle's stiffer in a brothel, eh? But I've already let in the first one."

With effort, Alex kept his lips spread in a smile. "How long ago?"

"Mayhap five minutes."

Thank heaven. Alex pressed another coin in Patsy's hand. "Make him wait."

Patsy peered at him. "What's your hurry? You could have had her at home."

Alex pulled out two more coins. "Like you said, the needle's stiff and ready."

Patsy hooted and dropped the money down her bodice, where it clinked with the other coins. "You've just made me a rich woman, Lord Drayton," she said. "That Katie, she's a spirited one. I sent in the biggest man to break her in."

It was all Alex could do to shove Patsy aside and race

into the house. But he didn't know where Katherine was.

"All afternoon she tried to talk to me in that squeaky voice, but I don't have time to be waiting on her like she's royalty," Patsy said, and finally led Alex through the front door. "I told her to keep her mouth shut. I'll get more money if the men think she can't talk at all."

The heavy smell of roses mixed with stale ale assaulted Alex as he followed Patsy past a lush pink parlor where several woman had gathered on the chairs and couches. When they spotted Alex, one spread her legs and ran her tongue around her lips. Another grasped her small breasts and lifted them.

"He wants the half-mute," Patsy called to them as she passed. She put up a hand toward Alex. "Wait here. I'll have to get the other one out."

Just then, a thick man with black hair and beard trudged down the hall, rattling the floorboards with each heavy step. "She's locked herself in her room, Miss Eberly," he said, his voice almost a whine. "She won't let me in. I didn't want to break down your door."

Alex almost laughed with relief. "I'll just go in," he offered to Patsy.

"Wait in the parlor, Garson," Patsy purred to the man. "Let those ladies give you some attention until she's ready for you."

"Not too long," he said, eyeing Alex suspiciously.

Alex hoped to God he wouldn't have to fight again. He hadn't the strength.

"Don't wear her out," Patsy said as she walked down the hall ahead of Alex. "Like I told Garson, some of those men outside want to tumble with her, too."

"I'll take care of her," Alex promised.

Patsy stopped midway down the hall and pushed at a door. "She's got something blocking it. Katie, open up."

There was no response.

Patsy banged on the door. "Katie! Open this door right now!"

"Katherine, 'tis Alex," he called softly. "Please, open the door."

There was a scraping sound inside the room, and then more silence.

"Spoiled bitch needs to learn her place here." Patsy

pushed at the door again, and this time it opened.

Katherine wasn't in sight.

"She gives you trouble, let me know. I told her I'll have her tied naked to her bed if she puts up a fuss. Have a go, Lord Drayton. I'll send the next one in thirty minutes."

Alex smiled at Patsy and waited until she had turned the corner to go down the hall, and then he pushed open the door and stepped inside. In a moment, he would have his wife out of here and heading home.

A blur of white greeted his vision before something hard crashed onto his head.

Chapter Twenty-nine

"Wake up, you mongrel." Katherine watched Alex's eyelids flutter as he moaned.

She hated him. Having her brought to this whorehouse and then coming to bed her was as vile and cruel an act as any he could carry out. And she'd married him. Loved him!

As his eyes slowly opened and focused on her, she picked up a shard of the broken vase.

"Katherine," he faltered, and tried to sit up.

She pressed the glass under his chin and saw a raw cut on his throat, but her fury wouldn't allow contemplation. "Stay down, you lecher. Why did you do this to me?"

Astonished, she watched the corners of his lips curve in a bare smile.

"You're speaking."

"Yes. Now hear me say that I am going to kill you." And afterward, she would hang herself. She'd sooner be dead than live a whore's life.

He grunted. "How much time has passed since you hit me?"

"You mean how much time do you have left to further violate me?" Her voice was frustratingly thin and weak, nothing like the outrage exploding in her heart. "You have no more time. You sent me here and now you want to play your sick game."

"I came to get you out. Please...how long?"

"Why? Did you think of a worse punishment?" He grasped her arm. She shook him off. "About twenty minutes."

"We have to leave."

"Not until you tell me why you did this to me, you contemptible worm."

"Mistake." He closed his eyes and took a deep, ragged breath. "You'll do me in if you cut me."

She hesitated, studying again the wound on his neck, his worn, pale face. His chest rose and fell with labored breaths. “What happened to you?”

“Shot.”

“Where?” She whipped aside the cloak and gasped at the blood that slicked his waistcoat and shirt. “Alex!”

His voice was a breathy grunt. “Help me up. We need to get out of here.”

Katherine tossed away the shard of glass. With effort, she helped him to his feet.

He sagged against the wall. “How...?”

“The window,” she said, rubbing her sore cheekbone. “That awful guard might be watching.”

Once outside, Alex lowered his head and leaned against the building.

“Alex?” In the daylight, he was positively gray.

“Hurry.” He roused, took Katherine’s hand, and led her behind two more buildings until they reached a boy who stood with Alex’s horse.

Alex handed him two coins, and the boy ran off. Amidst the pain on Alex’s face was sorrowful guilt. He kissed her. His lips felt much too warm.

“I’m sorry. I didn’t intend this.”

“You need a doctor. And then you need to explain yourself.”

Alex grunted as he knelt. “Step up. Mind my shoulder.”

A moment later, Katherine perched atop Neos, who simply had to be the tallest horse in England.

“Straddle him,” Alex said.

“Oh, mercy.” Mortified, Katherine spread her legs on either side of the horse and imagined the disapproving looks she’d receive from the townspeople. She made futile attempts to pull her skirts over her exposed ankles, realizing she had not even her cloak to cover her head. Behind her, Alex pulled himself up. He reached around her with his left hand and took the reins.

They ventured out onto the main road. Down the street behind them, the crowd of men in front of Patsy’s brothel had swelled. Katherine shivered.

“You can relax, my lady.” His uneven breath was warm in her hair. “The danger is behind you.”

The danger was behind her, yes, and she was much too close to it. She scooted forward.

"Move back toward me," he said hoarsely. "You don't have to sit so far forward."

"No. Not after what you did. Your—what did you call it? Mistake?" She stayed where she was and stared staunchly over the horse's head, unable to stem her hurt and anger. Her voice strained. "You sent me there because of my father's acts."

"No."

"Then why?"

Another pause. "'Twas my error. I'll deal with it."

"Your *error*?" She lowered her head, wanting both to lean back into him and run far, far away. "How could you do this?"

His voice, although weak, held a trace of its old arrogance. "'Twas a misjudgment I made."

"I don't believe you."

"Katherine—"

"Do not speak to me." She swiped tears from her eyes, then slapped at his hand when he slid his good arm around her. It had no effect. He shifted his thighs and pulled her closer to him.

"We'll talk about it when you're calm," he said, sounding so very forspent. "I can't guide Neos with you up on his neck."

"You may remove your arm from me, my lord," she said, hoping he heard her through her weak, wavering voice. She kept her back straight so as not to touch him. "Take me to the inn and leave me there. After you see a doctor, send someone for my trunks at the brothel. If they're still there."

"No. You'll come home with me."

"I will not. And...I don't know if I could look upon you without thinking of what my father did to your parents."

"You're my wife," he said. "Your place is at Drayton Castle."

"I never wish to see you again." Her voice ended on a half sob.

"Katherine, I won't go home without you." He sounded out of breath.

She didn't want him to go home without her, but didn't voice this. If he had any more feelings for her—if he loved her—he wouldn't have let her leave their home in the first place.

They fell into a long silence as they moved along the street, which had all but emptied of townspeople in the fading daylight and gathering black clouds overhead. On her right, huddled on the dirt next to a stable, shivered a girl who looked about eleven or twelve years old.

"Find shelter," Katherine said, hoping the girl could hear her. "'Twill rain soon."

She raised bleak eyes. "I have no shelter."

Katherine's attention was drawn to Alex's arm, which had slackened from her waist and now dropped to his side. His head lowered to her shoulder. "Take the reins. I cannot...."

Katherine bit her lip in worry. Who was she to be depended upon? Two neighbor children had died because she couldn't get to them. "What do I do?" she whispered.

Only his silence answered.

Neos snorted with the unfamiliar set of hands guiding him, but thankfully didn't test her.

She saw Lobb's Inn ahead on the left, and guided the horse to a waiting stable boy. "Get help," she rasped as loudly as she could. "This man is hurt."

Two men half-carried Alex to a room and lay him on a bed.

After sending for a doctor, Katherine sat on the bed and touched his feverish face, then helped him remove his jacket and shirt. "So much blood."

A shadow passed over his face. "I killed him."

"You were only protecting yourself."

The doctor arrived and, one hour after Alex's guttural groans of pain, held out an object. "Here's the bullet. It didn't hit the bone." The leeches made sucking sounds as he pulled them off the skin surrounding the wound. "I've done all I can. Use the poultices freely, but his fever is coming on. He may not last the night."

Katherine grabbed Alex's hand. He would die? "No. No. He'll be all right."

The doctor shrugged and snapped his bag closed. "We'll see. I noticed that your voice is quite hoarse. I've left some cinnamon drops on the table for you."

Katherine only half heard him. A deep trembling had taken hold of her, and after the doctor left she sat by Alex on the bed. "You can't die." She placed her hand on the side of his hot, pale face. "You can't. I won't let you."

Alex didn't answer. He was asleep, his breathing labored and slow. Bright red spots gradually bloomed on his cheeks. She lifted the poultice covering the bullet hole, made even larger by the doctor's probing fingers, and studied the tiny red streaks that had appeared around it.

"Alex," she whispered. "I love you. Stay strong for me."

She moved to a chair by the bed and watched his chest rise and fall, afraid to look away lest he took a last breath. Leaning down, she smoothed his hair and drifted her fingers over his purple eyelids, his cheeks, and the bristles on his jaw, and willed him not to die.

Two or three hours passed. Outside, a steady rain fell. The darkness pressed in on the single lit candle on the dressing table. After a time the storm let up, and eventually the moon peeked silver through breaking clouds.

Katherine turned the poultice on Alex's shoulder and pulled the covers over him, then pressed her cheek against his. Heat emanated from him in waves. He lay unmoving as if already dead. Yet he still breathed.

Footsteps sounded outside her door and then receded as someone walked past their room. Outside on the dark street, a raucous voice called to another. Later, a woman let forth a shrill laugh. Katherine drank of the ale and tried to swallow some of the bread and cheese the innkeeper had brought to the room.

Midnight passed. The moon had disappeared over the roof, leaving a black stillness broken only by occasional barking of dogs outside or the skittering of rats within the inn walls.

Her lids growing heavy, Katherine wrapped and wetted a fresh poultice. The wound had swollen and now oozed a watery, reddish fluid. The streaks had expanded, reaching out from the dirt-encrusted hole like spider legs. She studied it, and made a decision.

A moment later she banged on the innkeeper's door.

"Have you soap?"

"Have I what?" The innkeeper rubbed a hand over his weathered face and then straightened his crumpled nightcap.

"Soap. I need soap."

"Why? We have no one to draw water for a bath at this hour. You don't even need a bath, from the looks of you."

She fought the urge to rear back from his sour breath. "I just need soap. I'll pay." She held up a guinea.

The innkeeper shuffled down the hall and a moment later returned with a palm-sized bar. "For the laundry," he said. "Will it do?"

Katherine held the rough gray bar to the candlelight. "It will have to, if you have no Castile soap."

"You want that Spanish soap for whores, go to Spain. Take it or leave it."

Back in the room, she wrung water from a towel, then rubbed the soap onto it until it made a rich lather. Alex didn't awaken when she scrubbed the wound.

If the knowledgeable doctor knew what she was doing, he would call her an ignorant dolt, perhaps even accuse her of aiding in his death. Her mother had always told her to stop thinking up such outlandish notions as questioning the conviction that dirt was a shield against disease.

Now, as she rinsed the wound and then placed the fresh poultice on it, Katherine told herself that she had done her husband no harm.

After all, she had nothing else to lose.

She set the candle on the bedside table and undressed to her petticoat, then carefully climbed over him to lay on his left side. She ran her hands over his hot, still form. "Alex," she whispered. "I didn't mean what I said. I want to go home with you. To our home. Don't die. Don't."

Finally, she slept.

And awoke with a cry when she was slammed against the wall. She rubbed her head and looked around in confusion. The candle sputtered on the bedside table. Beside her, Alex thrashed about with rasping moans.

"Alex?" She touched his face, and gasped. He was burning up! The poultice had come off and in the dim light of the candle, blood was smeared over his shoulder and onto the sheet.

He lurched his body and flung out his arms, narrowly missing her face.

Katherine swung one leg over him to leave the bed.

He gripped her arm with shocking strength. "Who are you?"

"Katherine. Let go." She tried to pull away from the painful vice of his hand.

"Liar!"

She recoiled with fear at his blank, glassy stare.

"'Tis Katherine!" she cried. "Alex, you're hurting me!"

"She-devil! Trying to kill me!"

"Alex! Please!" Katherine jerked backwards but not soon enough; his other hand gripped her neck. Her gasp of pain was cut short by his thumb pressing into her windpipe.

Desperately she pulled at his fingers. He stared at her with flat, emotionless eyes, his pale lips contorted in a grimace. Spots filled her vision, a gray haze.

He would kill her.

Her hand left his and fumbled for the one thing that might stop him.

Her fingers found it. And drove into his torn flesh.

"Oh God!" With a roar, Alex released her throat and groped at his wound.

Katherine flung herself off the bed and crawled to the door, then stood on shaking legs, gasping and coughing.

Alex didn't come after her, and a moment later, his thrashing had ceased.

Shaking out a long breath, she crept toward him. His eyes were closed and his breathing was shallow. He moaned and moved in spasms, occasionally twisting his body and muttering garbled words.

Wearily, she poured water into the bowl and soaked a towel to lay across his fiery brow. After cleaning and dressing his wound again—all the while watching him for any sign of awakening—she moved the chair across the room near the door and sat, then leaned forward with her head in her hands.

Chapter Thirty

Alex awoke in listless stages to the pain in his shoulder. A linen cloth bag filled with a fragrant, green spongy concoction covered his wound.

He sat up slowly and rubbed his bristled face. Pink dawn touched the windows and illuminated Katherine, asleep and slumped in a chair by the door.

Bare sound came from his parched throat as he tried to call her name. The warm watered ale on the bedside table slaked his thirst for the moment and gave him a little strength to stumble across the floor toward her.

He knelt at her chair. Purple shadows under her eyes revealed her strain, and his heart twisted over what he'd put her through these past weeks.

She didn't want him. In the watery depths of his pain during their ride away from the brothel, he'd heard her say she never wished to see him again.

The old desolation, the longing to retreat into his emotional shell, threatened to engulf him. This time, he waged war. He wanted her to be happy, but by God, he'd bloody well not give her up without a fight.

"Katherine." Through waves of dizziness he rose and kissed her brow, then sank to his knees once more.

She stirred and opened bleary eyes. "Alex?" She studied him and smoothed back his hair. "You'll be all right," she breathed. "My husband. You'll be all right."

Alex spoke through the sudden roughness in his throat. "Come home. 'Tis where you belong."

"Yes." She leaned forward and wrapped her arms around his shoulders. Her breath was warm on his neck. "I was so afraid. I don't want to live without you."

"I swear to you that you will not." Clenching his jaw at the fire in his wound and the weakness in his legs, Alex stood and helped Katherine to her feet.

Much later, after they had slept again and eaten,

Katherine knelt by the tub brought to them by the innkeeper. She dipped a wet cloth into the steaming water and slid it across Alex's back. They hadn't discussed the reason she had been taken to the brothel, but she knew Alex would tell her when he was ready. Her trust in him was complete.

"Ah, good." He leaned forward with a great sigh.

"I'll bathe after you finish," Katherine said. His damp skin beckoned her, and she kissed his shoulder. His quick intake of breath was her only warning before he put his good arm around her and kissed her.

"Your lips and chin are wet from my shoulder, he teased.

"And the rest of me is getting soaked from your arm, my lord," Katherine said in mock disapproval.

"Then I suppose you need to take off that dress and join me." Alex ran one moist finger from her neck to her bodice.

Katherine shivered with the pleasure his touch caused in her, then eyed the small tub. "'Tis barely large enough for *you*. How will I fit?"

"I don't know," he said. "Forsooth, 'twill be enjoyable to try."

Katherine shook her head in doubt, but stood and undressed before him, relishing his roaming gaze. Never had she realized what pleasure she could give a man just by removing her clothing in front of him.

She stepped into the tub. Her legs had just enough room on either side of his hips. Alex grasped her waist with his good arm and guided her down. Her thighs slid delectably over his as she sat on his lap facing him

"There," he said with a smile. He took the cloth she had draped over the side of the tub, wetted it, and bathed her shoulders and back. Soaking it once again, he dripped the water over her chest, then lowered his head and moved his mouth and tongue over the moist beads of her nipples.

Katherine took in a final glimpse of their inn bedroom before she succumbed to her body's response.

His kiss was long and languid. Unhurriedly his hands, warm and wet, wandered over her body, touching her in places that made her gasp in pleasure. His fingers settled on her breasts.

"I want you," he murmured into her neck.

Katherine pulled back to look at him. "But you're wounded."

"Not where it counts." He guided her hand down.

"And we're in a tub little wider than a barrel," she added with a sensuous smile, and began to stroke him.

In answer, he sucked in a deep breath.

Katherine kissed his bristled jaw and smooth skin of his neck. Slowly she lifted herself and took him inside her.

"Yes," he breathed against the corner of her mouth.

Katherine closed her eyes and began to move, finding her own rhythm. She shifted her hips to take him in deeper.

Alex delighted in her fervent moans, watched her face tighten with intensity, her breaths come faster and faster, until she reared back and cried out his name. He released himself with a shout.

With soft gasps she slumped forward against him. "So good," she murmured.

"Pleasuring you is what's good," he said, kissing her soft earlobe.

After a time he helped her out onto the soaked floor. He led her to the bed and covered them with the quarter-pane, then hugged her to him for a time. He didn't want to leave his cloud of serenity after their lovemaking, but finally said, "We need to talk."

She stiffened in his arms, then sighed. "Yes. About your mistake."

"I didn't send you to the brothel, Katherine."

"Who did?"

"Agnes."

Katherine lifted her head, wide-eyed astonishment replacing her sleepy sensuality. "Agnes!"

"She told my coachman to take you there instead of the inn. My orders, she told him."

Katherine bolted to a sitting position, grabbed one of the pillows, and squeezed it between her hands. "Oh, that vixen. Wait until I see her." Then, she peered at Alex. "Why did you tell her to talk to the coachman instead of doing it yourself?"

Alex brushed his fingers through her damp, tousled

hair. "She offered to help."

"I'm sure she did." Katherine's brown eyes held the fire that he now knew well, but to hear her livid voice added a new depth to her. "She wished to help me right out of your life. She's in love with you, in case you hadn't noticed."

"I've never encouraged her. I blame myself for what happened. You could have been hurt."

"And you could have been killed."

"That woman will not enter our home again." Alex clenched his fist and released it slowly. "Mary seemed to like her, so I let her come as often as she wished. She saw Mary jump from her window."

"*Agnes* was with Mary?" Katherine stared at him.

"Yes. I had gone out to the corridor so that Mary might calm down. 'Twas not a good move."

Katherine lay back down, and her lips were warm and soft on his cheek. "The windows remind you of your guilt, so you keep them covered."

"Foolish of me, I know."

"No. We all have our demons. Put me in a closet and shut the door, and I'll show you mine."

Alex palmed her cheek and kissed her. "I love you."

Her face brightened with a moist-eyed smile. "Oh, Alex. How I've longed to hear you say that."

"Then I'll say it again. I love you. You're the most amazing woman I have ever met."

Her head lowered. "But can you forget? Will you always look upon me and see what my father did?"

He placed a finger under her chin and lifted it. "I will always look upon you, yes. And listen to your charming voice."

"My father was a spy. A murderer."

He lost himself in her eyes. "Yes. But he made you. And for that, I forgive him."

Katherine placed tender kisses on his cheeks, his brows, his lips. "I love you, dear Alex. My husband."

She loved him.

Suddenly, the last iron piece masking Alex's heart melted away. All he could do for a moment was struggle to maintain his emotions and not succumb to womanly tears. Needing something to drive away the lump in his throat, he took one of her rosy nipples and played it between his fingers. "We will speak of the dark past no more. Let us dress and return home. I want to make love to you in our bed."

"In time," Katherine said with a tiny, enchanting gasp. She trailed her hand down his chest and stomach, paused teasingly, and then went lower.

A throaty groan escaped Alex's lips. "Yes. In time."

A few hours before sunset, Katherine and Alex set out for home on Neos. In the middle of town, Katherine saw the ragged girl again with her hands out to passersby. Crying. Begging.

And not two doors down in front of her brothel, scrutinizing the waif, stood Patsy Eberly.

Katherine grabbed Alex's hand holding the reins and jerked Neos to a halt.

****

Lord Wiltshire's smile was wide and pleasant when Alex trudged past his parlor and saw him perched on the arm of a chair like a blasted parrot.

The man couldn't be satisfied with looking comelier than a woman—he also had to have the largest, most flamboyantly pink feather in his hat that Alex had ever seen.

Thomas Bliss stood and bowed, detaching the hat from his brown peruke with a flourish. When he bowed, the feather swept the Aubusson rug.

"Lord Drayton!" he began, and then his lips curled in distaste. "Have you been assisting in the birth as well?"

"What birth?" Alex asked, wanting nothing more than to retire to his bedchamber with Katherine.

Elizabeth stood, pale and red-eyed. "Clara is dead."

"Clara." Alex tried to think. "Clara? The sheepherder Thaddeus' wife?"

"Yes." Elizabeth approached him, her limp worse in her troubled state. "She gave birth late last night. The midwife grew impatient and pulled the babe from Clara's womb. Then she—she reached inside to get...." Elizabeth bent her head and sobbed.

Wiltshire, uncomfortable at either Elizabeth's distress or the subject at hand, settled into the chair.

Alex drew Elizabeth into his arms. "What happened?"

"The midwife ripped Clara's womb. "I—I've never seen so much blood."

Alex was silent for a moment. Then, "The babe?"

"Strong and healthy. But poor Pace is beside himself. For the first time Elizabeth seemed to notice the dried blood on his clothing. "You're hurt."

"The highwayman shot me."

"And?" Wiltshire stood once more.

"He's dead. I killed him."

"Well, good riddance, I say," the baron said with a tug on his gray bristled chin. "But you look a little peaked, Drayton. Best that you go to your bedchamber and rest for now. Elizabeth, would you like me to dispatch the servants to search for the boy?"

Alex tensed. "That won't be necessary, Wiltshire. I'll take care of it. You may want to leave now so my cousin can rest."

"Yes. I think I need to lie down," Elizabeth murmured, and turned to Wiltshire. "Forgive me, my lord."

"Of course," Wiltshire replied. When Elizabeth left the room, his smile curdled. "I do hope we can renew our acquaintance, Drayton. I realize we did not part on favorable circumstances."

Alex challenged Wiltshire with a glare. "And we will remain so unless you have the highest intentions toward my cousin."

"Oh, that I do," Wiltshire agreed with another flourishing bow. "She's to make her decision soon. I will cherish and protect her always. My servants will do all her walking for her and she'll only need to stand to come to my bed. She—"

Alex winced inwardly and put up a hand. "Enough. Elizabeth will make her decision when she's ready."

Chapter Thirty-one

"I'm considering what to do with Pace and baby Jason," Alex said a few days later during breakfast. "Clara has a sister, a poor farmer's wife, in Sheffield, but Pace tells me she already has seven children."

Katherine, smiling, toyed with her spoon. "Perhaps we could take them in as we did the orphan girl Carly."

Elizabeth's expression, bleak over Clara's death, brightened.

"They would have a better chance at life," Katherine said, trying not to spout everything that was on her mind. Her newfound voice had caused her to want to talk incessantly, just to glean the satisfaction of immediate response. "I believe they'd be happy here. Carly and Pace are already like brother and sister."

The corners of Alex's mouth curved up and he set an admiring gaze at Katherine. "You, who wanted no children because you felt you didn't deserve them, may gain two sons and a daughter. Have you forgiven yourself as well, then?"

"Yes," she said, and reached for his hand. "I will be a good mother to them."

"You'll be a fine mother, my love." He pushed back from the table and stood with a dramatic sigh. "My lonely castle," he muttered good-naturedly, "shall eventually be overrun by little feet. But they had better stay out of my tidy study." He bent down and kissed his wife.

****

"Isn't he wonderful?" gushed Elizabeth several days later as they sat in the parlor. She smiled down at Lord Wiltshire's rose-scented letter in her hand.

"Does Edward know?" Katherine asked.

"Edward? Oh. He is still my friend. Why do you ask?"

"He's *courting* you, isn't he?" Then, Katherine waved a hand. "I'm sorry. I'm as nosy as Agnes, whom I hope never to see again." She paused at the memory of the night she'd stood at her bedchamber window watching the Cookes leave. Now that she knew Agnes had been alone with Mary before her death, the vision of Agnes's calculated stare at her caused a foreboding chill.

"Neither do I," Elizabeth said. "Although I suppose if I marry Edward, Agnes will be my sister-in-law."

Katherine shook off the silly feeling. Agnes wouldn't dare attempt another ploy like the brothel to remove Katherine from Alex's life. "What do you want to do?"

"Elizabeth held the letter to her lips and then set it gently on the table beside her. "The baron seems so...full of life. I have never met anyone like him. Edward is nice, but he's just so cautious."

"There is nothing wrong with cautious. Give him time."

Alex entered the parlor. As always, his gaze sought out Katherine and took her in as if she were a cherished gift. "If you're speaking of cautious Edward, I'm on my way to his house," he said to Elizabeth. "Would you care to come along?"

"Oh...no, I don't think so," said Elizabeth. "I'll wait for Lord Wiltshire. He is paying a call to me this afternoon."

The upward curve of Alex's lips faltered. "You will allow him to court you, then."

"I—do not know as yet."

"As we discussed, 'tis your decision. I'll give Edward your salutations."

Alex led Katherine out into the Hall and kissed her. "I'll be back soon, my lovely lady."

Going with him to confront Agnes was out of the question. This was something Alex had to do alone.

Katherine kissed Alex back, and gave his bottom a subtle pinch.

"Saucy minx," Alex murmured in her ear. His hand slid up her waist to cup her breast. "Just you wait. I will lock you in my arms all night."

"'Twas only three days ago that you were shot," Katherine whispered back. "You're still weak as a babe."

"Am I now?" With his good arm, he encircled her waist. He lifted her off her feet and held her snug against the wall, pressing himself against her and giving her a long, deep kiss until she burned with need.

When he released her, she clung to him until sensation returned to her legs.

"You're gaining strength," she managed.

"Indeed."

A final kiss, a touch of his fingers to her cheek, and he was gone.

****

Elizabeth could make her own decisions, Alex thought as he trotted Neos across the green fields. Yet Edward deserved to know what was happening. He probably didn't even realize Elizabeth's thoughts had turned to another man.

And Agnes—Alex gritted his teeth at what she had done—needed to be found a suitor and married off. He would have to trust Robert to ensure that his daughter stopped her meddling ways.

He reached the house and dismounted. His boot heels crunched on the pebbled path up to Robert's door.

"God's pointy toenails!" cried a shrill voice above him.

Alex peered at an upstairs window. There, staring at him with both hands covering her mouth, stood Agnes.

One hour later, Alex left the house and set off over the hilly fields in the yellow-orange smolder of the setting sun.

Robert had never been his good friend, but as neighbors, they respected each another. The anger in Robert's eyes, after Alex had informed him of Agnes's actions of late, assured him that she would no longer trouble his household.

But it was the information passed privately to Edward that made Alex question his own judgment. He'd never seen the young man's eyes so bright with anger, nor the tension that made the cords stand out on his neck. Even Edward's voice had a razor sharp edge to it when he'd thanked Alex and walked him to the door after Robert, rod in hand, had gone to find Agnes.

If Alex had ever seen murder in a man's eyes, it was in Edward's.

Chapter Thirty-two

One month later, on the day of the Allerton ball, Millie curled Katherine's hair into delightful ringlets and clustered them on each side of her head with tiny green and white satin ribbons. The maid then shaped little curls across Katherine's forehead.

"Lovely, m'lady!" Millie exclaimed, clapping her hands in glee. "Now, the dress."

Carly, the copper-haired waif Katherine had found begging for food, jumped up from Alex's big chair. "I'll help." Her eyes shone as she assisted Millie in holding the dress over Katherine's head.

Light green satin slid coolly over Katherine's arms and down her body. Slit-open sleeves revealed delicate gold lace that exposed the skin of her arms. The round, low cut bodice, worn off the shoulders, was perfect for the pearl necklace that Alex had given her as a wedding gift.

Millie fastened the stomacher and helped her don a pair of gold-heeled dancing slippers. Then, Katherine turned in a slow circle while Millie surveyed her work with a broad smile. "The dress sets off your hair. You'll be the most beautiful lady at the Allerton's Ball."

"Yes," Carly breathed. She hugged herself and twirled around the room, her spindly ankles showing beneath her dress. "I want to go! I want to dance!"

Katherine laughed as she dabbed lavender scent behind her ears. "All in good time, dear heart." She checked herself in the mirror one last time and said, "I'd better get downstairs before Lord Drayton wonders what has become of me."

"He said earlier that we women have taken over his bedchamber," Carly said. "But I know he wasn't truly angry."

The three headed toward the stairs. Glancing down at the gold lace exposing her exquisite underskirt, Katherine remembered last year's spring parties held throughout London to start the Season. A new dress such as this would be made for her every few weeks, and her father spared no expense to please Ellis Potts.

Ellis. How long ago she'd thought she loved that wretch. What little she knew then about love.

The past weeks had shown her what true love meant. Contentment, happiness, pleasure—all wrapped up in the strong arms of a man who'd sworn off love but then opened his heart to her. Oh, how he had shown his love. For the first time since she could remember, Katherine freely expressed her desires and opinions, and Alex listened closely without chiding her for unfeminine candor.

They took long walks in the tidy garden, carriage rides in the country, and spent hours and hours in bed where he brought her to the pinnacle of passion over and over again.

Katherine pressed her arms to herself in a hug as she descended the steps to meet her husband in the parlor.

There he stood by the mantel, dressed in black velvet breeches and long vest, lifting a glass of brandy to his lips. He lowered the glass when she walked in. Jaw slack, he stared for a moment, then sucked in a quick breath.

"Have you forgotten to breathe?" Katherine asked, a tender warmth filling her as she walked into his arms. She reached back and fingered the black satin ribbon that secured his golden hair.

"How beautiful you are," Alex said. "And you smell so good. I want to have you in a field of lavender." He kissed her, then brushed a thumb across her lips. "You're a prize to be cherished."

"And you are my champion," she said, and met his kiss.

"Eww. Woman spit."

They turned to see Pace, a comical grimace on his face, watching them near the door.

"You might like it someday," Alex said to him.

"Never!" Pace declared. He then ducked away from Carly, who had snuck up behind him and kissed him on his cheek. With shouts of disgust from Pace and giggles from Carly, the two raced from the parlor, narrowly missing Elizabeth.

She hobbled in smiling, her slight body hidden beneath layers of blue and silver that brought out the shining gray of her eyes and ash blond of her hair.

Alex set down his glass and held out an arm for each. "Shall we depart?"

****

Lord and Lady Allerton's grand home, one hour's carriage ride from Drayton Castle, dazzled with neatly trimmed knot gardens that expanded the length of the drive and were interspersed by decorative pools and spring flowers.

Alex turned to Elizabeth when their carriage, in line with at least twenty others, halted in front of the mansion. "Wiltshire and Edward will both be here, Bethie. And they'll expect a decision from you."

Elizabeth plucked at the silver ribbons ornamenting her gown. "I know," she whispered. "I know."

Inside, it wasn't the echoing din of many voices or the brilliantly colored clothing of the guests that struck Katherine, but rather the sharp contrast of the Allerton's brightly lit home with their shadowy castle. Instead of dark planked floors and gray stone walls, The Allerton home gleamed with ivory colored paneling and polished green marble floor tiles that echoed the heels of the strolling merrymakers. Overhead, a silver chandelier holding dozens of blazing white candles hung between twin white curved staircases that led up to grand parlor. Right at the center of the balustrade between the two sets of stairs stood an impeccably dressed man and woman greeting their guests.

Having grown accustomed—nay, tolerant—toward her window-covered home, Katherine thought the sun reflecting on the walls seemed almost too bright. She paused, however, looking wistfully at all the drapes pulled back from the windows. Alex followed her gaze. Without a word, she continued on toward the stairway, knowing that to ask her husband to open the drapes in their home might be akin to tormenting him. Would he never end his aversion to windows?

Alex gave introductions to Lord and Lady Allerton, whose quick scrutiny of Katherine seemed filled with approval.

"Lady Drayton, 'tis nice to see you," Lord Allerton boomed as he kissed her hand. "How sad that you lost your family in the Plague and the fire. I knew your father well."

Katherine stiffened and gave a sidelong glance toward Alex. But by Lord Allerton's warm smile and Lady Allerton's sympathetic eyes, it was obvious that they knew nothing of her father's treachery. She relaxed. "Thank you for your condolences."

"Indeed," said Lady Allerton. "I am so glad you could come." She gave Alex's arm an affectionate pat. "'Tis good to see you so happy, Lord Drayton. You two have found new life in each other, it seems. And you look superbly happy. What brought you together?"

"My father," Katherine said simply.

After greetings to Elizabeth, the Allertons turned to meet their next guests, and the three moved along the balustrade toward the parlor. Katherine paused after a moment, patted Elizabeth's shoulder, and pointed toward the door. "Elizabeth, there is Edward just arrived. He's splendid in his yellow vest and breeches, don't you think?"

Elizabeth's gaze wandered toward the grand white entrance doors. "Yes...splendid."

"Why don't we wait for him here, and then we can all go into the parlor together?" Katherine suggested.

"Oh. I don't think...." Elizabeth turned away and continued her awkward limp toward the parlor.

Alex and Katherine watched Edward move toward one of the curved stairways with his family.

"See the scowl on his face," said Katherine. "He seems so very angry. You never did tell me how he reacted to the news of Lord Wiltshire."

"Like that," Alex said, gesturing toward him. "Bloodthirsty."

"I do hope he doesn't try anything. He's not a fighter."

Alex's hand slid lightly up Katherine's back. "Edward has more sense than that. Still, 'twill be interesting to see what comes of this night. My shy cousin is unused to two men wanting her."

Katherine looked past Edward, then smiled up at Alex. "And are you used to two women wanting you?"

He smiled. "I don't understand."

She pointed to where Agnes, stunning in pink and purple satin, floated regally up the steps behind her brother. Agnes had paused and stared at Alex with wide eyes outlined in dark pencil. Her gaze then moved to Katherine.

Katherine fought off a strange chill. She concentrated on the fact that although Agnes's bodice, which exposed the tops of her nipples, was at the height of fashion, her dress would be more acceptable within the crowds at Whitehall Palace. However, she had taken great care with her appearance. Her yellow hair swept out from her head in curls and ribbons, and the white powder on her face accentuated her red painted lips and pink cheeks.

"Bah! I do not wish to see that woman." Alex stationed Katherine's hand on his forearm. "Come. We shall dance. If I remember how."

With arched brows Katherine tugged her hand away, and observed his frown.

"What? You think I should I speak to her?"

"Gads, no. What I think is that you should not present our first dance to me thus, my lord. 'Tis a *request* you should make of your lady to dance, not a command."

"Ah." His expression relaxed into a smile. "There I go again. Allow me to get it right this time."

He touched her bare shoulder, and it tingled with the gentle caress of his fingers. His hand stroked a sizzling path down her arm and over the exposed skin under the open slits of her sleeve before settling over her hand. This he lifted and brought to his lips. The breath caught in her throat, and for a moment it seemed everyone around them disappeared.

"Would you care to dance with me, my lady?"

Katherine took a forgotten breath. "I would be honored, my lord."

****

Allerton liked white, Alex concluded as he surveyed the gleaming white walls, tiled floor, and heavily carved oak furniture of the magnificent parlor. He had forgotten the brightness of this place compared to his dark home.

Seeing all this light plucked at some strange ache within him. He'd never spoken to Katherine about her pulling the drapes open in the parlor on the day he took her to the keep.

He knew she yearned for the sun to enter their home. Katherine's hand, as always, left his arm warm. She smiled up at him, and within Alex welled a surge of love.

Laughter and perfumed body heat assailed them as they walked toward Elizabeth standing near the corner, her eyes on the people who danced the Saraband to the musicians' harpsichord and violins.

He began to tell Elizabeth that they would be right back, but then the crowd parted for a second and he spotted Lord Wiltshire sitting on a chair across the room, a drink in one hand, his other waving in jerky movements. He seemed to be in hot debate with a man sitting across from him.

Elizabeth saw him now, too. Even over the music and hordes of guests, Alex heard her audible gasp of pleasure.

"Elizabeth, may I speak to you?" he said, leaning close to her ear. She needed to be very careful right now with her display of emotions.

"Yes, of course," Elizabeth replied, "but in a little while, if you don't mind. I see Lord Wiltshire—oh! He has just noticed me." She waved gaily and smiled, and Alex watched as Wiltshire gave a satisfied return smile, nodded to the other man, and rose.

Wiltshire lumbered toward her in his outlandish red and orange breeches and vest. They met in the middle of the room and were swallowed up by the crowd.

Katherine's hand tensed on his arm. "Edward just entered the parlor."

Behind Edward—whose gaze darted around the room, no doubt, to find Elizabeth—Robert, Sarah, and Agnes nodded to the crowd with wide smiles. Agnes eyes again met his before she averted her gaze.

He turned toward the dancers. "Come," he said to Katherine. "Let us leave others to their own devices. A new dance begins."

They took positions in the center of the room, ladies on one side, men on the other. The violins began, controlled and rhythmic, for the three short steps each line took toward the other. All dancers paused, bent slightly at the knees with toes turned out, and then straightened and continued on for four more steps until each man and woman stood directly in front of the other.

It had been years since he'd performed the jigg, and Alex concentrated on the movement of his stiff hands and feet and noted Katherine's poise and skill.

"Relax," she whispered to him. She, like the other ladies, disappeared around the men's backs and reappeared on the other side, arms out in front, hands moving gracefully as she took the first of three steps backward.

"I used to be good at this," he whispered back as he stepped backward, damnably clumsy, and considered that his own arms resembled two rigid canes.

When the dance finally ended, they sat on one of the couches. Alex accepted two glasses of wine from a servant and gave one to Katherine. "To my beautiful wife," he said, kissing her cheek. "I want you to keep that pearl necklace on later."

Katherine touched the pearls. "You want me to wear it with my nightclothes?"

"'Tis the only thing I want you to wear."

Katherine's mouth opened slightly. Her cheeks turned pink and her eyes grew dark with a desire that made him want to carry her off to the nearest bedchamber.

Alex fingered one of the soft curls at her neck, then looked beyond to see a man staring at them. He stood with his bejeweled hands perched on his waist, a voluminous white silk shirt hanging over his bright blue-green breeches. Alex met Katherine's eyes. "What did you ever see in the Earl of Rochester?"

Katherine shrugged. "Father wanted the match. I thought he meant to gain lands and power from the union. But now I know he hoped Ellis might tell me secrets."

"But you said you loved the earl."

Katherine touched his cheek. "I never knew what love was. That is, not until I fell in love with you."

"And I said there could be no love in marriage," Alex replied softly. "How wrong I was."

Through the crowd, Rochester moved across the room. He acknowledged neither Alex nor Katherine as he passed, but instead preyed on Agnes, who stood near the food table watching him with a bright smile.

Katherine saw him then. "Ah, and there he is. I wondered why you suddenly asked about him. Do you think him angry at you for telling King Charles of his whereabouts with Mrs. Mallet?"

"I do. He spent two days in the Tower for it. I believe he'd like to put a sword through me."

Katherine nodded toward Agnes, who had cocked her head and laughed too loudly at something Ellis said. "She knows not she'll only be a plaything to him,".

They both watched as, a moment later, Ellis and Agnes left the room.

"Perhaps I should warn her about him," Katherine said, tapping a finger to her lips.

Alex laughed and helped Katherine to her feet as the music swelled for the next dance. "You are too kind. I believe *he's* the one to be warned."

After four more dances, Katherine, feeling the satin bodice of her gown beginning to stick to her skin, went to the rooms reserved for the ladies to freshen up.

Afterward, she noted to her left a balcony, empty of people, that beckoned her with its silence and early evening air. She would just slip outside for a moment to fan her face.

The gardens in the back of the manor were splendid in their size and color. In the fading daylight, Katherine studied the layout and gleaned ideas for her own flower gardens.

"Here we are," said a voice below her. "This is more private. We can sit and talk without having to shout to be heard."

The voice sounded familiar, raucous and boyish at the same time. Katherine moved to the side of the rail and peered below. There, directly below her, Ellis led Agnes to a stone bench. No one else was about.

"This is nice," Agnes said in a sultry purr as she took a seat. "Although I would like to dance with you at least once, my lord."

"We shall. Soon." Ellis sat beside her and immediately traced his finger over the top of one exposed nipple.

"Oh! My lord!" Agnes jumped to her feet and unfolded her fan with a snap. She waved it over her face with rapid strokes, but made no move to leave.

"Please, sit," Ellis said in the innocent voice that had initially charmed Katherine. "I couldn't help myself. You are the most beautiful woman I've ever seen."

Katherine twisted her lips. How often had she heard that from the men at Court who pursued the women? She should leave them alone, but curiosity kept her rooted.

"Am I?" Agnes sat, and Ellis put an arm over her bare shoulders.

"You are. I can't believe my good fortune. But I shall always regret that you're betrothed to another."

Agnes fell right into his trap. "Oh, but I'm not betrothed to anyone," she simpered.

"But you might be," he said, and Katherine had to strain to hear his voice. "If you're so inclined."

"What-what do you mean? T-to you?"

Ellis' hand slipped into Agnes's bodice and cupped one large breast. Since most of it was exposed anyway, it didn't take much effort to pull it free. It hung exposed, a white melon in the moonlight.

Agnes gasped. "My-my lord!"

Ellis palmed her breast, and leaned his face toward hers. "Have you ever had a man's tongue in your mouth?"

"I—well—"

Her words became muffled when Ellis kissed her. Katherine shook her head. For all Agnes's vile ways, she was no match for a gentleman of the king's bedchamber, who had boasted of sampling each of the king's mistresses and half the wives at Court.

She took a last peek at Ellis sliding Agnes's skirts up over her knees, and then went back inside.

Lady Sarah Cooke was just exiting the powder room.

"Lady Cooke," Katherine nodded in greeting. "Oh, if you're seeking Agnes, she and Lord Rochester are sitting right outside below that balcony there. Be very quiet lest you disturb them. They're in deep discussion over the human body."

A moment later, Lady Cooke's squawks of outrage rang down the corridor.

Alex, waiting for Katherine, leaned casually against the wall near the parlor door. His questioning smile over her quiet laughter, however, froze when a cry, shrill and thin, sliced across the room through the din of the packed parlor.

"No! Edward!"

Alex shoved himself straight and swung his head toward the sound. "Bethie?"

Piercing the sudden, stunned silence was an agonized scream.

Chapter Thirty-three

Blood bloomed over the delicate silver lace of Elizabeth's bodice. She lay on the long gaming table at one end of the Allerton's now-empty parlor.

Her hand slowly cooled, but Katherine still gripped it, willing the warmth of her body to fill Elizabeth with life again. Alex, his own face pale and his mouth in a thin line, gently stroked Elizabeth's forehead and hair.

In a nearby chair, Edward sat bent with his head in his hands, sobbing in uncontrolled gasps. "I killed her," he moaned. "My God, I killed her."

"'Twas an accident, Edward," Alex consoled, his voice breaking. "Her hip twisted and she fell between you."

"'Twas the baron I wanted, I swear it," Edward said.

Some time later Robert took his family home. Wiltshire had disappeared after giving Alex his condolences and claiming he was certainly not at fault for Edward's clumsy sword thrust.

Lord Allerton accompanied Katherine and Alex, who cradled Elizabeth's body wrapped in his cloak, back to Drayton Castle.

Alex seemed to lock himself up within his mind. He wouldn't speak, but spent the ride staring down at his cousin with a pinched, anguished face.

When the moon was high and bright, the carriage creaked to a stop. The front door crashed open. Pace and Carly, their laughter shrill in the night air, raced down the front steps.

"Alex, the children shouldn't see this," Katherine said. "Stay here and I'll get them inside."

"Yes," Alex said.

However, Pace had flung open the door and poked in his head. "I beat Carly to the carriage!" His grin faded as he saw Elizabeth's limp body in Alex's arms.

"Step back, Pace," Katherine said as she guided the

boy from the carriage. Alex emerged with Elizabeth. Millie and Sam, their faces creased in concern, had come down the front steps.

"Lord Drayton?" Carly asked. "Who are you carrying?"

Alex's voice hitched. "'Tis Elizabeth. Please go to your bedchambers, you and Pace. I'll be up to talk to you soon."

"But what happened?" Pace asked. He shrugged from Katherine's arms and reached out to touch Elizabeth's cheek, then drew it back quickly. "She's cold." His tone heightened in pitch. "Is Lady Liz dead?"

Alex stopped and faced him. "Yes," he said flatly. "She is dead."

Carly came toward them, her eyes wide and dark. "What—what happened?"

"Why?" Tears glistened in Pace's eyes. "Why is she dead?"

"Millie, take them to their rooms," Katherine said.

Pace was crying openly now. "I want to stay with him. He's gone sad again. Please, Lord Drayton, let me stay with you."

Alex's face crumpled. "Come with me, then," he said to Pace. "You can help me watch over her."

Katherine took Carly's hand as Pace walked with Alex through the door and to the long table in the Hall.

Alex remained aloof and silent all the next day, coming out of his study only to gaze upon his white-clothed cousin lying in her coffin with her hands crossed over her chest. He remained apart from Katherine through the night.

Katherine didn't seek him out, knowing that Alex's way of dealing with death was to enclose himself within his grief. When he was ready, he would come to her.

The next evening, looking exhausted, he joined her in their bed, and she held his tense body close. She stroked his warm skin and pressed her face to the soft, springy hair of his chest. She said nothing, knowing her touch was what he needed.

At length he responded, turning on his side and pulling her into his arms. "I couldn't save her," he said, his voice muffled on her neck.

"You're not to blame," she whispered. "Nothing could

be done."

His arms tightened around her like rings of iron. "I loved her. I don't think she knew. I never told her."

"She knew," Katherine said softly, and kissed his mouth. "She loved you, too."

For a time he was silent. Then, his hands began to slide roughly over her back and buttocks and between her thighs.

"I need you." His breath was warm against her breasts. He raised his head and engulfed her in the sad blue of his eyes. "'Tis wrong, I know."

"No, Alex. Not wrong." She curled on her side and kissed him, then boldly ran the tip of her tongue across his bottom lip. In her hand she took him and slid her fingers down his length. He quickly grew hard under her coaxing. "Let me comfort you."

Alex needed no further persuading, and relished her gasp of pleasure when he rolled her on her back and slid over top of her. He sealed her lips with his. Raw, rough emotions coursed through him as he thrust his tongue into her mouth and brusquely ran his hands over her warm silky skin until he thought he would go wild with desire. He kissed his way down her breasts and stomach, smelled her sweet, musky scent, tasted and teased the nub at her center with his lips and tongue until her thighs quivered in his hands. She was wet and ready for him.

He moved up and laid claim to her willing mouth while he positioned himself and pushed into her. He pulled almost all the way out and then drove into her again, and again, faster and faster.

He thought he was being too rough. But she arched her back and wrapped her legs around his hips and clutched his back with her hands. Her soft, sexy whimpers turned into throaty cries of bliss. In her eyes, he saw her love for him.

Katherine took in the hot desire in Alex's eyes. She ran her fingers through his loose, soft hair and let him ride out his pent up emotions, his raw male power. His weight on her was a sensual confinement, his tongue and hands and hard-driving thrusts the luscious restraints that held her captive.

He filled her, made her complete. He drove into her

and touched a hidden place that built up a crescendo of sensation, sending her straight to the summit. She clutched him, dug her fingers into his back as she went over the edge, and he leaned into her and drove all the harder.

"I love you," he whispered savagely. "Love you."

Abruptly Katherine shattered into a million delightful bits and then melted away into paradise.

Alex shuddered and released himself into her, his breaths hard and fast. He relaxed slowly, and then kissed her for a time, his lips moist and hot. Gradually he slid off, and his arms loosened around her. His breathing slowed.

After he was asleep, Katherine pulled away bit by bit so as not to wake him, and rose to check on the children.

With a joy that caught her breath in her throat as she walked down the dark corridor, she passed her hand over her lower belly. It wasn't definite, but she had missed her monthly time. And deep within a primitive part of her, she knew instinctively that it was true.

She carried Alex's child.

****

Alex had only allowed Agnes in his home to pay her respects to Elizabeth. Now, her eyes wet and reddened, she stood with Edward beside Elizabeth's coffin.

"Edward, you have to stop crying," she said with a sniffle.

Edward dragged his eyes from the coffin. He pointed to a bench against the wall. "I sat there with her. I first kissed her on that bench."

"Ah, Ed," Agnes said. "Where is your mouchoir? You need to wipe your nose."

"I don't want to soil it," Edward said. 'Twas a gift from Elizabeth on Twelfth Night."

Agnes made a comforting sound and removed a square of white linen from her sleeve. With it came a tiny vial, which tumbled down her black dress to the floor. The stopper rolled off and yellow-brown liquid spilled from the vial.

Edward leaned down to get it.

"Wintergreen," Agnes said lightly. "For my headache. I mix it with my ale."

"Doesn't look like wintergreen tincture," Edward muttered thickly. "But I can't smell it. My nose is stopped up." He corked what was left of the liquid and handed the vial back to his sister. Then, he turned back to Alex. "I'm sorry she's dead. I loved her. I wanted her to be my wife."

"Don't blame yourself." Alex patted Edward on his shoulder harder than he intended. He wanted them gone, was sick of hearing Edward's tearful confessions. The man had not stopped crying since arriving early this morning. Agnes, thankfully, had walked away.

"Do you need more whiskey?" Katherine asked. "I can get some for you."

Edward pulled a wrinkled piece of paper from his pocket. "No. I want to be sober when I read my poem during the burial. I wrote it last week asking her to marry me."

Alex swallowed and patted Edward's shoulder again, this time with more gentleness. While Lord Wiltshire had not bothered to show, Edward was overwhelmed with grief. Alex turned to Katherine. "I could use some whiskey," he said tiredly. "If you're offering."

"Of course," Katherine said. "I need to check on the food anyway."

She gave him a poignant smile, squeezed his hand, and left his side.

****

As expected, the servants were keeping up with the fast-emptying platters of food and jugs of ale. The new cook Katherine had hired ran the kitchen like a well-tuned orchestra. Katherine moved on to note fresh barrels of ale and whiskey being tapped. Townspeople and neighbors milled about eating and drinking. She greeted several of them, then poured Alex his whiskey.

"You're pale, Katherine. Are you well?"

Katherine turned toward the voice. "Why, Agnes?" she asked. "Do you wish me in that coffin instead of Elizabeth?"

Agnes lips spread in a warm, weary smile. "Of course not," she said, holding out a tankard of ale for Katherine. "I brought this for you, and one for me. Can we talk?"

Katherine kept her hands at her sides. "No. I have nothing to say to you. After we bury Elizabeth, I never want to see you again."

"Katherine, I've been a horrible person," said Agnes, lowering her gaze to the floor. "I am so sorry for what I've done to you."

"I'm sure." Katherine began to walk away.

Agnes's voice cracked and rose in pitch. "Please. I'm falling apart. Elizabeth was my friend, and now she's dead. My brother wants to kill himself. My father beat me after Alexander told him that I sent you to the brothel." Her lips trembled and a tear slid down her cheek. "I feel so alone. My own family has forsaken me."

Katherine tried to put aside her intense dislike of the woman. Clearly, Agnes needed someone to talk to. "All right. What did you want to speak to me about?"

Agnes's gaze darted around the vast Hall. "Can we go somewhere quiet?"

Katherine glanced again at the food and drink. The servants were doing fine. "We can go to the parlor. Or walk the grounds."

"I do need some air." Agnes fanned herself. "Perhaps 'tis cooler outside."

"One moment. I need to take a drink to Alex." Katherine began to turn away, but when Agnes dabbed at her eyes, she decided to have a servant take it to him. The sooner she got this conversation with Agnes out of the way, the better.

She led the way through the Hall and outside to the stone bench in the middle of the flower garden. The sun in a cloudless sky poured over the green lawn. Pace's excited voice reached her as he dashed with the other children through the tidied boxwood maze.

The child's resilience and immediacy of the moment astounded her. Like Alex, Pace had grieved in his own fashion.

"How lovely," Agnes said as she took a seat. "I didn't know those pink roses grew over there. They must have been covered by weeds for years." She handed Katherine her tankard of ale.

"Thank you." Katherine took a drink and noted an off-taste. Had the ale been improperly brewed?

Agnes chatted on about flowers and herbs for a few minutes, telling Katherine of the variety that Edward dried in his herbarium. Just when Katherine began to grow impatient, Agnes said, "You need to be strong for Alexander. I've never seen him so sad. Even when Mary died...but that was a relief, I think. Near the end, he had to tie her wrists to her bedposts to keep her from hurting herself."

"I know." Katherine sipped at her ale, now barely noting the faint bitterness over the image of an out-of-control woman bound to the bed she herself had occupied. She shivered, then shut out the thought, determined to get on with the conversation.

"Poor Elizabeth," Agnes said with a shake of her head.

Katherine scoffed. "You truly mourn for her? You used her shamelessly to get to Alex."

"I'm over Alexander," Agnes said with a dismissive flick of her wrist. "Do you know that the Earl of Rochester will court me?"

Katherine started. "*Ellis*?"

"Yes. Mother said she made sure of that after he—well—"

"What did he do?" Surely he hadn't ruined Agnes in the seconds it took Katherine to speak to Sarah. She took a last sip, then set the tankard on the bench. She would have to direct the servants to change the ale barrel when she returned to the Hall.

"He did nothing, really." Agnes blushed. "Just kissed me." She raised her tankard to her lips.

"Don't drink that, Agnes. There's something wrong with it."

"Oh, no. 'Tis fine."

"The earl has questionable intentions," Katherine said. "He's only after money. I know this because—"

Agnes's lips, wet with drink, curled into an ugly sneer that took Katherine aback. "You *dare* to ruin my life even more than you have? You took Alexander away from me right at the time when he could end his mourning for his worthless wife. Now you're trying to talk me out of a rich earl's attentions!"

"No, I'm not." Katherine touched her forehead in an attempt to quell the sudden dizziness sweeping through her. "Ellis Potts wants wealth. You...don't have it. He just...wants to...." What was she saying?

"Ellis wants *me*. He didn't want a hatchet faced slattern like you."

Katherine flicked her gaze back and forth and tried to figure out where she was. In the garden. Talking to...Agnes.

"Katherine, are you all right?"

"Don't know...feel faint." The blue flowers near her feet blurred into a gently rocking sea.

"You're just tired. Drink."

Katherine tried to lift the tankard. "Heavy."

"Here, let me help." Agnes raised it to Katherine's lips.

Katherine swallowed with effort. "I'll...go inside."

"In a moment. I'm not finished talking to you." The movement of Agnes's arm left a trail of shimmering black as she tossed the remains of Katherine's ale onto a shrub.

Katherine tried mightily to keep her eyes open. The children's voices in the boxwood maze echoed in a trill of fading waves. "Get Alex," she whispered.

"No."

"Please."

"You should have married the baron," Agnes said, her voice raspy with hatred. "Then Edward would have Elizabeth." She gripped Katherine's shoulders with clawed fingers. "*You* killed Elizabeth by coming here. And you've ruined everything I planned. Alexander was meant for me, *me*!"

"I...what have you done...I'm with child."

Agnes's voice pounded in echoing waves. "Mary always drank down all the laudanum I gave her in her brandy. That and the mercury made her miscarry. The clodpoll believed me when I told her it was Alex who poisoned her." She laughed, a tinkling sound like tiny dancing bells. "I've no time to make you go mad, and you're too strong to push out of a window. What I gave you will work much faster, although most of it got spilled because of my poor brother's sniveling." Her hands released Katherine's shoulders.

Katherine could no longer move her mouth to speak. Through weighted lids she saw the ground rush up to meet her.

A sing-song voice came from far away. "At last. *I* shall be Lady Drayton."

Chapter Thirty-four

Where was Katherine? Alex looked around, his height making it easy to see over the crowd. She seemed not to be in the Hall.

Sarah Cooke had led the still-crying Edward away. Robert stood near the whiskey barrel talking to some of the other men who seemed intent on getting drunk before Elizabeth's burial at dawn tomorrow morning.

Agnes appeared on the other side of the coffin. "Lord Drayton, I am truly sorry for your loss."

Alex took in her tear-streaked face and trembling chin. "I know you were good friends."

"I wish to be your friend, too."

Alex held back from barking out a bitter, sardonic laugh. "Thank you for coming today, Agnes."

A commotion turned Alex's attention toward the front door. "What's all the to-do?"

"Lord Drayton!" came Pace's shrill, alarmed voice. "Lady Drayton's lying on the ground!"

****

"Dear God," Alex moaned as he lifted his limp, unresponsive wife and carried her into the house at a run. "Oh, dear God."

He lay her on the couch in the parlor. "I don't think she's breathing."

Robert knelt, his whiskey breath wafting over Alex's shoulder. "Whatever could have happened?"

Alex couldn't answer. A deep trembling had taken hold of him. His throat seemed to clamp shut as he watched her not breathing, not moving. His heart shredded. "Breathe, Katherine. *Breathe*!"

Agnes leaned into his line of vision. "Father, is everything all right?"

He heard Sarah's shaky reply. "Agnes, didn't you see Lady Drayton just a while ago? You two went out the front door together."

"Yes, we went outside to talk, and then I came back in," Agnes said with a catch in her voice. "She seemed fine when I left her."

Alex swung toward her. "Did you see anyone? Was she alone? Where is Pace?"

"He's here." Carly crouched in one corner with a white-faced Pace, her arms wrapped around him.

"I saw no one," Pace said, his voice quavering. "I came out of the maze and there she was. Is she dead? Is she dead, too?"

Agnes straightened, her eyes riveted on Katherine, and tapped her chin. "I did speak with her briefly," she said. "She wanted to remain alone after accepting my apology. She did mention something about being with child. I wonder what happened?"

"She's with child?" The old, black fear slammed into Alex. He grabbed Katherine's shoulders. "Awaken! You must awaken!"

No response. Her lips were pale, her eyes shut tight.

He lowered his head to her chest. "You can't be dead. I can't go through this. Please. Katherine, please. I love you so much. Wake up." He seized her to him, willing her to breathe, yearning his own life into her.

Her head sagged back. Hopelessness slithered into him like a thousand cold snakes.

She was dead. As was his child. He couldn't save them.

Hands gently gripped his shoulders. He paid no heed. They gradually tightened, then tugged, and still he clutched Katherine to his chest.

"Alex," Sam said into his ear.

Alex lurched to his feet with Katherine in his arms. People surrounded him, drunk and sober and confused. Their faces swam before him. "I shall burn this castle to the ground!" he cried to all. "'Tis cursed with death." He set his gaze on Carly and Pace still huddled in the corner. "We will leave this place. And never return."

Chapter Thirty-five

Alex slumped in the great chair in his bedchamber. His wild anger had dissolved, and its place lay a chillingly familiar desolation. "I can't do it, Sam," he said, his head in his hands. "This is tearing me up inside. Everyone I've ever loved has died. I can't look at her dead in a coffin for three days. She had so much life in her. I can't do it."

Sam touched his shoulder. "Do you wish to...."

"Yes." Alex raked stiff fingers through his hair. "'Tis not proper, I know. But I can't do it."

"We'll bury her tomorrow with Elizabeth, then," Sam said.

"Tomorrow. Yes."

The next morning, Alex stood in the family graveyard and stared around him with bleak eyes. Four little stones stood in a neat row. His babes, all dead before they'd left Mary's sick womb, lay within the ground wrapped in their tiny white shrouds. To their left, Mary's tombstone stood, and those of his parents.

At his feet, two fresh holes in the ground now held the coffins of Elizabeth and Katherine.

Katherine. His throat tightened with sorrow. His wife. His lover, mother of his child. He wanted to follow her into the ground. She had left him an empty shell.

He'd thought he could never love again, but she had taken his icy heart in her soft warm hand, and melted it.

"My lord, we can go back now if you wish. The rest of the mourners are returning to the house."

Alex turned to Sam on legs that felt years older. "Yes."

****

Scattered scrape and tumbling sounds reached her ears. With a gasp, Katherine opened her eyes to full blackness. Groggy with sleep, she tried to sit up. Her forehead met with something hard. Her headboard, perhaps? Was it night? She widened her eyes to see, but it didn't help.

Her hands skated down something smooth and solid above her. Shifting, she felt her elbows connect with the same at her sides. Icy knives of steel cut through the last of her dazed mind. She was trapped in some sort of box.

What was happening? She sucked in breath, and the smell of freshly hewn wood and dank earth assailed her nostrils. The sound above her came again, flat and thick.

Her lungs wouldn't fill. "Alex!" Her voice was weak, too weak for anyone to hear. She pushed at the top and sides of the box. "Alex!"

The dull thump sounded again above her. Suddenly an image rushed into her head of a day filled with the stench of a city burned to the ground, of a day when she slumped at her father's grave, unable to block out the sound of dirt falling onto his coffin.

The same sound resonated above her right now. Katherine went rigid.

Dear God! Did they think her dead? Were they burying her?

She gasped for breath and began to pound on the lid. "Alex! Help me!"

Perspiration beaded her face. She couldn't think. Couldn't breathe. Blackness stuffed itself into her nose and mouth and would smother her, make her go utterly and completely mad. She thrashed and sobbed, trying to tuck up her legs and rock her body from side to side.

No! NO! She had to get out—get out—God! She was in hell—worse than any torment the devil himself could concoct.

"Alex...." Her heart crashed against her chest and her lungs burned in their effort to suck in air.

I'm not dead!

With all her strength, she slammed at the walls of her prison.

****

Alex turned to take a last look at Katherine's coffin, now partially covered with dirt. He would return home now, put Pace and Carly and Jason into the carriage, and go as far away from this demon-plagued hell as possible.

To the sea, perhaps, where he could sit on a cliff and watch the sun set on his life.

Somewhere a faint, rapid knock sounded. He glanced at the burial man beating dirt from his shovel with his boot.

"Lord Drayton?"

Agnes. Alex barely glanced at her.

As she hurried up to him, she stumbled and gave a small, alarmed cry, and caught his arm. "Gramercy, my lord. 'Tis a wonder you were standing here to catch me. May I walk back with you?"

Alex nodded absently. He took a step away from the gravesite, but then heard the sound again. A muted thumping, as if someone with thickly gloved hands were knocking on a door. "What is that I hear?"

Agnes blinked and glanced around. "I hear nothing." She shivered and drew closer to him. "I've a chill today, and you are so warm. And...I would like to comfort you."

"I don't want your comfort."

"Is there no chance for us, then?"

Alex's grief pinpointed in a flash of fury. "What is wrong with you? There never *was* a chance with us."

"Oh, Alexander." Her moist-eyed gaze slid left and right, and she licked her lips. "I want to be your wife. I—I love you."

Alex wasn't listening. There it was again, that knocking sound, but fainter now and slowing in cadence. He fell to his knees and peered down into the hole where Katherine's coffin rested, covered now by a thickening layer of dirt.

Thump. Thump. Then, silence.

The man with the shovel had stopped and was staring down into the hole.

A sudden, sick tilting in Alex's gut made his hands clammy. The breath left his lungs. Edward's words rushed back, words he'd spoken to Agnes on the day Alex stood outside the herbarium with his book.

Don't touch that. It's mandrake root. Makes one sleep like the dead.

Words tore from Alex's throat as he leaped into the hole and frantically dug away at the dirt. "Oh, God. She's alive. She's alive!"

****

Voices. Murmurs. Dank earth smell and inky blackness.

Death slithered through her mind.

Shouting. God's angels had come to fetch her.

A scraping, then, furious and fast, as if the world around her were falling apart. And more shouts, these frantic. And clearer.

The pounding above her grew horrendous. These were no angels. Hell must be her destination.

Screaming. "Agnes, what have you done?"

"We're almost there."

"Open it!"

A grating along the top edge spilled sudden light into her prison. Katherine opened her mouth and sucked in life.

A face drew close to her. "Katherine. My love."

Large hands cradled her cheeks. Warm lips pressed to hers.

Alex.

Chapter Thirty-six

He couldn't stop watching her. Katherine slumbered peacefully next to him on their bed, one hand curled loosely into a fist on her chest. Gently, Alex skimmed his hand over the back of hers and followed the curve of her fingers.

The purple shadows under her eyes would fade. Healthy color would return to her smooth cheeks.

She stirred beside him.

He looked past her at the slivers of golden afternoon sun that rimmed his heavy drapes. His heart had been like those drapes, shutting out whatever bright hope and love that had tried to break through.

But now his heart had opened, and the light streaming into it was Katherine. She had given him a second chance at happiness.

"I love you," he whispered in her ear.

Katherine opened her eyes, stretched, and smiled at her husband. "I love you. What hour is it?"

"Almost four of the clock."

"I could fairly sleep the day away." Katherine brushed a stray hair from Alex's forehead. "Do you think our child will be all right?"

Alex lay a hand on her belly. "The doctor seems to think so. You continued to breathe throughout your sleep although no one could see it. And he said anyone daft enough to use soap on an injury such as mine had to be too stubborn to die."

Katherine gave Alex a pensive look. "Agnes. Is she...?"

"Gone," Alex said, handing Katherine a goblet of watered honey with orange. He tried to keep the venom from his voice. "For so long I thought it was my fault. She did all those things to Mary, my children, to you—so she could be my wife. They took her away this afternoon."

Katherine sat up and sipped the drink. “What will become of her?”

Alex shrugged. “Mayhap Rochester will step in.”

“Mayhap not. I’m sure he’s gone on to his next conquest.” Katherine placed her cup on the bedside table and snuggled into Alex’s arms.

His heart began a fast thump with her soft kisses on his chest. “How are you feeling?” he asked, his voice hoarse, and hopeful.

Reaching down, she stroked him. “Very good. And I know how you’re feeling.”

Alex turned her on her back and lay over her, giving her a slow, tender kiss. She tasted of honey. His lips trailed over her cheek and forehead. Raising his head, he saw her shadowed as usual by the dimness of the room.

“Don’t move.” He got out of bed and walked to the windows. One by one, he flung open the drapes.

The sun spilled in like a beacon of hope.

He turned to look at her. “You’re so beautiful.”

Katherine opened her mouth in astonishment and propped herself up on one elbow. “But the drapes. You want them closed.”

“No more.” Alex went to her. “The past is finished. I want no darkness in our home.”

“Our home,” Katherine sighed happily as he lay down and took her in his arms. “Joy and light. And children to fill it.”

“And love,” Alex said as his lips met hers. “Always love.”

A word about the author...

Born in Caribou, Maine, Pamela Roller grew up an Air Force brat, residing in several U.S. states and in Europe. Upon graduating from Longwood University in 1983 with a teaching degree, she followed her heart and moved to Virginia's Shenandoah Valley.

Before authoring her first book, she worked as a waitress, restaurant co-manager, retail manager, bar bouncer, Mary Kay consultant, rent-a-cop, poultry plant sanitation worker, karate instructor, quality control technician, production supervisor, and teacher's aide. She currently teaches public school English and credits her students with driving her to escape reality by writing fiction.

Pamela resides in Virginia with one son, her real-life hero husband, and a myriad of SPCA pets.

Visit Pam at www.pamelaroller.com

Printed in the United States
80943LV00004B/1-3